"I just wanted to thank you for saving my life."

"I don't want your gratitude," Nick said.

"What *do* you want?"

The quiet question, no less intense for its lack of volume, snared his attention. Slowly his gaze met hers. "I think you already know the answer to that."

To her credit, she didn't flinch. "I told you once..."

"That you wouldn't sleep with me."

"It's not fair...."

"If you're concerned for my feelings, don't be. I rarely do anything for altruistic reasons." His words served a twofold purpose. They held a warning for her, one she would be wise to heed.

And they served as a reminder to himself....

Dear Reader,

Happy New Year! And happy reading, too—starting with the wonderful Ruth Langan and *Return of the Prodigal Son*, the latest in her newest miniseries, THE LASSITER LAW. When this burned-out ex-agent comes home looking for some R and R, what he finds instead is a beautiful widow with irresistible children and a heart ready for love. *His* love.

This is also the month when we set out on a twelve-book adventure called ROMANCING THE CROWN. Linda Turner starts things off with *The Man Who Would Be King*. Return with her to the island kingdom of Montebello, where lives—and hearts—are about to be changed forever.

The rest of the month is terrific, too. Kylie Brant's CHARMED AND DANGEROUS concludes with *Hard To Tame*, Carla Cassidy continues THE DELANEY HEIRS with *To Wed and Protect*, Debra Cowan offers a hero who knows the heroine is *Still the One,* and Monica McLean tells us *The Nanny's Secret*. And, of course, we'll be back next month with six more of the best and most exciting romances around.

Enjoy!

Leslie J. Wainger
Executive Senior Editor

Please address questions and book requests to:
Silhouette Reader Service
U.S.: 3010 Walden Ave., P.O. Box 1325, Buffalo, NY 14269
Canadian: P.O. Box 609, Fort Erie, Ont. L2A 5X3

Hard To Tame
KYLIE BRANT

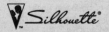

INTIMATE MOMENTS™
Published by Silhouette Books
America's Publisher of Contemporary Romance

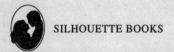 SILHOUETTE BOOKS

ISBN 0-373-27195-6

HARD TO TAME

Copyright © 2002 by Kimberly Bahnsen

Printed in U.S.A.

Books by Kylie Brant

Silhouette Intimate Moments

McLain's Law #528
Rancher's Choice #552
An Irresistible Man #622
Guarding Raine #693
Bringing Benjy Home #735
Friday's Child #862
*Undercover Lover #882
*Heartbreak Ranch #910
**Falling Hard and Fast* #959
Undercover Bride #1022
†*Hard To Handle* #1108
Born in Secret #1112
†*Hard To Resist* #1119
†*Hard To Tame* #1125

*The Sullivan Brothers
†Charmed and Dangerous

KYLIE BRANT

lives with her husband and five children in Iowa. She works full-time as a teacher of learning disabled students. Much of her free time is spent in her role as professional spectator at her kids' sporting events.

An avid reader, Kylie enjoys stories of love, mystery and suspense—and she insists on happy endings! When her youngest children, a set of twins, turned four, she decided to try her hand at writing. Now most weekends and all summer she can be found at the computer, spinning her own tales of romance and happily-ever-afters.

Kylie invites readers to write to her at P.O. Box 231, Charles City, IA 50616.

For Mary Ann and Harris—
because it's hard being the "out-laws"!

Prologue

They were dead. Every one of them.

With an unnatural strength borne of terror, Sara Parker tore away from the female U.S. Marshal and pushed through the apartment door.

"Get her out of here!" Agent Carlson shouted from his position on the floor. Sara felt arms grabbing at her shoulders, trying to yank her away from the bloody carnage.

She fought like a wild thing, adrenaline giving her the power to break free. She rushed into the compact kitchen, stumbling over the bodies on the floor. Carlson was checking one of the agents for a pulse, but Sara knew, in some numb, distant area of her mind, that he wouldn't find one. Just as she knew the futility of the hope she still harbored.

"Sean!" She dropped to her knees beside the blond man's chair and took his hand in hers, refusing to consider what the coldness of his fingers meant. He could have been asleep but for the fact that his eyes were open. The round hole in the center of his forehead was a horrifying contrast to his choirboy countenance. Somehow he still managed to exude that sad sweetness that was so much a part of him. Even in death.

There was a soft keening sound that Sara didn't recognize as coming from her. Unmindful of his blood-soaked shirt, she slipped her arms around his waist, pressed her face to his form. *I'm sorry.* The words echoed endlessly in her mind. *I'm so sorry.*

And then the hands were at her shoulders again, drawing her to her feet. Her unnatural strength of a few moments ago had drained away as quickly as it had surged, leaving her feeling empty and weak.

"Don't. Try not to look at them." Agent Reindl's voice was unusually compassionate. "We've got to get you out of here."

Sara allowed the woman to guide her out of the apartment, only half aware of the sharp exchange between the two agents, the cell phone conversation between Carlson and his superior. She took no note of the different route they took to the car. Made no observation of her surroundings before Reindl forced her to lie down in the back seat.

The vehicle started, pulled away. Sara lay motionless, her cheek pressed against the cool leather of the seat, eyes open, yet unseeing.

Another safe house. More agents. Leak in the department, had to be. Dammit, Dobbs had four kids.

The words eddied and swirled around her, surreal and unrelated. They made no sense. Nothing did anymore. She started trembling, the shudders racking her body. She could have told them that they were wasting their time. Finding another safe house was pointless.

She'd never be safe again.

* * *

"We'll move you tomorrow, once we get word from the department. You'll be fine here for tonight."

Sara gave a listless nod at Reindl's words, and continued to stare at the wall of the motel room. Carlson was on his cell phone again, after which he'd hold another whispered conversation with his partner. Both were doing their best to maintain at least an outward appearance of control. But Sara knew the truth. The only one in control was Victor Mannen, and he'd just had six people massacred.

She would be next.

The knowledge washed over her like a wave, and fear circled. How had security at the apartment been breached? How had two U.S. Marshals and four young adults been dispatched with such chilling efficiency? Useless to wonder about, really, just as it was useless to harbor a macabre fascination in how she would meet *her* death. A gun again, or a blade slipped into her back as she walked into the courthouse flanked by guards?

Swallowing hard, Sara barely noticed the concerned glance Carlson sent her way. There was something outrageously self-centered in worrying about her own demise when the deaths of six other people rested on her shoulders. A part of her wondered why she even cared. There was nothing worth living for, at any rate. Not since Sean…

She choked on the boulder-sized knot that lodged in her throat, and pressed a fist to her lips. Agent Carlson ended his conversation and looked at her. "How you doing?" he asked, not unkindly. The big, bespectacled agent had been the favorite of all of them. He'd always been ready with a joke or a quick remark. But now he was as grim-faced as his partner. Two agents and four witnesses dead meant Sara had a target on her back. And so did anyone unfortunate enough to be guarding her.

Launching herself out of the chair, she hurtled toward him, her arms going around his waist, taking him by surprise. After an instant he brought a hand to her back, patted her awkwardly. "Don't worry, kid. It'll be okay."

She appreciated his attempt at reassurance, even as she recognized the lie. Stepping away from him, she avoided his gaze. "I think I'll take a hot shower."

He shot a quick glance at Reindl, and when the woman nodded, he said, "Sure. Probably a good idea."

Crossing to the bathroom, Sara shut the door, leaned against it limply. Then, with a sigh, she reached up her sleeve and withdrew the wallet she'd just lifted from Carlson. She forced herself not to think as she rifled through it, taking out the cash. Folding the bills, she shoved them in her pocket and then laid the wallet on the vanity.

Her actions automatic, she turned the shower faucets on full blast and then climbed up on the vanity, unlocked the window. It was easier, far easier, to act without considering the sense of déjà vu she felt. But as she climbed through the open window it occurred to her that she was following her set pattern for dealing with trouble.

She was running.

Chapter 1

Six Years Later

He was back again. Watching her.

Sara noted the man's entrance and her muscles tightened, even as she fought to remain expressionless. She laughed at something one of her customers said, made a quick remark, but the awareness, the heightened sensitivity, was already creeping down her spine.

This was the third day he'd come into the café on her shift. The restaurant had plenty of regulars, but none who looked like this man. None who projected a darkly seductive threat merely by his presence. None who moved as though an untamed animal prowled below his smooth, sophisticated exterior.

Moving away, she checked with the people seated at the next table, then turned to go to the kitchen. En route, Candy, another waitress, sidled up to her.

"Your admirer's back."

Sara didn't smile at the woman's teasing tone. "Promise if he sits in my section you'll switch with me."

"Glad to, but we both know it's not me he keeps returning for."

Giving her new orders to the cook, Sara loitered as some of her other orders came up. Candy shot another indiscreet look at the dark stranger and lowered her voice even further. "I discovered some information about him, in case you're interested."

Loading her arms with plates of steaming food, Sara didn't look up. "I'm not." She'd been packed since the first day she'd seen the man—ready, if necessary, to flee at a moment's notice. The man unnerved her, had from the first. She couldn't decide whether it was her well-developed survival instincts that quivered to life around him, or something much more elemental. Both were equally dangerous—to her.

Without missing a beat, the woman went on. "He's a hometown boy by the name of Nick Doucet. Yes, dear—" she began gathering up her own filled orders "—that's of *the* Doucet family, from Soileau Street. *Very* old name, not to mention old money. Comes back to New Orleans a few times a year for a visit, and this time he's been home over a week."

"Naw 'Leans." The woman's pronunciation pegged her as a native. And even though Sara had lived there only a month, she recognized the family name Candy had mentioned. She wound her way back to her tables fighting a sense of relief. The mysterious stranger had a reason to be here. He hadn't been sent after her. She wouldn't have to leave again. Not yet.

With swift precision she unloaded the dishes before four customers seated outside under the awning. It was early, barely seven-thirty, but the air was already thick with a sticky heat. By noon it would be nearly unbearable, and the only ones who would choose seats on the patio would be tourists and other masochists.

"Hey, Amber, you're sure lookin' fine this mornin'." The compliment came from Douglas, fortyish and graying. With no consideration for his bulging middle, he'd ordered steak and eggs with a mound of potatoes covered in cheese. There was a chorus of agreement from the other men. Sara smiled and seamlessly shifted back into her role.

"And how are the fab four doing this morning? Douglas, how're the twins? Michael, the haircut looks great." She swapped banter with the men even as she was aware, much too aware, of Doucet seated several tables away, speaking with the manager, Lowell Francis.

"When you gonna run away with me, Amber, huh?" This from Baldwin, the youngest member of the group of businessmen. With his slicked-back brown hair and soulful eyes, he reminded her of a hound dog begging for affection. She didn't bother telling him that when she ran away, she always ran alone.

"I guess when your wife gives you permission to leave town without her, Baldwin."

At the others' laughter, Sara leaned closer and said soothingly, "If I was married to a fellow like you, I'd keep you on a short rein, too." She left the table amid their good-natured ribbing, and made a studious effort to ignore the man sitting nearby.

"It won't work this time." The words were low and smooth, and Sara's stomach quivered. Even before turning she knew who the voice belonged to. Nick Doucet. Fixing a smile on her face, she met his dark gaze and said, "Someone will be back in just a moment to take your order, sir."

She lost no time reentering the restaurant, scanning the place for Candy. But when she found the woman, the other waitress shook her head and threw a look over her shoulder at the manager. "Francis just warned me about staying in my own area. Sorry, girlfriend." Catching the frown on the manager's face, she hurried away, and Sara slowly went to the kitchen to check on her orders.

So she wouldn't be able to avoid Doucet any longer. A shiver worked down her spine as she picked up plates at the kitchen window. The threat she sensed from the man wasn't directed at her, that much seemed apparent. And so his interest must be personal, and could be dismissed easily. She was an expert at rejecting men, could even, when the spirit moved her, do it without crushing their egos.

But somehow she knew that nothing in her experience had prepared her for a man like Nick Doucet.

After delivering the dishes to customers, she moved to his table, donned her bright waitress smile and took out her pad. "Are you ready to order, sir?"

"Are you angry with me, Amber?"

Her smile froze, but she managed a quizzical lift to her brow. "Why would I be angry with you?"

"For not letting you ignore me any longer."

Nerves kicked in her stomach. A mental image of the conversation she'd witnessed between him and the manager flickered across her mind. "We rarely allow our customers to starve. Someone would have been along to take care of you."

"But I wanted you." The words hung in the air, quivering like a plucked harp string, and that unwelcome shiver shimmied down her spine again. She had the impression that he knew the effect he had on her, which made her all the more determined to hide it.

She reeled off the specials, ending with, "If you'd like variety, the buffet is always good. Ten ninety-five for all you can eat."

"Just fruit. Wheat toast and coffee. Black." The ordinary words had greater impact when delivered in that

smoky tone, coupled with the intent look in his fathomless
ebony eyes. There was nothing ordinary about this man.
A well-developed intuition told her that.

He had a presence that commanded attention. Slightly
over six feet tall, his broad-shouldered form was lean
rather than bulky, with the dangerous stillness of a bomb
waiting to detonate. His hair, as dark as his eyes, swept
back from a slight widow's peak. The slashes at either
corner of his mouth could have been etched in granite. His
brutal handsomeness gave the impression of lethal power,
ruthlessly harnessed. And Sara was more grateful than
she'd like to admit when she was able to move away from
him.

The swelling number of customers in the café gave her
a ready excuse should he try to speak to her again. But he
seemed content to lounge in his chair, regarding her silently. And no matter how busy her job kept her, that uncomfortable awareness wouldn't fade.

It was several minutes before she noticed that Doucet
had garnered his own share of attention. Candy's wasn't
the only unsubtle look sent his way, and more than one
table of patrons was holding a whispered conversation in
which his name figured. As Sara slid plates onto the table
before three elderly men, one of their murmured remarks
hung suspended in the air.

Bastard. It was impossible to tell whether the word was
meant in the figurative or literal sense. She felt an unwilling flicker of sympathy for Doucet, one that was totally
unnecessary. If he experienced the same sense of unease
that she did at being the recipient of such attention, it certainly didn't show. The only emotions reflected on his face
were ones he allowed to appear there.

And all that showed right now was his continued interest
in her.

It took more fortitude than it should have to collect his

order from the kitchen, approach his table with it. But
when she entered the patio area Doucet was no longer
alone. Douglas Fairmont had left his party to address him,
and she felt a ridiculous wave of relief that his presence
would provide a buffer between them.

"I'd really like to lay it all out for you." At a gesture
from Nick, Douglas looked around, saw Sara. He shifted
his girth to allow her room to set the plates in front of the
man, but it was clear he had no intention of leaving. "If
I could have just a half hour of your time, I promise you'll
see for yourself the possibilities for future growth."

She quickly unloaded the tray, giving far more concentration to the act than was warranted. As she set down the
linen-wrapped silverware, Doucet reached for it. Their
hands touched and she snatched hers back with a sudden-
ness that had his attention shifting from Fairmont to her.

"I might be interested." Although still addressing the
other man, his dark gaze was fixed on Sara. "You can stop
by and give me the details this evening, say, at seven?"
Nick's eyes traced her features as Fairmont stuttered out
an agreement. "On the condition, of course, that you bring
Amber with you."

"No way, Douglas." Sara gripped her purse and hurried
more quickly down the sidewalk, unmindful of the heat.
She worked a split shift that day, with a couple hours off
before she was needed for the lunch crowd. She'd planned
to spend that time dropping by the library, maybe picking
up a few groceries. But the man glued to her side wouldn't
be dissuaded.

"Be reasonable. And slow down, for God's sake." He
pulled out an embroidered handkerchief and wiped his
broad forehead, which was already gleaming. "All I'm
asking for is an hour of your time."

"How many ways can I say it?" She never broke stride. "I'm not going."

"There's a hundred dollars in it for you."

That stopped her. The look she fixed on him was fierce enough to have him backing away a step, raising his hands in mute surrender. "I meant no disrespect, Amber, honest."

Forcing a lid on her roiling emotions, Sara took a deep breath, reached for calm. "I don't mind doing you a favor, Douglas, but Nick Doucet..." She shook her head. "I don't want to have anything to do with him."

"But you won't. Not really." Seizing the opportunity to make his case again, Douglas went on eagerly. "My appointment is for seven. We'll arrive, maybe have a drink, then he and I will discuss some business. Afterward, I'll take you home. You won't even have to talk to him if you don't want to."

Sara started walking again. The man's wheedling tone couldn't begin to quiet the alarm shrilling in her mind. Doucet was trouble. Maybe not the kind of trouble she'd originally imagined. At least she no longer feared he'd been sent to kill her. But he presented a different kind of danger. She was much too aware of the man for it to be otherwise. "You can just show up without me. He heard me say I wasn't coming. He won't blame you."

"I can't take that chance." Fairmount reached out to take her arm, and she pulled away in an involuntary response that no amount of acting could effectively disguise.

He balled up the handkerchief in his hand, his fingers clenching and unclenching around it. "This is important to me. I have a deal in mind that could make my career—all I need to do is line up the financing. I've been to everyone else in town, but Nick Doucet might be the only one with the vision to take a risk on my venture. I know you don't owe me a thing, but he may be my last chance. C'mon, Amber, whaddya say?''

People strolled past them on the sidewalk, parting for the drama being carried out between the pair. Seeing the cautious hope mirrored on Fairmont's face, Sara felt suddenly ancient. She could have told him that hope was as dangerous an emotion as need or trust. Far better to have no expectations at all than to risk having them shattered.

She took a deep breath and steeled herself to do just that. "I'm sorry, Douglas. I'd like to help you. If it were anybody else…but there's no way I'm going to have anything to do with Nick Doucet. Not even for you.''

An hour later she was ensconced in a comfortable chair near the entrance of the New Orleans main library, reading the newest selection from a popular horror writer. The cool, quiet environment was a welcome balm after the outdoor heat, and from the nerves that quivered to life whenever Nick Doucet got too close.

Sara turned a page, squelching a twinge of conscience as she remembered the crestfallen look on Douglas's face when he'd realized that no amount of persuasion was going to convince her to change her mind. But she'd learned long ago the folly of allowing emotion to dictate her actions. Her instincts were keen, honed by years on the streets, and those instincts came screaming to life every time Doucet was in the vicinity. She knew better than to ignore them.

A woman hurried by, grasping a young child by the hand. She spared Sara only a cursory glance, a fact that relieved a measure of the tension that had been building in her for the last several days. She knew what the woman saw when she looked at her—a medium tall, slender woman with badly cut hair, twisting a cheap locket around her index finger as she read the latest offering from a popular horror author. The picture was exactly the one Sara meant to present, accentuated by the gaudy, obviously cheap costume jewelry. The image fit Amber Jennings, and would be easily shed when she decided to move on to another city. Another state. She never kept any of her identities more than a few months.

The next half hour meandered by, the pace a welcome contrast to her usually hectic work schedule. When voices interrupted her concentration, she looked up, frowned slightly. A group of women in filmy, flowery dresses was trooping out of an inner room toward the exit, their good-byes disturbing the relative quiet of her sanctuary. They strolled out the door, trailing expensive perfume in their wake.

Returning to her book, Sara was once again lost in the author's imaginary world when a slight movement to her left disturbed her again. This time it was a solitary female, upwards of eighty, she'd guess, with the patrician bone structure that reflected beauty regardless of age, and pale, almost translucent skin.

But it wasn't the older woman's beauty that held Sara's attention; it was the way she was clutching the edge of a table, swaying slightly on her feet.

Hesitantly, Sara asked, "Are you all right?"

"Quite all right, thank you." The crisp words were delivered with just an air of haughtiness, and usually would have been enough to deter Sara from inquiring further. She guarded her own privacy too zealously to be at ease poking into others'. But for some reason memories picked that moment to swarm to the surface. Sean had had a grandmother he'd loved dearly. She'd been, he'd often claimed, the only member of his family who'd given a damn about him. Hundreds of times over the years Sara had reached for a phone, longing to dial that rest home in Illinois just to hear someone else mention his name. Each time realization of the risk had overpowered the emotion. Sara still made sure the woman knew she hadn't been forgotten, but she did so anonymously. It was safer, far safer for all involved.

The flicker of memory was enough to have her rising. Pulling up a chair, she said, "Why don't you sit down until it passes?"

The elderly lady aimed one fierce look at her, visibly battling her infirmity through sheer force of will. Then, the struggle obviously decided for her, she sank into the chair with a frustrated sigh. "Darn dizzy spells," she muttered, her eyes closing for an instant. "There's little I despise as much as the weakness that comes with the years."

"I suppose none of us like to show our vulnerabilities, regardless of age."

The woman's eyes snapped open again. "No," she murmured, studying Sara closely. "I imagine not. What's your name, young lady?"

"Amber."

"I'm Celeste. And since I've inconvenienced you this much, perhaps you wouldn't mind lending me your arm and walking me to my car."

Sara leaned forward and Celeste rose, clinging to her arm for support. "You aren't expecting to drive, are you?" she asked dubiously.

The older woman gave a surprisingly strong laugh. "Good heavens, no. My husband considered it extremely gauche for women to drive themselves, and although times have certainly changed, I suppose it's a bit late for me to learn driving skills." As they spoke they moved slowly through the door and down the wide steps outside. At their appearance, a gleaming black Rolls pulled to a stop beside the curb, and a uniformed driver got out, opening the back passenger door to the vehicle.

Once Celeste was ensconced in the back seat, she looked

up at Sara. "I'd like to repay you for your kindness. Would you care to accompany me home for tea?"

The invitation took Sara aback. "I…I'd better not. I have to get back to work soon."

Celeste waved a hand and the driver went around to the other side of the car, opening the passenger door. "I'll have Benjamin drive you when you have to go. Please don't waste time arguing, dear. I make it a point to get my own way. It's one of the few pleasures left to me."

Studying the woman, Sara noted the flush in her cheeks, which couldn't be blamed on the heat. They'd merely exchanged one air-conditioned environment for another. No doubt Celeste had a full staff and a family at home to see to her health. But Sara still felt compelled to accept, if only to see her home safely. There was little risk. Surely this sweet, frail woman wouldn't lead her to danger.

So she engaged in uncharacteristic small talk with the woman as the car made its way across town. After several minutes it turned off the street through an open gate and up a long winding driveway.

Sara fell silent in something approaching awe. The sprawling, ancient mansion was white, with small dormers marching along the roofline proclaiming its French architecture. She could almost imagine the centuries falling away to reveal hoopskirted ladies and gentlemen in cutaway coats sipping mint juleps on the wide veranda.

"Impressive, is it not?" Celeste said as the car drew to a stop before the house. "It was built by my ancestor Claude in 1722 for his wife, Pauline Fontenot." Simple pride rang in the woman's voice as she was helped from the car by the driver. Sara rounded the vehicle, and Celeste set her hand lightly on her arm as they climbed the steps. "Claude brought his young bride to New Orleans, after it was settled for King Louis XV. This house was damaged by the fire in 1794, but my great-great-grandfather, Jean-

Paul, presided over the restoration himself, and made sure the structure was duplicated exactly, rather than allowing the Spanish style of architecture to influence the rebuilding. My grandson is the ninth generation to live here, although—'' she made a moue of disappointment ''—he doesn't spend nearly enough time here.''

The long lineage the woman cited was difficult for Sara to comprehend. She hadn't known her own grandparents. Family hadn't meant a whole lot to her mother. Janie Parker had been most concerned with good times and handsome, fast-talking men. She'd made it her business to fill her life with both.

When they reached the huge, double front doors, Celeste showed Sara inside to a graceful tiled hall with vaulted ceilings supported by carved beams. After ordering iced tea from the servant who met them at the door, the older woman led Sara into an old-fashioned parlor, complete with furniture that looked as though it had traveled from France with Claude himself.

Celeste waved her to a chair facing the tall narrow windows gracing one wall. ''This is my favorite room, partly because of its view of the gardens. If I were feeling more stable today I'd take you on a tour of them. It's this awful blood pressure medication I'm on, of course. It sometimes causes the worst dizzy spells.''

''The gardens look lovely.'' There was a note of wistfulness in Sara's tone.

''They can be very peaceful.''

''Sometimes peace can be hard to find.''

''You are quite young, I think, to be so wise.''

''I'm twenty-one.'' The lie came to her lips automatically as she shaved two years off her age. Amber Jennings was twenty-one. And Sara Parker's age no longer mattered, since she'd ceased to exist six years ago.

''Ah, to be twenty-one again.'' Celeste smiled at her, a

dazzling display of charm that transcended her years. "I would be tempted to envy such youth had I many regrets."

"But you have no regrets, have you?" The words came from behind them, the voice amused. Sara stilled, finding something about it ominously familiar. "Shall we credit that to clean living or a convenient conscience?"

"Nicky!" Delight sounded in Celeste's tone, sparkled in her eyes. As the older woman offered a cheek for the tall, dark-haired newcomer to kiss, Sara stared, her feeling of foreboding changing to disbelief. Life, she'd often found, contained the cruelest of ironies. That had never been so apparent as right now.

Because the man straightening to greet her was none other than Nick Doucet.

"Amber, I'm thrilled that you will get to meet my grandson. Nicky, this is—"

"Amber Jennings," Nick murmured, an arrested look on his face. Sara's pulse tripped, and it didn't escape her that he used the last name she was currently going by. She had little time to reflect on that fact, however. With his dark gaze fixed on her, he crossed to her chair, took her hand in his. Raising it, he brushed his lips across her knuckles. "What a delightful surprise." The old-fashioned courtliness of his gesture was at odds with the pure wickedness in his eyes. "Welcome to my home."

Heat flashed through her, owing nothing to the temperature and everything to the simmering, latent sexuality he exuded. His voice was as smooth as velvet, meant for dark steamy rooms and rumpled satin sheets. The image that description conjured up was just a little too real, and had tension spiking through Sara's muscles.

"You know each other?" Puzzlement was evident in Celeste's voice as she watched their byplay.

"No."

"Yes."

Their simultaneous but contradictory responses had the older woman's brows climbing.

Sara felt compelled to explain, "Your grandson has come to the café where I work on a few occasions. That's all."

"For some reason Amber seems anxious to avoid me," Nick added, taking a seat next to his grandmother. "What a delightful surprise to find her here this afternoon, especially after she turned down my earlier invitation."

She gazed at him with genuine dislike. "If I'd had any idea that you were related to Celeste, you can be sure I wouldn't have come." In the next moment she flushed, realizing how that sounded, and sent an apologetic glance to the older woman. She needn't have bothered. Nick's grandmother gave all appearances of finding their conversation highly entertaining.

"So Amber rejected an invitation from you? How... fascinating."

"She appears to have a strange, and totally unnecessary, compulsion to avoid me." He broke off as a servant entered with a tray of iced tea.

Celeste accepted a glass and drank deeply from the cool beverage with obvious enjoyment. "Amber, please forgive my grandson. He has been outrageously spoiled by women, myself included. It does him good to be thwarted by one now and again."

Sara took a drink of her tea. "I have a feeling he's more in need of it than most."

The woman's eyes crinkled. "Again you are correct."

"I'm sitting right here," Nick pointed out. Lazily, he reached out to pick up his glass. As he drank, he took the opportunity to survey his grandmother critically for signs of fatigue. She looked frailer every time he came home, so he'd made his visits more frequent. Watching the indomitable matriarch of his family fade with each passing year was perhaps the only thing capable of touching his heart. "Why don't you tell me how the two of you happened to meet up?"

"Oh, I just met Amber at the library and we hit it off," his grandmother said airily. She was an accomplished liar, but not accomplished enough to fool him. Her color was high, and there was a slight tremor in her hand as she set down her glass. He thought he could guess something close to the truth, even if it wasn't forthcoming from his fiercely independent grandmother.

"I've enjoyed seeing your home." His attention shifted to Amber, who was studiously avoiding looking at him as she spoke to his grandmother. "But I really have to get going or I'll be late for work."

His brows skimmed upward when Celeste took Amber's hand in hers and gave it an affectionate squeeze. "It was such a pleasure, my dear. Thank you so much for everything." With the mantle of age, his grandmother had abandoned some of the niceties of polite society. She didn't waste time, or civility, on anyone she didn't hold in some esteem.

"I enjoyed meeting you." Amber's smile was the first genuine one Nick had seen from her, and his hand faltered for an instant in the act of raising his glass. As if she felt his gaze on her, her smile quickly faded, to be replaced with her more familiar wary mask.

"Perhaps we'll meet again. I think I would enjoy getting to know the woman who can hold her own with my grandson." Eyes twinkling, Celeste rose. "I'll tell Benjamin that you're ready to leave." With careful steps she left the parlor.

Nick took the opportunity to refill Amber's glass, noting the way she stilled as he drew closer. He could almost see the effort it took for her not to move away, and felt an element of admiration, tinged with amusement. She was determined not to show him even that small weakness. He understood that kind of control, possessed it himself. He wondered what kind of experiences had forged hers.

"Are you going to meet with Douglas tonight?" she asked.

She'd managed to surprise him. Taking his time setting the pitcher down and settling into his chair once more, he studied her. "Why?"

Her fingers worried the earring at her lobe. The nervous gesture was at odds with the defiance in her eyes. "It wasn't fair of you to make the meeting conditional upon my accompanying him."

"I don't play fair, Amber." A thought occurred to him then, and wouldn't be quieted. "What's your relationship with Fairmont?" He was adept at eliciting the information he wanted with far more finesse, but her answer mattered more than it should have.

"Are you asking if I serve him more than breakfast?"

"Do you?"

Silence stretched, while their gazes did battle. "No."

The elastic tension inside him that had stretched taut while he waited for her answer slowly relaxed. He hadn't thought so, but her defense of the man had had him reconsidering. "Good."

"Why do you care?"

"Because..." he paused to sip his iced tea "...I have no intention of entering into a business arrangement with a man I would later have to destroy."

Shock flickered across Sara's expression. Her hand clutching her glass, she rubbed her thumb over the condensation collected on it. "And I have no intention of accompanying him here tonight. Will you still help him?"

"I may. It depends on the figures he shows me."

"So...you're into investments?"

Smiles didn't come easily to him, but he felt one on his

lips now. "I make all sorts of investments. Some more lucrative than others."

From her expression it was obvious that his cryptic response failed to satisfy. But she didn't press him for details as other women might have done. Instead she said in a very matter-of-fact voice, "I won't sleep with you, you know."

The tea had difficulty passing the sudden knot in his throat. He hadn't expected such forthrightness from her, but then, he really didn't know Amber Jennings. Not at all. "I reserve the right to try and change your mind about that." He noted with interest the way her fingers flexed on her glass, and wondered if the action reflected anxiety or annoyance.

"You don't look like a man who enjoys wasting his time."

"I'm not."

Her glass made a small clink on the marble tabletop as she set it down, then rose. "I'd like to leave now."

"I'm sure Benjamin has the car ready."

She hesitated, then gave a nod. Turning to go, she halted a moment later, and said, "Please tell your grandmother again how much I enjoyed meeting her. She's a wonderful lady."

He made no effort to disguise the affection in his voice. "She is, yes." Strolling along beside her, he opened the front door for her when they'd crossed the hallway. The car was pulled up front, waiting. She started toward it without another word, and Nick followed her out onto the porch, watched her descend the steps. "Amber?"

She halted in the act of sliding into the car, and looked at him.

Raising his glass to her, he said, "I'll see you soon."

She made no comment, and he'd expected none. The car door slammed, and the vehicle pulled away. He was contemplating the winking taillights when he heard his grandmother's voice behind him.

"I like that girl, Nicky." She tucked her arm into his and he covered her fingers absently with his own. "You will leave her out of those games you play, *n'est-ce pas?*"

Broodingly, he watched the car as it turned out of the drive. "I'm not playing, *Grand-mère*. Not this time."

Chapter 2

Sleep could be unkind to those with blood on their hands. Nick tossed on the sweat-dampened sheets while faces loomed in his unconscious, each receding, to be replaced by yet another. And when an all too familiar shot ricocheted through his dreams, shattering his slumber, he woke with a start, his heart jackhammering in his chest.

He hauled in a deep breath, then another. He was used to the nightmares, but lately they'd become more frequent. More relentless. After wiping his perspiring face with the sheet, he tossed it aside, got out of bed.

Despite the darkness, his steps were sure as he crossed the room that had been his since childhood. Unmindful of his nudity, he opened the terrace doors and stepped out onto the little balcony that overlooked his grandmother's beloved gardens. There was a hint of a breeze, but it did little to cool his heated skin. The air was heavy with moisture. It would rain by tomorrow.

His muscles still quivered with the aftershocks of the

nightmare. From long practice he kept his breathing deep and steady, fighting off the sensation of suffocating. At one time that feeling had been a constant in his life. But those days were over, reenacted only in his dreams.

The scent of gardenias drifted toward him and his fingers clenched on the railing as he filled his lungs. But it wasn't the gardens he thought of this time, but the woman who hovered at the edge of his unconscious.

Amber. With her wide, catlike eyes and long sleek body, she reminded him of a feline, begging to be stroked. But that one wouldn't welcome petting, and most definitely not from him. She did everything in her power to avoid being touched by him at all.

Nick worked his shoulders, impatient with himself. He'd never been one to obsess over a woman, and if he wasn't careful, that's what Amber would become. An obsession. One that filled the mind and absorbed the senses. One that caused a man to forget all about obligation and focus solely on her.

She was a puzzle, with her badly cut hair and quick, nervous movements. Her anxious mannerisms, when she toyed with her earring or her necklace, were at odds with the cool, measuring look in her eye. It was intriguing to wonder which was the real woman—the nervous waif or the wary combatant. Whichever she was, she'd made no secret of her distrust of him.

If he were a better man, a kinder one, he'd forget all about Amber Jennings and leave her alone to live her life as she chose. But because he was neither, he knew he'd do nothing of the sort.

The promised rain hung low in the clouds, doing little more than releasing the occasional fat drop and keeping a miserable mugginess in the air. Sara waved to Candy as they parted ways for a few hours. She wasn't expected back until the dinner shift today, and the freedom of the next few hours beckoned. She'd been on edge all morning, and it was tempting to blame that fact on the weather. But in truth, Nick Doucet was at the root of the feeling.

Without meaning to, she'd watched for him all morning, his words from yesterday ringing in her mind.

I'll see you soon. Her memory all too accurately recalled the promise in his voice, the predatory, masculine intent in his eyes.

Her experience with men in recent years had been kept to a minimum, by her choice. There had been the waiter in Seattle, the one who had reminded her, in some slight way, of Sean. The resemblance had only been physical, and their encounter brief. She'd left town shortly after their relationship had started, and there had been no one since.

Dispassionately, she'd wondered from time to time if she was capable of feeling the type of desire that books rhapsodized over and movies glorified. Wondered if something vital in her had been broken years ago and could never work correctly again. She'd never regarded her lack with much regret. From what she'd witnessed, passion was an excuse, a weakness...and in the hands of some, a weapon.

But that didn't account for the razor sharp awareness that flared to life every time Doucet came close. And her own unfamiliar reaction was just one more reason for her to steer clear of him.

Ignoring the sullen threat in the clouds, she walked several more blocks until she came to a small market on the corner. Going inside, she selected some necessities and paused over the produce. She could take all her meals at the café on the days she worked, but she liked to have fresh fruit in her room for an occasional snack.

Thunder rumbled ominously, and with one eye on the sky, she paid for her purchases and hurried from the store.

"You took a chance coming out on a day like today without an umbrella."

Her spine stiffened as she recognized the voice. Without turning, she hurried even faster, to no avail. Nick merely fell into step beside her.

"Can I carry something?"

"No." A few drops of rain hit the pavement before her. It was too much to ask that, given no encouragement, he'd disappear. He was much too tenacious for that.

With his hands tucked into the pockets of his custom-fit linen trousers, he strolled along, seeming unconcerned as the drops fell with increasing urgency. "Perhaps it's difficult for you to believe, but I was raised as a Southern gentleman." He reached over to pry one of the bags from her fingers. "It's my duty to at least give the appearance of being helpful."

It was her reluctance to touch him, not his perseverance, that caused her to relinquish her grip on the bag. The nerves were back, flickering just below the surface of her skin, and she damned them almost as fiercely as she damned the man beside her. "Do Southern gentlemen normally stalk women who have made their disinterest clear?"

"Stalk?" He seemed to give the word consideration. "That seems a harsh conclusion, given the fact that the market you were shopping at is directly across the street from my family's offices." She looked at the nondescript brick building he indicated. "We could dodge in over there, and wait out the rain."

"Go ahead," she invited, walking faster. The precipitation was growing heavier. She'd be soaked by the time she reached her apartment. But there was no way she was going anywhere with him.

"Now what kind of gentleman would I be, Amber, if I didn't see a lady to her door?"

At the teasing words she whirled on him, wiping the rain from her face with a hunched shoulder. "It appears you would be a dense one, Doucet. Or maybe you're the type who can't stand the fact a woman isn't interested. Is that it, huh? Is it the challenge you enjoy?"

He'd stopped when she did, met her gaze with his enigmatic one. "I enjoy *you*."

Lightning sizzled, and Sara was unable to discern whether it was from the darkening sky or the chemistry sparking between them. She couldn't look away from him. She was inexperienced, but not stupid. It would be impossible to misidentify the predatory gleam of male intent in his eyes, or the corresponding frisson of pleasure shooting down her spine.

The sky opened up then, and the ensuing downpour succeeded in dispelling their silent communication. "C'mon." Nick cupped her elbow in his hand. The feel of his fingers on her chilled skin sent tendrils of warmth curling through her system, and although she tried to dislodge him, he held her firmly. Guiding her to a deep doorway up ahead, he allowed her to step beneath the protection it provided, then crowded in after her.

He was too close. Sara shrank back as far as she could, but if anything, he seemed to loom nearer. He didn't seem to notice her discomfiture at his proximity. He shook the moisture from his dark hair, finger combed it carelessly.

Her throat clogged. The white shirt he wore was plastered against his body, and she could see through it to his chest, with its covering of dark hair. His soaked trousers clung to his hard thighs, leaving no doubt about the muscular strength of his body. She moistened her lips, which had gone inexplicably dry. Thunder boomed, and she glanced out at the street. All the other pedestrians had taken cover, and even as she registered the logic of the action, there was a part of her that was tempted to bolt, to take her chances with the elements in an effort to escape this man. These feelings.

"Amber."

She didn't want to respond to that low raspy tone, didn't want to see the desire that would be stamped on his face. But her gaze raised of its own volition. And immediately the storm around them paled in comparison to the tempest between them.

Despite his earlier efforts, a lock of black hair had fallen across his forehead. His eyes were heavy-lidded, intent, and there was no mistaking the stamp of arousal on his face. It was there in the flare of his nostrils, in the skin stretched taut over his cheekbones. Her pulse leaped once before settling into a hard staccato beat.

His head lowered. There was no room to pull away. And even if she'd had the will to make a run for the street, it was doubtful that her legs would have obeyed the command to move. A strange lethargy had invaded her limbs, turning them weak and boneless.

She felt his breath warm her throat before his lips brushed against the pulse that was pounding there. Then that same barely perceptible caress whispered across her jaw, her eyelids, the corner of her mouth. He didn't touch her anywhere else, and that fact somehow made the light contact more sensual. Restrained, but full of promise. She shivered against him, but not from the dampness. Heat flashed between them, enough that she imagined the air around them should fill with steam.

The world narrowed, to include only this moment. This man. She thought he could surely hear her heart slamming against her chest. Imagined she could hear his. Her lips parted as his mouth hovered above hers.

The tip of his tongue traced the seam of her lips, with a light deft stroke that had her shuddering. He rubbed his mouth against hers savoringly, as if he wanted to absorb her flavor and brand her with his own.

And because he was close, all too close, to succeeding, she found the strength to turn her head.

"I have to go." She could barely form the words.

"Amber."

She used her elbows to wedge herself past him, not daring to look in the direction of that dulcet voice.

"I want to see you tonight."

The words sounded as though they'd been dragged from somewhere deep inside him. The blood pumped through her veins, and she struggled for composure. She'd never been in greater need of it. "I have to work."

"Then I'll come by for dinner."

Without responding, she walked away as swiftly as she could without running. Running would have been useless, at any rate. There was no way to outpace the emotions that even now were churning and crashing inside her like white water. No way to escape the certainty that she'd made a very grave mistake indeed by allowing Nick Doucet to touch her. To taste her.

She walked faster to outpace the memories. His flavor still lingered in her senses, and she felt oddly disoriented. Her thoughts were a jumble, and it wasn't until she heard the blare of a horn that she realized she'd nearly stepped off a curb in front of an oncoming car. Jumping back, she ignored the driver's rude suggestion and tried to control a shudder at her recent narrow escape. Both of them.

The rain was steady now, falling gently. Her grocery bags were plastic, so she didn't have to worry about them ripping, but everything she'd bought would have to be dried off before she put it away in her apartment. She looked forward to the task. Any distraction would be a welcome respite from her tumultuous thoughts.

Turning into a wide alley, she ducked her head against

the dampness as she headed for her apartment. The place barely qualified as such; located above a seafood market, it had rarely represented a haven to her. The smell of fish was impossible to erase, and the room was barely big enough for her bed, table and couch. The three-quarters bath attached was little more than a converted closet. But Sara felt an unusual eagerness to return to the place. Alone.

Slogging through the puddles, she kept her eye trained on the outside staircase that would take her to blessed peace, not to mention dryness. She passed a man who, despite his black rain slicker, looked almost as drenched as she was. The rest of the alley was deserted. Most people had more sense than to stroll the New Orleans streets in a storm.

"Sara Parker."

The words turned the rivers of rain on her skin into instant sheets of ice. For the space of an instant she almost convinced herself that she'd imagined them.

Until they were repeated.

"Sara Parker from Chicago." The voice was louder this time. The man was right behind her.

After a barely imperceptible hesitation, she quickly masked her reaction. Survival instincts, well honed, surged to the surface.

She schooled her expression to a politely quizzical mask before she turned. "If you're talking to me, you've got the wrong person."

The man smiled, a menacing grimace. "I don't think so." His arm raised and her throat seized. Her focus narrowed to the yawning black muzzle of the gun he had pointed at her head. "Victor Mannen sends his regards."

Time slowed, then froze. "I don't know what you're talking about." Distantly, she heard a shout, but didn't look away. She couldn't. The slow-motion sequence of death had her in its grip.

She was oddly unsurprised at the way she'd meet her end. It had only been a matter of time. Hadn't she always known it? But it seemed curiously ironic that only a few minutes ago in Nick's arms she'd felt more alive than she had in years, and now she was going to die.

The man's words were almost gentle. "Goodbye, Sara."

Tearing her gaze away from the finger squeezing the trigger, she ducked, swung one of her bags, hitting his gun hand. She heard a shot as she stumbled away, waited for the agonizing pain to tear through her.

And instead staggered as the man tumbled forward against her, his hands clutching at her before he crumpled at her feet.

She stared, transfixed by the crimson stain spreading from the tear in his slicker. Heard the groans emanating from him as he struggled to his knees. And then her mind flashed back to the scene in the safe house in Chicago. The bodies crumpled on the floor, soaked in blood. And Sean, sweet sad Sean, with his eyes wide and lifeless.

Abruptly, she dropped her bags, her purse, and ran. Blindly. Wildly. Away from her attacker and away from the images still vivid and raw after six years. And when strong arms came around her, halting her flight, she reacted like a thing possessed, struggling madly.

"Amber, it's over. It's over now."

It was the soothing tone that registered, rather than the words themselves. Nick. She sagged against him, unable to control the shudders racking her body. His arms were a safe harbor in a storm-tossed sea. Her mind grappled with incomprehensionable fragments. His presence in the alley. The gun still clasped in his hand. And the words he murmured over and over as his lips brushed her hair.

"Nothing will be allowed to hurt you, *ma petite*. No one. I promise you that."

* * *

"And you didn't recognize this guy? Had never seen him hanging around the café, on the street...?" Detective Matt Chatfield's narrowed blue regard was unwavering.

Sara shook her head. Someone had found a wool blanket for her and draped it around her soaked form. She huddled into it now, wishing its warmth could banish the chill in her veins.

The detective's gaze flicked to the man beside her. "How about you, Mr. Doucet?"

"I never got a look at him." Nick reached over, took one of Sara's icy hands in both of his. She gave it a discreet tug, but he held it firmly. "He never turned around."

"So you shot him in the back."

The detective's voice was carefully expressionless. Nick's was not. "I shot him in the center of the right shoulder blade so he'd drop the gun he had aimed at Amber. He did."

Sensing some undertone at play between the two men, Sara gave up the struggle to free her hand and studied them. Physically, they were almost opposites. They may have been around the same age, but Chatfield was taller, broader. His face was as enigmatic as Nick's, just as hard, but he was blond and blue eyed, in contrast to Nick's darkness. There was no mistaking the cop's toughness, but for some reason it was Nick who seemed the more dangerous.

"I suppose you have a permit to carry concealed?"

Silently Nick rose, withdrew his wallet and flipped it open. He passed it to the other man, who studied the permit before nodding, handing it back. "Where's your weapon now?"

"I gave it to the first uniform on the scene."

Chatfield raked him with a quick glance. "Ankle holster?" He waited for Nick's nod before asking, "What did you say you were doing in the alley, Mr. Doucet?"

There was an unsettling glitter in Nick's eyes, but his

tone was civil enough. ''Amber and I had parted several minutes earlier. I'd forgotten to give her back one of her bags.''

She looked at him, surprised. In her hurry to get away from him earlier that day she'd completely forgotten the sack of fruit he'd insisted on carrying for her. An involuntary shudder worked through her. If Nick's kisses hadn't completely shattered her logic, if she'd been capable of remembering to collect the bag before leaving him, she'd be dead right now. The cold certainty of that fact formed a brick of ice in her chest.

Settling back in his chair, Nick said, ''Wouldn't your time be better spent trying to find the guy who tried to kill her instead of going over all this information again?''

Imperturbably, Chatfield picked up his pen. ''I've got uniforms canvassing the area. From the amount of blood he lost, I doubt he got far.'' His gaze shifted to Sara again. ''Ms. Jennings, let's go over your statement again. You said the man didn't ask for your purse, for money. Did he say anything?''

Her chest squeezed tight as she sensed the minefield ahead. ''He said something, but I couldn't understand it. I thought he was talking to someone else. When I turned around, I saw his gun.''

The detective scribbled a note. ''Did you catch any of it at all?''

She manufactured a tired smile, strove to hide the tension in her body. ''When I noticed the gun I didn't pay attention to much else.''

''I think he mistook Amber for someone else. The name he called out was Sara. Sara Parker.''

Nick's words sent a slice of panic tearing through her. She hadn't guessed that he'd been close enough to hear the gunman's words. It took effort to keep her features impassive as Chatfield raised his brows, looked at her. "Do you know who this Sara Parker is?"

She shook her head, but the detective didn't look convinced. "She's not a friend of yours, maybe? Someone who has an enemy? 'Cuz maybe this guy didn't mistake you for her, after all. Maybe he thought you could lead him to her."

"I don't know anyone by that name." Her voice was firm, and her words were at least partially true. It had been a long time since she'd been Sara Parker. She'd left that identity half a country away, at least a lifetime ago.

"You're on the wrong track," Nick said bluntly. His fingers squeezed hers lightly, a reminder that he was holding her hand. "This guy wasn't after anyone else. He thought Amber was Parker, and she was going to die for it."

The detective made another notation on his pad. "Did he say anything else?"

Nick paused, glanced at Sara. When she didn't answer he said, "I couldn't make out everything. But I could have sworn I heard him mention Chicago."

Chatfield lifted a shoulder. "Well, who knows. We'll tug on those strings, see if they lead anywhere." His gaze shifted to a point behind them, and he rose. "Excuse me for a minute, would you, please?"

Sara's well-defined flight instinct was screaming at her, urging her to flee. She quelled it with effort. She couldn't stay in New Orleans now, of course. Her story, her identity, wouldn't stand up to scrutiny. If anyone started digging they'd find that Amber Jennings from Detroit, Michigan, had died twenty years ago. And it wouldn't be long before that discovery led to the next, far more risky one.

She didn't intend to stick around that long. She'd be packed and headed out of the state within an hour of leaving the station. It wasn't as though she lacked experience disappearing. She'd vanished dozens of times before.

But rarely had the thought left her feeling this desolated. And she didn't want to examine the source of that feeling too closely.

"Are you warming up, *chérie?*" Nick's voice sounded low and caressing in her ear, and she nodded, despite the chill that seemed to permeate her system. "Your hands are still like ice."

"Well, I can't say that I'm not looking forward to a hot shower."

"The detective should have enough for today. I'll tell him I'm taking you home. You could always come back in tomorrow." Nick rose and crossed the room before she could protest. She'd have to devise a way to dislodge him so she could make her escape. But for now, at least, she was grateful for a few moments to herself. The stress of the pretense she was engaged in, on top of her brush with death, was overloading a system already taxed by her unfamiliar reaction to Doucet.

"What the hell do you mean, there's no trace of him?"

Sara jerked, startled by the note of menace in Nick's voice. She turned to see him standing nearby with two police officers she didn't recognize, and the detective. Chatfield ushered them all to the table. "The gunman hasn't been found, Miss Jennings. I'm sorry."

Her stomach dropped at the detective's words. Moistening her lips, she said, "But... he was wounded. How could he have...''

"We think he may have had a car waiting nearby. But that doesn't mean we're not going to find him. If he shows up at a clinic or hospital, we'll get word of it."

If. The word reverberated in her mind. And surely the gunman would avoid seeking medical attention for that very reason. Which made it all the more imperative that she vanish quickly. Completely. She'd escaped the hit man in Phoenix three years ago, hadn't she? It was more comfortable to ignore the niggling inner voice that suggested maybe her escape that time had been sheer luck.

And maybe her luck was running out.

With a flick of his hand, Chatfield dismissed the officers and sank down in a chair opposite Sara, studying her gravely. "Miss Jennings, I want you to know there's still a good chance we're gonna catch this guy. I want you to go through a few books of mug shots, see if you recognize him. And I'll follow up on that mistaken-identity lead, because it seems like we might have hit the jackpot on that one."

Slowly, she raised her chin to look at him, dread circling in her stomach. "What do you mean?"

"I made a couple phone calls, checked some databases. There was a murder case about six years ago in Chicago, where the prime witness for the Justice Department disappeared. Her name was Sara Parker."

Over the last half-dozen years Sara had become an accomplished actress, but it took all her abilities now to gaze steadily at the man, to fight the fear and panic welling up inside her. "So you think this guy today came hunting for that witness and almost killed me instead?"

Chatfield gave a slow nod. "It seems possible. But I don't want you to worry. We're giving this close attention, and we'll have someone posted outside your apartment until we bring this guy in. Every effort will be made to guarantee your safety."

She gave an unamused laugh. "You can't really guarantee anything of the sort, can you, Detective? Nobody can."

"We'll do our best, ma'am." He got up and crossed the room, came back carrying a stack of books. She didn't bother telling him that his department's best wouldn't be enough. If the Department of Justice had failed so horribly, what could the New Orleans Police Department do? The answer was bleakly apparent.

Nothing.

Two hours later she flipped one of the books closed and rubbed her eyes. Chatfield looked up from his desk nearby. "Nobody familiar in there?"

"They're starting to all look alike. Maybe we could finish this tomorrow."

He got up and came to the table. "Sure. You've been through a lot today. I'll have a uniform drive you home and I'll tell Mr. Doucet you're leaving." Nick had stepped out to make some phone calls a few minutes earlier. It occurred to Sara that her departure couldn't come at a better time.

She let the blanket slip from her shoulders, and concentrated on folding it neatly. "I'll take the ride, but you don't need to bother Mr. Doucet."

The detective's shrewd blue eyes observed her carefully. "Okay. I just thought…I guess I figured the two of you were together."

"No." Sara lay the folded blanket over the chair and reached for her purse. "We're not together."

The policeman who took her home went into her apartment ahead of her, checked it for intruders, then turned to go. The process reminded Sara of the precariousness of her position here, the need for a swift escape.

"Thank you for the ride, Officer." Nerves stretched to the snapping point, she could barely conceal her impatience to have the man gone.

He seemed impervious to her tension, lingering in the doorway. "There'll be a car right outside, ma'am. You don't have to worry about a thing."

She managed a wan smile, waited for him to close the

door, and locked it after him. Then she flew into action. Her suitcase was dragged from beneath the bed, drawers opened, emptied into the bag. She spent little time on packing niceties; speed was of the essence. Swiftly, she cleared the closet of clothes. She didn't have much. It didn't make sense to spend the little money she had on things she'd only wear for a matter of months.

Each personality demanded a different wardrobe. She left the belly-showing sweaters and low-riding jeans. Amber Jennings had had an affection for the skimpy garments. Sara's next identity would be Amber's opposite.

For the same reason, she ignored the collection of cat statues placed carefully on the windowsills. She'd picked the whole set up at a flea market. Hailey, Carla, Amy—whoever she became next—wouldn't be a cat lover, but perhaps an avid sports fan.

On her hands and knees, she reached for the hem of the comforter, flipped it up. Searching for the pocket she'd carefully sewn in the fabric, she withdrew the bills she'd stuffed inside and jammed them in her purse.

Still on her knees, she froze when a knock sounded at the door. She wasn't proud of the first blinding wave of panic that washed over her. Nor the second emotion, which followed closely when she heard a voice call out, "Amber, it's Nick."

She closed her eyes, let her breath out with a rush. *Nick.* It was too much to ask that he wouldn't follow her home, but another five minutes and she could have missed him completely. It was also useless to damn fate. She'd learned that years ago.

Closing the suitcase, she shoved it beneath the bed, out of sight. "I'm getting ready to turn in."

"I need to talk to you, Amber. Open the door."

Sara threw a quick glance around to check that there was nothing to give her plans away, and then resigned herself to the inevitable. Moving swiftly, she went to the door, unlocked it. He hadn't changed his clothes; he'd come directly from the police station. For the first time it occurred to her that before they'd been caught in the storm, she'd never seen him look less than immaculate. His obviously custom-tailored clothes were wrinkled now, his expensive shoes probably ruined. But it didn't lessen the impact of his appearance. Didn't detract from the aura of latent power that surrounded him.

He pressed the flat of his hand against the door, as if expecting her to try to keep it closed against him. The idea had merit, but she knew it would be futile to try. Letting him push it open, she stepped back, and he followed her in. Immediately he shrank the apartment with his presence, and she knew that if she hadn't been leaving, she would have been reminded of him in this space each time she was in it.

"You haven't changed." His gaze raked her soggy clothes, then made a quick survey of the apartment, before returning to her. "Have you eaten?"

"I…no. I'm not hungry."

He let the door latch behind him, came farther into the room. "So if you haven't been eating or standing under a hot shower, what have you been doing?"

Because she didn't want to answer the question, she asked one of her own. "Why are you here, Nick?"

He slipped his hands in his pockets. "I'm not sure you should be left alone tonight."

She deliberately misunderstood his words. "I'm not alone. The officer who brought me home said there would be a car out front." She was counting on that, in fact, when she slipped out the back. "It's been a long day, and I'm exhausted."

He paid no attention to her words. "This room is freezing." Crossing the room, he went to close the window near her bed she routinely kept open. When his hands went to the sash she blurted, "Don't shut that!"

The alarm in her voice was unmistakable, so she swallowed, forced a calmer tone. "I like it open." She didn't miss the assessing look in his eyes as he stepped away from it slowly, nor the shift in his attention when he saw the flipped-up comforter that she'd forgotten to smooth back into place.

With a feeling of inevitability, she watched him go down on one knee, look at the edge of the suitcase partially revealed. Glancing at her again, he cocked an eyebrow. "Going somewhere?"

"Where would I be going?" Her shrug was deliberately casual. "I keep some of my clothes in that, because the space in here is limited…Nick!" He was pulling the suitcase out, popping its lid. He surveyed its full contents for a moment before rising, turning to her.

His voice was soft, almost inaudible. "Where are you going, Amber?"

She'd always had the ability to recognize when to cut her losses. Her chin tipped upward. "I'm not sticking around to be used as target practice in some crazy man's six-year-old vendetta."

He seemed to choose his words carefully. "If they find the guy they'll need you to identify him."

"They have to find him first, though, don't they?" She wasn't acting now. The words, the situation, was all too real. "Excuse me for not being a dutiful citizen. I have no intention of being used as live bait for a killer."

"And you were expecting to sneak by the NOPD with suitcase in hand?"

"There's a back door," she snapped.

"And another car posted there."

His words struck her hard in the chest. Stunned, she could only stare at him.

"They've got three officers posted around this building. You aren't going to be allowed to go anywhere. The department is taking this very seriously, especially while they think the gunman might have been related to a high profile case in Chicago."

Reaction set in, and she began to shake. There had to be a way out of here. She'd been in tighter spots than this and had always found an escape. But rarely had she already been this shaken, this stressed. "I won't stay, wondering when he's going to find me again. I can't."

"All right."

His words made no sense to her, especially with her mind already whirling with plans. "What? What do you mean?"

"I mean," he said calmly, bending to pick up the suitcase, "that if you really want to leave, I'll take you."

"You'll take me?" Distrust filtered through her panic. "You'll take me where?"

He regarded her patiently. "I'll get you out of the city. That's what you want, isn't it?"

Of course it was. And at the moment Sara was unable to think of a way to accomplish that on her own. A measure of cool reason returned. It would be easy enough to slip away from Nick once he'd gotten her out of New Orleans. Her choices right now were depressingly limited.

"All right." If her agreement surprised him there was no sign of it on his face. He merely turned and headed toward the door, leaving her to follow. And as she trailed after him, she tried to quiet the inner alarm that warned her she was only exchanging one kind of danger for another.

Chapter 3

Nick sat in a plush armchair in his private jet and studied Sara as she slept on the couch opposite him. To watch the even rise and fall of her chest, the softness that came over features usually kept in an expressionless mask, seemed curiously intimate, even intrusive.

Since he wasn't a man to grow fascinated by a woman, he excused his interest by telling himself there could be quite a bit to learn from the act. A person with no fears and nothing to hide might well sleep spread out, arms flung wide. It was telling that Amber slept curled up in a ball, burrowed into the softness of the couch.

And it was disturbing to him to feel this primal surge of protectiveness just watching her.

Frowning slightly, he considered the unfamiliar emotion. With the exception of his grandmother, people didn't get close enough to him to touch him in any way. The one time he'd relaxed his guard had resulted in tragedy. It was a lesson he'd never forgotten. He didn't even know this woman, and it was maddening to have to keep reminding himself of that. Maddening to know just how much he wanted to.

He shifted a bit, strangely uncomfortable with the fact. However, he wasn't one to dodge the truth, even when it was pointed straight at him. He didn't make the mistake of thinking it would be easy to gain her trust. She'd accepted his help only because she'd had no other options. He realized that. But he was a man who knew women— knew how to strip away the layers of complexities and defenses to bare the essential woman beneath.

Nature had given him one gift toward that end, and birth had determined another. Women were attracted to his looks and intrigued by his money. But if Nick was interested, they gained far more from him than the superficial. He truly enjoyed females—their minds, their softness, the little quirks that made each an individual. Despite their differences, all wanted the same thing, and he gave it freely—his attention, his respect, if not his heart. He enjoyed watching a woman warm under his care. Perhaps it was overcompensation for feeling little or nothing himself. It didn't matter. Because as he watched Amber sleep he thought he had never seen a woman more in need of a man's attention. Nor one more determined to fight it.

She stirred a bit, capturing his gaze again. Her eyelids didn't flutter; awareness didn't return slowly. Her eyes just opened in the next moment, and she appeared instantly alert. He imagined he awakened much the same way, even without the nightmares to rouse him. And when the familiar guarded mask slipped over her features, he was struck, not for the first time, of that similarity between them, as well.

''What time is it?'' She sat up, raked her fingers through her hair. She'd showered once they'd boarded the jet, and changed her clothes. Now she was tilting her head, peering across the aisle.

Raising his wrist, he looked at his watch. "About 3:00 a.m. We're nearly there, but you could have slept a bit longer."

She didn't respond, and he wondered if she felt a bit dazed by the rapid series of shocks she'd undergone in the last twelve hours. It would be enough to sucker punch most other people. But if Amber was stunned at all it didn't show. Instead, she looked at him steadily. "This could get you into trouble with Chatfield and the NOPD, couldn't it?"

Her words gave him pause. Was she actually concerned about him? "I'll call from the house in the Keys when we get there. I imagine they'll be unhappy, but as long as I agree to bring you back when they catch the suspect, I don't anticipate a problem." At least, not a problem he'd concern himself with.

"The Keys?"

"A series of small islands off the coast of Florida. I've got a place on Key Largo. Have you ever been there?"

She merely shook her head, and he felt a flicker of impatience, one he ruthlessly squashed. She was as close-mouthed as any woman he'd ever met, determined to reveal nothing personal about herself at all. And because he recognized that her reticence mirrored his own, he also realized it was a wedge she used to prevent him from getting too close.

"Approaching the island. Landing in minutes."

At the pilot's voice, Nick gestured toward a chair. "We'll need to put our seat belts back on."

She did as he bade without comment, settling into the seat. Thoughtfully, his gaze lingered on the death grip she exerted on the armrests. Fear of flying? Or just of landings? He didn't know, and already knew better than to ask.

Abruptly, his earlier impatience drained away. Getting to know Amber was a process of fitting miniscule pieces together in an effort to construct a bigger, constantly shifting picture. He fastened his own seat belt, feeling a flicker of anticipation. Before they left the island again, he vowed, he'd know everything there was to know about the woman.

"There are four bedrooms. Mine is the front one. You may take your pick from the other three."

Rather than demurring politely, Amber took Nick at his word and followed him from one room to the other. She didn't merely peek into the bedrooms, but walked inside and seemed to pay an inordinate amount of attention to the windows.

The scene from her apartment flashed into his mind. *Don't shut that! I like it open.* And again he found himself wondering whether her desire for the open window was induced by preference or need.

"I'll take this one," she finally decided, after looking at the three selections. The one she'd chosen was across the hall from his, and faced the ocean. But he had a feeling it was the porch roof right below the window, rather than the spectacular view it afforded, that had decided her.

He didn't comment on her choice, merely set her suitcase down near the closet. Then he turned to face her, hands tucked into his pockets. "There's an adjoining bath, and I called ahead, had the kitchen fully stocked. Sleep as late as you want. I'll see you in the morning. We'll have a big breakfast."

A small smile flickered across her mouth. "It's already morning, and I rarely eat breakfast."

He was striding to the door. "You'll need your strength tomorrow. I'm going to start showing you some self-defense tactics. Do you know how to shoot a gun?"

At her silence he glanced back, saw her jaw hanging open. "No. Why would you want to do that?"

He reached the door, rested a hand on the jamb. "So you'll feel safe, Amber." While she was still regarding him from rounded eyes, he gently closed the door behind him, but didn't walk away. Not yet. He waited. One minute. Two. Then he heard her footsteps, a pause, the slight scrape of wood against wood.

She'd opened the window.

From the position of the sun in the sky, Sara concluded that she'd slept far later than normal. She rarely had the opportunity to sleep late, and even more rarely, the inclination. Sleep meant dreaming, and her dreams had never made for restful nights.

As she showered and dressed, she considered the surreal sequence of events that had brought her here. Nick had managed their escape with ruthless efficiency. With her elbow in one hand and her suitcase in the other, he'd walked her out the front door of her apartment building, right up to the cruiser parked at the curb. He'd informed the officer inside that he planned to take Sara home with him, even inviting him to contact Chatfield about the idea. Nick had given him his address, then guided Sara to the car he'd parked illegally on the other side of the street.

Back at his family home, he had gently coerced her to eat a light dinner, and to speak with his grandmother again. Although it was obvious that Celeste was curious about her sudden reappearance, this time with Nick, she made no mention of it.

Then, following a timeline known only to himself, he'd risen, kissed his grandmother's cheek and guided Sara out the back, across the grounds. When she'd seen the chopper on the pad waiting for them, the whole scene had taken on a James Bondish aura.

Mansions. Helicopters. Private jets. Beach homes. She'd lived in dozens of states over the last few years, donned as many identities. But her lifestyle had remained constant. With no friends or family to help her, no education, and credentials that wouldn't stand up to scrutiny, she worked minimum-wage jobs, staying in clean but cramped apartments. It was no surprise to her that money could make a great many things possible. But it did surprise her that Nick Doucet would use his to help her.

Toweling her hair with one hand now, she walked to the window. The sun turned the water a shattering blue that hurt the eyes even as it beckoned the body. She cupped a hand to shield her gaze and watched as a figure swam up to shore, then rose out of the ocean.

Nick. Her blood pumped warm and molten. He strode naked out of the water, like a mythical god rising from the waves. With his hair slicked back and that glorious body gilded by the sun, every bone, sinew and muscle was highlighted in sensuous detail.

Her mouth went abruptly dry. The day in the rainstorm…yesterday?…she'd guessed at the power in his lean hard body, but nothing in her experience would have led her to imagine the reality. She was unused to such imaginings, in any case.

At that moment he looked up, and their gazes met for an instant. An echo of the electricity that had flowed between them the day before flickered to life. Dismayed by the intensity of her reaction, she stepped away, strangely shaken. She was almost convinced that she had nothing to fear from the man.

But she was no longer certain she could make the same claim about herself.

When Nick offered her another Belgian waffle, she pushed her plate out of reach. "No, thanks. I usually work through breakfast, remember?"

"We're going to have to change your eating habits. You need to build muscle."

His casual assessment of her needs annoyed her. "I prefer my weak useless build, thanks."

His dark eyes met hers. For an instant, she was reminded of the look they'd exchanged earlier when he'd caught her watching him come out of the ocean. When she'd admired *his* build. To hide her response at the memory, she reached for her orange juice.

"I was serious last night, Amber. For your own peace of mind you need to learn to defend yourself. I'm not suggesting it will help in every situation, but having some skills in that regard will make you feel more secure.

"I can manage on my own."

"Really?" He matched her challenging tone. "How'd you sleep last night?"

Her hand faltered, very slightly, in the act of setting down her glass. "Fine, why?"

His smile was faint. "Liar. But that will change. You'll be tired enough from our daily workouts to get a decent night's rest. Sleep is important to overall health, too."

She was starting to get a really bad feeling about all this. "What did you have in mind?"

The wariness in her voice seemed to amuse him. "Nothing too diabolical. Daily running. Conditioning. Self-defense tactics. Have you been following any sort of fitness regime?"

It was all she could do not to laugh. "No, I've been kept rather busy working for a living." And staying alive.

Imperturbably, he wiped his mouth with his napkin and rose. "Put on a pair of tennis shoes and meet me outside." He left the room, seemingly unaware of her glare. She really shouldn't be surprised that he was a man used to issuing orders. But she'd never been particularly fond of following someone else's directives. The time was nearing for Nick Doucet to find that out for himself.

An hour later she was bent over, hands resting on her knees, breath sawing in and out of tortured lungs. She hated running, always had. Wasn't this why she'd failed gym in ninth grade? Well, that, and the fact she'd skipped the class most weeks. Even then development of a healthy lifestyle had been the least of her worries.

She heard footsteps approaching, then a pair of hard masculine legs filled her vision. Refusing to look up, she willed her breathing to even out.

"Not bad for the first time. We'll try again after supper, see if you can push it a little farther."

Without changing position, she slowly raised her head. "You have got to be kidding." Didn't he realize that she'd felt like dropping ten minutes ago? It had taken sheer stubborn pride to get her this far, and she knew darn well they hadn't been jogging for more than twenty minutes.

"C'mon. You can walk back."

Crawling was more her speed at this point, but it seemed she had more pride than sense. She straightened, turned back toward his house. "Look," she said, when she could speak without wheezing. "I appreciate the thought you've put into this."

That put another of those faint smiles on his lips. "No, you don't. But you will."

He wanted honesty? Fine. "You're right, I don't. I also don't see the point."

"Running is good conditioning, and speed can also come in handy if someone is after you."

"Why didn't I think of that?" she asked, not bothering to disguise the sarcasm in her tone. "I could have outrun that bullet yesterday."

He was showing an irritating ability to ignore her. "If

you're in shape, you can fight back. I don't mean like taking on a guy twice your size, but having some moves that can injure him so you can get away." He cast a critical gaze up and down her form. "You've got a good stride and you don't run like a girl. Those are two factors in your favor."

She wondered what she ran like if it wasn't a girl, but wisely refrained from asking. Her breath was better saved for getting back to his place without embarrassing herself.

He allowed her to collapse for half an hour in one of the chairs on his deck, and drink two glasses of ice water, before nudging her again. "All right. It's time for the next round."

She didn't bother to open her eyes. "No."

A moment ticked by. And then another. It took effort not to look at him. She could feel his calm perusal of her still form. But in the next moment her eyes flew open, in alarm, as she found herself being carried off in his arms. "Nick! Put me down."

"Of course." Despite the agreeable tone, he didn't set her on her feet until they'd reached the destination he'd obviously had in mind. The room at the back of the house held various pieces of weight training equipment, with a plastic-encased foam mat on the floor.

Her patience snapped. "I'm not doing this, do you understand? I have no interest in learning karate or whatever the heck you want to teach me."

He slipped out of his shoes. "Teaching you the martial arts would require a bit more time than we have to spend. All I'm going to do is show you some basic defense maneuvers that might buy you some time or scare off a mugger."

A mugger? She almost gave an incredulous laugh. As if a mugger was at the top of her worries. Victor Mannen hadn't hired muggers to stalk her for the last six years. It wasn't losing her purse that she feared every time she walked down the street. Nick might think he was helping her with this crazy self-defense and conditioning course he was embarked on, but she'd found the best defense was not to get caught in the first place. She preferred to expend her energies to that end.

"Take off your shoes and socks."

"No. I'm not doing this."

With a shrug he approached her on the mat, and she warily backed away. "Let's start with the basics. If you see the guy before he grabs you, you've got the chance to run. But what if he comes up on you from behind?" With one smooth movement he stepped in back of her, clasped one arm lightly around her neck. "Show me what you would do to escape from this hold."

Ice splintered in her veins. She didn't move. Couldn't. "Let me go." The demand wasn't as strong as she would have liked, but its message was clear.

"There are three ways to break a hold like this, and I'll teach you all of them."

She knew that low voice in her ear belonged to Nick. Logically she knew it. But logic didn't always dictate emotion.

"I mean it, Nick. Let me go, *now!*"

"Show me what you'd do, Amber. The guy has you like this, leaving his other hand free to—"

His words were cut off as she erupted in a flurry of motion. Blinded by panic as she was, there was no strategy in her movements. Only instinct, raw and primal, screaming for release. She was a whirlwind of biting, kicking, scratching, gouging actions, with real fear as the impetus. It was long moments before she became aware that she was free; even longer before Nick's voice, soothing, with an underlying note of grimness, registered. "It's all right, Amber. It's all right. No one's touching you, see? There's no one here." He used the same rhythmic cadence he would use to calm a frightened animal. "Take my hand." She stared at it, outstretched toward her. There were angry scratches on the back of his wrist. Scratches she'd put there. She shuddered, wrapped her arms around herself.

"Take my hand, Amber. I'm not going to hurt you. Look at me."

But she couldn't. She didn't want to see his expression, whether it be one of horrified fascination, or something even worse. Didn't want to stand before him, raw and more exposed than she'd been in years. Demons could lurk inside for any number of years, partially hidden, tempting one to believe they didn't exist anymore. It made it all the more bitter when they sprang forth, mocking her efforts to keep them buried.

She lurched forward, not sure her feet would work, half-surprised when they did. Brushing past his outstretched hand, she crossed the room, praying for the strength to make it upstairs. And wishing with all her heart that she'd never accepted Nick Doucet's offer of help.

Nick made no move to stop her. When she'd turned toward him again he'd been prepared for tears, would have preferred them to the haunted look in her eyes. That look had hit him with a force far greater than any of the blows she'd managed to land.

He rubbed his hand over his jaw, more shaken than he'd like to admit. The woman was having too great an effect on him, so much so that he couldn't even predict his own reactions. It was a totally unfamiliar occurrence, and it couldn't be allowed to continue.

He knew from brutal experience what happened when he lost his objectivity on a case. People wound up dead. Letting down his guard, even a fraction, increased the danger. So he was going to have to find a way to manage this…connection to Amber Jennings, without compromising the assignment. The reminder stiffened his resolve, but the fact that he'd needed it at all was worrisome.

Hearing a sound in the doorway, he slowly raised his gaze. She was watching him, her face ashen, but otherwise composed.

"I'm…sorry for what just happened."

Her words released something fierce inside him. "You don't owe me an apology."

She didn't argue, just continued standing there with ramrod straight posture that almost completely hid the trembling in her limbs. "I…I want to learn what you tried to teach me." She attempted a smile, but couldn't quite manage to pull it off. "I want to learn how to defend myself. And how to shoot."

For a man who'd just considered the importance of governing his reactions to the woman, he was doing a damn poor job of taking his own advice now. She looked like a strong wind would knock her over. It was all he could do not to go to her, lend her his support. And knowing what his touch had done to her only a few minutes earlier made him long to put his fist through a wall. "All right." His voice was clipped. "We'll start again tomorrow."

"No, today." If his tone was grim, so was hers. "I won't freak again, I promise."

He stared at her, recognizing the barely smoothed nerves and the savage determination in her expression. And realized the courage it had taken her to approach her own fears head-on. "All right. Let's try it again." He wasn't about to make the same mistake he'd made earlier, so he led her to the body-size punching bag hanging in the corner. "Back up against the bag. It's the attacker." With effort he kept his voice brisk and impersonal. "If your hands are free, you clasp them together—" he demonstrated "—and drive your elbows back into his stomach."

He watched, issued suggestions, and she practiced with a stoic sense of purpose that had been missing earlier. He showed her how to place her fingers together in one straight line, and how to use them to jab someone in the throat to disable him. He bent his wrist back and demonstrated how to use the heel of the palm beneath an attacker's nose with enough force to drive him back, giving her opportunity to flee.

"We'll concentrate on defensive moves, techniques that will buy you enough time to turn and run."

"Can't you teach me how to take an opponent down?"

He shook his head, reached out and repositioned her hands. "Your build and strength are against you. You just need enough moves to take the attacker by surprise and cause some serious pain." His lips curled briefly. Far from the wild, frantic woman who had run from the room earlier, she was hanging on his words now with a fierce purpose that was impossible to miss. He didn't have the faintest idea what had caused the change, but he promised himself that soon he'd find out.

When she was perspiring from her exertions, he said, "That's enough for today."

She didn't argue. Bending her head, she wiped her forehead with the edge of her T-shirt, revealing a band of soft, smooth skin. "Now we'll practice shooting."

"I think we've done enough for one day."

"I want to learn."

He was beginning to observe a rather noticeable stubborn streak in her. With a mental shrug, he acquiesced, and drove her across the island to a shooting range.

Half an hour later, with his hands on his hips, Nick surveyed the target outline she was practicing on. She'd listened to his instructions carefully before emptying the clip in her gun, but there wasn't a mark on the cardboard.

Cocking an eyebrow, he strolled back to her. "That was an interesting start," he said through his headset.

She glowered at the weapon she held. "I don't like guns."

That was easy enough to discern. It showed in the way she looked at them, full of suspicion and perhaps a glimmer of fear. Despite his repeated suggestions, she still held the weapon gingerly, instead of clasping it firmly in her hand.

With more patience than he would have dreamed he possessed, Nick reloaded her weapon, handed it back to her. "Okay, let's start again. Show me your stance." At least she'd gotten that part right, he noted. "Good. Feet shoulder width apart, and remember, the gun is an extension of your arm. Use your other hand to brace it." If she'd been anyone else he would have stepped up behind her, guided her hands into the proper position with his own. Instead, he reached over, attempted to arrange them correctly as he murmured directions. "All right. Try it again and don't close your eyes this time."

Her second attempt was slightly more accurate than the first. There was a hole squarely in the center of the outline, which he chalked up to luck, and a few others scattered around the outer edge.

"Better. Want to try it again?"

She relinquished the gun to him just a little too eagerly. "Tomorrow, all right?"

He nodded and took off his headset. When he would have turned away, she caught his sleeve to stop him. His gaze dropped to her slim hand for a second before she let it fall to her side. "I just wanted...to thank you, I guess. For everything. Yesterday...helping me leave last night...and today. I guess I never did thank you for saving my life."

The words sounded as though they were hard for her to

form. They were harder, much harder, for him to hear. He ejected the spent cartridge from her weapon with savage force. "I don't want your gratitude, Amber."

"What do you want?"

The quiet question, no less intense for its lack of volume, snared his attention. Slowly his gaze raised to hers. "I think you already know the answer to that."

To her credit, she didn't flinch. "I told you once…"

"That you wouldn't sleep with me." He shifted his focus once more to the gun, prepared to hand it in.

"It's not fair…"

"If you're concerned for my feelings, don't be." He gestured for a nearby employee to come and get the weapon and ear guards. "I rarely do anything for altruistic reasons." His words served a twofold purpose. They should hold a warning for her, one she'd be wise to heed.

And they should serve as a warning to him.

Chapter 4

Victor Mannen straightened one tailored suit sleeve and suppressed the rage throbbing at his temples. Control was the true mark of breeding, and above all else he considered himself well-bred. The battle, however, was difficult. There were few things more infuriating than incompetence.

When he returned his attention to his phone conversation again, he made certain that nothing but polite interest sounded in his voice. "You disappoint me, Robert. You've given me nothing new."

Special Agent Robert Thorson's tone was entirely too casual for Victor's liking. "There's nothing else to tell. And believe me, I put my ass on the line keeping you updated."

Mannen thought disparagingly of the man's ample form. "A substantial danger, to be sure, but you are compensated for being accurate and in-depth. This information is neither."

"I can appreciate your concern, sir, but if there were

anything else to tell, I'd know about it. Nothing happens in the Department of Justice without coming through my office first. Like I said, they're close to shutting Golden Enterprises down. We've got agents tugging at every string they can find in your operation, and if nothing else, they intend to keep you tied up fighting our lawyers. If you can liquefy, you should pull your money out now.''

Bringing the seventeenth-century wine flute to his lips, Victor sipped from the fine crystal and resisted the urge to snap its slender stem. If incompetence was offensive, stupidity was intolerable.

With practice, he kept his voice smoothly melodious. ''How gracious you are to offer me the benefit of your advice. You can't imagine how I value it.''

Wariness threaded the agent's words. ''Of course, you know the police are looking to pin the Delgado murder on you. But as far as I've been able to discover, they've got nothing solid to trace him to you.''

''Delgado was a vicious criminal who overdosed in jail on his own heart medication. What could that possibly have to do with me?'' Mannen paused. The delicious irony of the man's demise still managed to amuse him. ''I'm more concerned about any renewed interest at Justice regarding that irritating murder charge your department leveled at me six years ago.''

The silence that stretched following his words gave him his answer, even if it wasn't the one he'd hoped for. The agent hadn't heard of it. Yet Mannen had no reason to disbelieve the report from the new source he'd cultivated. Thorson's ignorance of the matter indicated that either Justice suspected him of leaking information, or that he didn't wield as much power in the department as he once had. Either way, the man had outlived his usefulness.

''There hasn't been any talk to that effect. How could

there be? The only surviving witness hasn't surfaced for years."

"Perhaps you're right." Victor sipped again. "I'm worrying excessively." He set the wine flute on the table and prepared to end the conversation. "You'll contact me if you hear more."

"Of course."

Victor hung up the phone and studied the expensive wine in his glass, admiring the way the chandelier overhead laced the liquid with shards of color. It wasn't enough to savor the taste of the wine, he reflected. One really needed to experience it with all the senses. After several moments, he murmured, "Franklin." The massive man who was his new assistant came to attention. "I fear our friend is no longer of assistance to me."

"Shall I take care of that for you?"

"Please do so. Allow him to return to D.C. first. The city has such a nasty reputation for violence, his death will make fewer waves there."

The other man nodded and disappeared into the next room.

Mannen contemplated his surroundings in the penthouse he'd rented for the day. When traveling he always liked to take some of his own things with him to maximize comfort. Hence the antique crystal, the rare wine and the exquisite lace tablecloth. Certain standards must be upheld to consider oneself civilized.

His lip curled slightly. Despite his ire with Thorson, he had of course divested himself of as many of his connections to Golden Enterprises as possible. But with the huge conglomerate inoperable, it had become necessary to find other ways to supplement his finances. Fortunately, he'd never lacked ingenuity. His newest venture might well be the most lucrative to date.

Smiling at the thought, he brought the glass to his lips

again. He didn't spare a thought for any obstacles in his
path. Obstacles were no deterrent to a man of his means.
He simply eliminated them.

Sara pushed herself harder, even though her thigh muscles screamed in protest. It wasn't an innate competitive
streak that made her reluctant to fall too far behind Nick,
at least not completely. The man was obviously in superb
condition, whereas her idea of running was to seek the
nearest shelter from rain. But it was a matter of pride that
she improve the time and distance she'd accomplished yesterday. And the day before that.

"Let's take a breather."

Since he didn't even appear winded yet, she knew the
suggestion was more for her benefit than for his own. She
ignored it, but settled into a slower pace that would give
her hammering heart a rest. And as she had the two previous days, she used the opportunity to study her surroundings.

Out of habit and necessity she'd made mental notes of
escape routes off the island. Nick had been right on one
point—she needed to learn to defend herself. She'd become an expert on how to create new, believable identities,
how to get jobs when references weren't available, how to
recognize when it was time to leave one place and start
over in another. Survival techniques, all of them. But the
lessons Nick was providing involved survival of another
kind. And they offered an opportunity she could ill afford
to pass up.

That was the only reason she hadn't left yet, but that
didn't mean she hadn't prepared for her departure. Their
runs had given her a chance to scout the area, as had her
nightly forays when she'd climb out her window onto the
porch roof and shimmy down the drain spout. She'd made
note of which of the nearest houses had boats, but the

knowledge probably wouldn't help her. She'd yet to discover one that had the keys left in it. And since her skills didn't extend to hot-wiring engines, she'd start checking cars in the proximity tonight.

She suppressed a prickle of conscience. Conscience was a luxury for someone who lived by her wits. There was no need to waste sympathy on Doucet, at any rate. Whatever his reasons for bringing her here, she doubted her absence would disturb him for long.

Sending the man a sidelong glance, she noted that he ran as he did everything else—effortlessly. The sight of him in running clothes was always disconcerting. He was usually beautifully dressed in tailored, obviously expensive garments. The garb failed to mask his danger, but did lend it a polished edge. When he ran, however, he wore a sweatshirt with the sleeves torn out, shorts that showed the muscles bunching and releasing in his lean legs. Without the sheen of civility the more formal clothes afforded, he projected an aura of certain menace. One she'd do well to heed.

He slowed, his hand reaching out to clasp her wrist, forcing her to stop. "You need a break. If you push your body too hard you'll have a difficult time getting out of bed in the morning."

It was hard to protest when her muscles were quivering like Jell-O. "I have to cool down."

He nodded and released her, then adjusted his stride to hers as she set a fast walking pace. "You're really not in bad shape for someone who hasn't exercised regularly."

The compliment amused her. "Well, waitressing has me walking miles a day between the kitchen and tables, and the trays I carry aren't exactly light."

"Is that what you've always done? Wait tables?"

Deeply ingrained caution had her delivering a lie. "The

only jobs I've ever held. With tips, the salary allows me to get by.''

''And is that all you want? Just to get by?''

His question scraped a nerve. It had been a lifetime since she'd been able to consider what *she* wanted. Her long ago dream of helping others through nursing or social work seemed peculiarly ironic. It was all she could manage each day just to stay alive. ''We can't all be handed businesses that have been in the family for generations.''

Nick didn't seem to take offense at the caustic observation. ''I suppose not.'' There wasn't a hint of impatience in his tone, and not for the first time Sara wondered where he'd learned his control. Because if she was guarded, this man had a regular force field around him.

Squelching her curiosity, she concentrated on her stride. It wouldn't do to let herself wonder about him. She wasn't planning on staying long enough to ask the questions that plagued her. And she certainly wasn't expecting to let him get close enough for the answers to matter.

''Actually, my grandfather still has a tight grip on the family import business, with the occasional aid of my father. I'm not in New Orleans often enough to do the job justice.''

''Ah, that's right. I suppose you're tending to those investments you mentioned.'' The conversation almost distracted Sara from the burning of her sore muscles.

''Among other things, yes.''

''You don't get to be as good as you are in martial arts, conditioning and shooting from dealing with stocks and bonds.'' She noted the abrupt stillness that came over his features. ''I mean, I hear Wall Street is tough, but not that tough.''

He was silent for so long she thought he wouldn't answer. She didn't know which of them was more surprised when he finally said, "Perhaps not, but Army Special Ops is."

Her heart, which had been beating so furiously a moment ago, seemed to stop. "You're in the army?" She tried to imagine him as a recruit taking orders, and failed to do so.

He nudged her, one hand to the small of her back, to get her moving again. "I *used* to be in the army. The Green Berets. A lifetime ago."

She couldn't seem to tear her gaze away from him. Yes, that would explain his extraordinary control, his well-conditioned body, and the subtle threat he projected. The Green Berets. She might not have a high school diploma, but even she had heard of the highly trained unconventional warfare team. They were the forces given the most perilous assignments, in the riskiest places. No wonder he'd seemed to overshadow even the tough NOPD detective. She couldn't imagine the situations Nick had been in. Or the things he'd done.

Her palms had dampened, and she rubbed them on the tail of her shirt. "How long have you been out?"

"Five years."

His voice was clipped, as though he was already regretting the disclosure. But Sara didn't heed the warning signs. "Why did you leave?"

An imperceptible flame leaped in his eyes, which were fixed on her own. "Deep cover can be reality altering. It's easy to lose sight of what's real, what's important." His voice, his gaze, were hypnotic. "There comes a time when it's impossible to tell where your false identity begins and where you end. When you start to question your motives, your goals... If you're lucky, you get out before you make a mistake that someone else ends up paying for."

He didn't voice the words left unsaid. He didn't have to. She knew what happened when innocents were drawn into situations not of their own making. She swallowed hard, his low, rough words striking a chord within her. Because he'd just described how she'd spent the last six years of her life. She recognized the look of haunting regret in his eyes.

She faced it in the mirror every day.

"Eat. You need the fuel."

At Nick's command, Sara set down the fork she'd been using to disinterestedly stir her food, and shot him an irritated look. "You give a lot of orders."

Although he didn't smile, his face lightened a fraction. "Most of which you ignore."

She now knew where that innate authority of his stemmed from, but the knowledge didn't make her any more amenable to being told what to do. "I've never been much for following directions."

"If you don't care for the shrimp, I can have Marta make you something else."

Sara shook her head. "The food's fine. It's just the heat and exercise. I'm finding our daily routines affecting my appetite, that's all."

His dark gaze on her, he said, "Exercise can depress the appetite, but you have to feed muscle to build it."

"I don't need to be an Amazon to excel at the lessons you're teaching."

"No, but you need stamina and strength to disable an opponent long enough to get away from him." He considered her for a moment longer. "Was that experience in New Orleans the first time you've been attacked?"

The ground had just become treacherous. She'd developed a remarkable aptitude for spinning plausible falsehoods. But lying to Nick, in the face of what he'd done for her, was growing increasingly unpalatable. "I don't suppose many people come that close to violence. At least not more than once.''

He speared a shrimp. ''Fortunately not. But from what I've heard of Detroit, it can be a pretty tough town. If you escaped there without once needing to defend yourself, you were probably lucky.''

Sara froze. ''Detroit?'' Her current identity was from Detroit, but she'd never mentioned the town to Nick. Had she?

His face was quizzical. ''Isn't that where you told Detective Chatfield you were from?''

Tension seeped out of her, and the hand she stretched toward her glass wasn't quite steady. ''Yes. But you can hardly compare fending off hormone-laden teenage boys with meeting up with someone intent on killing you.''

This time a faint smile crossed his lips, but his eyes remained watchful. ''I think you'll find your self-defense lessons equally useful in both cases. If someone tries to take something from you, you should do your damnedest to prevent it.''

''Does that apply to you, Nick?'' Her tone, her gaze was direct. ''Just what is it, exactly, that you're interested in taking from me?''

He reached for his wine, drank, never looking away from her. ''Yes, I suppose in one sense it does apply to me.'' His voice was sleek and smooth, sliding over her like a lover's caress. ''Because I'll take...as much as you'll give me.''

He watched the moon rise from the ocean to hang low and heavy in the star-studded sky. The night was silent. Not a sound emerged from Amber's room. Not the faint scrabbling noises she made when she climbed out onto the roof night after night. Not the creak of the drainpipe when she climbed down it. Perhaps she was too tired to engage in any nocturnal journeys tonight. But then, it was barely past midnight. She didn't usually stir until after two.

He brought the slim cheroot to his mouth and filled his lungs. He wasn't a man accustomed to peace, but here he experienced at least a sliver of it. Sitting outside on the small balcony of his bedroom, contemplating the shimmer of moonlight on the water, inhaling nicotine. And thinking of the woman in the other room.

He'd thought…he'd *hoped* that proximity would have lessened his fascination with her. It'd been his experience that most women tended to wear badly, given enough time. But not this one. Not yet. The realization brought both caution and pleasure. There were too many facets to Amber Jennings, too many complexities that both intrigued and maddened him. He was beginning to wonder if he would ever discover all of them.

There was danger in that line of thinking, a danger he'd be wise to heed. He knew what he had to do in this assignment, and letting Amber matter too much would only haze his thinking. He was too much of a professional to let that happen.

Contemplating the trio of perfect smoke rings he'd exhaled, he considered the reason for her nightly forays. She didn't trust him, of course. Rightly so. He wouldn't allow the realization to burn. She had as much reason to maintain defenses as did he, would never have survived on the streets without them.

Nick didn't know how long he spent sending smoke rings to join the low-hanging clouds, but when a small noise reached him he straightened, senses heightening. It came again, and it didn't come from the direction of the porch roof, as he'd half expected.

Reaching down, he ground out the cigar in the ashtray he'd brought out with him, and then rose, strode into his room. Grabbing his discarded trousers, he pulled them on without bothering to button them.

He stood still in the hallway, waiting until the noise reoccurred. It sounded like a small wounded animal in distress. And it was coming from Amber's room.

Pressing his hand flat on her door, he pushed it open a ways. She was lying on her stomach amid a tangle of covers, wearing a cropped cotton top and matching boxers. There was nothing in the least bit erotic about her lingerie, but inexplicably, his mouth went dry.

"No." Her low moan was accompanied by a swing of her arm, and her head turned on her pillow restlessly. For a moment he was tempted to slip away. There was something strangely intimate about watching the woman sleep. And dream.

But he knew better than most how nightmares preyed on the unconscious, how it felt to jolt awake, sweaty and shaken. And how the ghosts that picked the midnight hours to haunt could fade with time, but never completely disappear. Without making a conscious decision, Nick approached the bed.

She whimpered again, her hands clenched into fists. Her legs jerked, as if to take flight. But there was no escaping the mental movie in her mind, except by waking.

He knew better than to touch her and take her by surprise. Instead he pulled the overstuffed armchair closer to the side of the bed and sat on the edge of it, leaning toward her. "Amber. Wake up."

Although she stilled, her eyes didn't open.

"Open your eyes, *chérie*. Look at me." Nick kept his low tones soothing, with the barest hint of command. "Come to me, *ma petite*. Don't let the bastards win. Open your eyes and fight back." He barely noted what he was saying—his attention was focused on her, as if he could awaken her by sheer force of will. And then he stopped, staggered, when her eyes opened abruptly and stared directly into his.

"Nick." She levered herself away from the mattress, pushed her hand through her hair. "What are you doing in here?" The quaver in her voice was at odds with the defensive words.

"You were having a bad dream. Don't you remember?" He leaned back in the chair, watching her carefully. And then could have yanked his tongue out when her eyes grew shuttered.

"I'm sorry. Did I wake you?" It was disturbing to watch her try to tuck away the tatters of the dream, attempt to resurrect that famous guard of hers.

"No, I was awake." He gave her a few moments to collect herself, observed the effort it took. "Do you have nightmares often?"

She rolled one shoulder, the movement jerky. "Everyone has bad dreams, right? Look, I appreciate the concern, but I'd like to get back to sleep."

He recognized the lie in her words. It only made him more intent on discovering the truth. "How long have you been having them? Since New Orleans?"

Her hand stilled in the act of raking through her hair, and she shot him a startled look. "New Orleans?" Comprehension seemed to follow sluggishly. "No. Not that. I mean...I don't remember what the dream was even about, actually." She shook her head. "It doesn't matter, does it?" The shudders that still worked through her mocked her question. It obviously mattered to her. Too much.

He leaned forward, reached for her. She reared back. "What are you...Nick!"

As an answer he hauled her into his arms and onto his lap. Remaining rigid in his embrace, she said, "I've never been a lap sitter."

"Something else you'll have to work on." He cupped

her nape in one hand, kneading rhythmically. "Relax. You're never going to get back to sleep while you're this upset."

Her tone was caustic. "I'm not going back to sleep at any rate with you in the room."

"Then don't sleep." His lips brushed her hair as he spoke. "But give your body a chance to recover." He ignored the way she remained stiff in his embrace, and waited for his heat to transfer to her, warming the chill from her skin. And was rewarded long minutes later when a bit of the tension seeped from her limbs and she arched her neck back against his hand.

"You're good at that."

"I've thought of hiring out."

A smile sounded in her voice. "I'm sure your services would be in great demand."

A final tremor worked through her body, and he frowned, shifting her weight a bit closer. When he was a child and awakened from a dream brought about by fears of monsters and ghosts, he'd had his grandmother to comfort him. He wondered who had comforted Amber. Once he got older he'd learned that some monsters were not the figment of a childish imagination, but very real, and the ghosts that haunted were the intensely personal kind. Somehow both were more frightening than anything his imagination had managed to conjure up as a kid.

The darkness shrouded them, wrapping them in a cocoon of intimacy, one Amber would never have allowed under other circumstances. Her eyelids closed, and a small sigh escaped her. This time it was she who curved her body nearer to his, and his heart slowed, steadied to a heavy thudding.

Comfort turned ever so gradually to awareness. He watched her eyelids raise slowly, and her gaze fix on his. The tip of her tongue crept out, moistened her lips.

"I don't understand you." Her words were nearly soundless. He took her fingers, warm now, in his hand, brought them to his lips.

"I know." How could she, when he struggled at times to understand himself? He wasn't an analytical man. He trusted gut instinct over emotion. There was safety in maintaining emotional distance from others, in avoiding any kind of ties. But there was no denying that this woman drew unusual feelings from him, had from the start. She couldn't know how uneasy that made him.

"I can't stay in Florida much longer."

He stilled, aware she'd just offered him a painful bit of truth. "No."

Her gaze searched his, for something he couldn't give. But then she shifted to a more upright position. Her face was inches away. Gazes still meshed, she slid a hand around the back of his neck and slowly, tentatively, pressed her lips against his.

All it took was that first light taste. Her flavor rioted through his senses, sparking memories of the only other kiss they'd shared, at a time that somehow seemed less complicated. Desire, too long ruthlessly suppressed, kicked instantly to life. There were few women he could remember wanting this badly. And none he could recall denying himself.

His mouth slanted over hers, parting her lips, and he drank in her warm sweetness. Her small gasp was lost as his tongue glided along hers. Arms banding around her, he brought her closer, until she was pressed tightly against his bare chest.

His palm slid beneath her pajama top to settle on smooth, satiny skin. The contact was electric. She jerked against him, bringing her hip into closer proximity with his aching groin. He smoothed his hand along the curve of her waist, his fingers caressing the expanse.

She was slender, almost delicately made. He pushed up her top and raised his lips from hers, his eyes slitted. In the shadows her skin shone like marble, but pulsed with warm, supple life. The sight made it impossible to think, to weigh risks and consequences. Without considering the ramifications, he pushed the top higher to expose her breasts.

They were small, high and exquisitely shaped. His throat went dry and whatever remained of reason abruptly vanished. He cupped one in his hand and bent down to take it in his mouth.

A shattered cry escaped her as his lips pulled and tugged there. He used his other hand to cover her other breast, teasing her nipple into a small tight knot. Her breasts were firm, arousingly so, inviting a man to linger. To explore. But no, he thought savagely, not any man. Just him.

Her breathing was coming in ragged spurts when he switched his attentions to her other breast. Her fingers were entwined in his hair, exerting pressure, and he welcomed the slight pain. This time he caught her nipple between his teeth and teased it lightly, while his hand dropped to her thigh, inched up slowly.

She arched beneath the sensual assault. He flexed his cheeks, drawing strongly from her as his hand slid inside her baggy boxers and cupped her warm dampness.

Her body jolted in his arms. He parted her slick cleft and worked a finger deep inside her, using his thumb to apply rhythmic pressure to the sensitive bundle of nerves beneath his hand.

Heat suffused him, burning him from the inside out. She clutched his shoulders, her nails biting into his skin. He could feel the tightening of her body, and increased the pressure of his mouth, his fingers.

He felt her convulse, and a bolt of primal satisfaction coursed through him. He'd wanted this, and more, since the first moment he'd seen her. Wanted her naked and wet and moaning his name. Wanted to mount her, to take her without any preliminaries, and ride her hard and hot until they both collapsed in a sweaty tangle.

The strength of the wanting still managed to amaze him. And yes, to alarm him. His touch turned caressing as she lay beneath his hand, spent and soft. Clinging desperately to a remnant of tattered reason, he removed his hand, lifted his mouth. He'd long since lost any illusions about honor, so it certainly wasn't nobility that drove his actions. No, it was common sense. Logic. He could think the words even as a part of him scoffed at them.

He rose with one smooth movement and carried her to the bed. Laying her down, he climbed in beside her, drew the sheet over them both.

Curling his body to hers, he kept his hand on her stomach, keeping her firmly pressed against him. "And now, *mon ange*—" he kissed her shoulder "—you will sleep."

Her body was still, but lacked the rigidity it had held after the nightmare. "Nick…you—"

"Go to sleep." The command was as much for himself as it was for her. He had just enough control left to wrestle with his frustration, to tuck away his raging hormones. She wouldn't easily forget what had happened between them. But if he made love to her the way he wanted to, he knew she'd never forgive him. The fact that that mattered at all was an issue he'd deal with later.

Maybe he hadn't completely lost his soul, after all. Because for the first time in years, he attempted to abide by a long-forgotten whisper of conscience. And the hellish night he had ahead of him was only a sliver of what he deserved.

"Don't worry." Hearing Nick's voice, Sara headed into his office, stopping short in the doorway when she saw him at his desk using his cell phone. He looked up and saw her, and a glimpse of something unidentifiable flickered in his eyes before being quickly extinguished. The middle desk drawer was open, and she saw a snub-nosed revolver in there. The sight was hardly surprising. Although she'd yet to feel comfortable around firearms despite the daily practice he'd given her, the ease with which he handled them hadn't escaped her.

His attention had returned to his conversation. "Everything is set then. Yes, you can count on it. I'll be in touch." He broke the connection and gestured for Sara to come inside. He set the phone in the open drawer and then closed it. "I thought you were on the beach."

"I was. I came back for some bottled water. Were you working?"

"Working? No. I just called Detective Chatfield to get an update on his progress."

The reminder of the search for the gunman who'd come so close to catching up with her in New Orleans cast an unexpected chill over her sun-warmed skin. "Did he have anything to report?"

Nick shook his head. "I'm sorry, *chérie.* There's been no trace of the man who attacked you. But the search continues. Chatfield is still following some leads."

The chill deepened, glazing her insides with ice. If her attacker had managed to elude the police for this long, chances were he'd never be found at all. Which meant he might be on her trail even now.

"You're safe here, Amber." Nick's words closely echoed her thoughts. "My pilot didn't include this stopover in his flight plan. There's no way for anyone to trace your whereabouts."

She scrubbed one hand up and down her opposite arm in an effort to chase away the goose bumps. "I'll bet the Federal Aviation Administration frowns on that."

A corner of his mouth lifted slightly and he inclined his head. "I'm told they do."

She shook her head, bewildered. "Why would you risk alienating the NOPD? Chance trouble with the FAA? You don't even know me."

His eyes were hooded. "I'm beginning to, I think."

Although his words could have had another meaning, her cheeks flushed. He had known her intimately last night, when he'd brought her body to shattering completion. And then held her while she slept. "Why, Nick?"

He crossed to her, his steps slow and deliberate. Reaching out, he trailed his fingers over her jawline. "I care for you."

Eyes wide, she gazed into his and wished, not for the first time, that she could read what was in those ebony depths. How could he profess to care about her, when he didn't know who she was? What she was? She barely knew herself, anymore.

"Mr. Doucet."

Nick dropped his hand, but didn't move. His gaze searched Sara's, and despite her experience at keeping her emotions shielded, she was afraid of what he might see there. When his name was repeated, he slowly turned to survey Marta, who was standing nervously in the doorway.

"I need to go to the market for food."

He nodded, then flicked a glance back at Sara. "Let me get some money for Marta. Then…you and I need to talk."

Feeling a combination of relief and shock, she watched him stride from the room. Her knees had gone maddeningly weak. In need of support, she crossed to his desk, clutched its edge. It occurred to her that in allowing Nick to help her flee New Orleans, she'd merely exchanged one problem for another. She had nothing to offer a man like Nick Doucet, or any other man, save the obvious.

Her plan to slip away from him rather than return to New Orleans was seeming increasingly shabby in light of what he'd done for her. And while she couldn't afford to rethink her plan, perhaps she could discover for herself what kind of situation she'd be placing him in. If there was any way she could minimize the risk he'd be exposed to by her disappearance, she owed it to him to find it.

With that thought in mind, she reached for the drawer where he'd placed the phone, and took it out. He was nothing if not careful. Calls made on this cell phone couldn't be traced, or he would never have chosen the service. He wouldn't take any chances on the detective locating them. She hit the power button, then Redial. If Chatfield was still in the district headquarters, she could talk to him herself. She could find out directly if Nick was softening the news he'd gotten from the detective. She wouldn't put it past the man to keep any upsetting information to himself. And she could also discover the detective's feelings about Nick taking her away. Once she vanished again, she didn't want to leave him facing possible trouble with the NOPD. He deserved better than that from her.

When the call was picked up, she straightened, prepared to ask for the detective by name. But instead of the Southern accent she'd expected, the disembodied voice on the other end of the line held a flat, Midwestern cadence. The floor tilted beneath Sara's feet and she sank, boneless, against the desk again. The person on the other end repeated her greeting, a note of impatience entering her voice.

"Victor Mannen's office."

Chapter 5

The blood congealed in Sara's veins. Then it surged to her head with a dizzying rush that had her grasping the edge of the desk to prevent herself from sliding to the floor.

Nick hadn't called Chatfield at all. He'd been talking to Mannen.

A locomotive raced through her chest and she had to fight to get air into her lungs. Each individual event that had transpired since she'd met Nick Doucet jelled into one abstract collage. The picture it formed was horrifying, but there was no escaping the reality.

Nick knew Mannen. And since Mannen had spent the last six years trying to have her killed, the next logical assumption was that Nick was his latest weapon of choice. It was shatteringly bitter to recognize just how potent a weapon the man had become.

Questions whirled in her mind, flavored with the familiar but bitter taste of betrayal. She let loose a wild laugh.

How could he betray her when she hadn't let down her guard? But of course, she had. He'd seen to that. That provocative scene in her bedroom took on new meaning and burned like poison. For some reason it was important to Nick for her to trust him. Last night was just one more step toward ensuring that she did so. The fact that he hadn't killed her yet was a curiosity to be examined from the distance of thousands of miles. Right now only escape mattered.

She pulled back his desk chair, slowly sank into it. By the time she heard his footsteps in the hallway, an unnatural feeling of calm had descended over her. She'd survived worse betrayals than this. She would survive Nick Doucet, as well.

He stuck his head into the room, his gaze noting her position at his desk. Perhaps something about her stillness roused his instincts, because he stepped into the room, considered her carefully. "Ready?"

"Did you and Marta decide on dinner?" Sara's voice was casual.

He nodded. "We'll have fresh clams and linguini tonight."

"Something tells me I won't have much of an appetite."

"You can tell that already?"

"Yes." Her entire system was numb; it aided in maintaining a detached air. She knew from experience that shock would set in later. "At any rate, I make it a habit to avoid dining with hired killers."

His expression grew puzzled, but she thought she could see the caution blooming in his eyes. His lying, murderous eyes. Approaching her, he said, "Amber, what are you—"

His pace abruptly halted when she raised her hands, pointed his gun directly at his chest. "Step back."

He wasn't a stupid man, she noted resentfully, despite his lack of morals. He obeyed, not stopping until his shoul-

ders were against the wall. She didn't think he was armed,
but that still left his voice, a lethal weapon in itself, hypnotic in its power. "Tell me what you're thinking, Amber.
Surely you don't believe—"

"That you're working for Victor Mannen?" she in-
quired dispassionately. She watched Nick's gaze jump between her and the desk drawer, and mentally congratulated
him for not wasting time on denials. Instead he moved
swiftly to damage control.

"I just spoke to him, yes, but it's not like it looks, Amber. I'm—"

"Let's dispense with at least one of the pretenses between us, shall we?" She despised the note of emotion
that had entered her voice. "I think we both know who I
am."

He paused for a moment, his dark gaze fathomless. Then
he said, with the air of a man tasting the words, "Sara
Parker."

Her name quivered in the air between them, enveloped
in the tension, the knowing. His soft voice was imbued
with warmth, a heated touch sliding down her spine. It
shouldn't have an effect. Wouldn't be allowed to.

"Yes. Sara Parker. Now let's talk about who you are.
Or rather, *what* you are."

"You're leaping to conclusions." Gone was the seductive tone; his words were edged in hardness. "Don't allow
emotion to dictate your actions. You can't afford to."

"Emotion, Nick?" She cocked her head quizzically, her
hands holding the gun steady. "Do I look like I'm ready
to collapse in a shuddering heap? I can assure you, I'll be
quite emotionless when I shoot you."

There was a leap of flame in his eyes, a note of certainty
in his voice. "You won't do that."

With a movement that trembled only slightly, she
thumbed off the safety the way she'd seen him do a dozen

times. And his expression altered, either from the deft movement or the look on her face.

It was a measure of the man that he didn't show even a flicker of nerves. But then, she'd never had any doubt that Nick wasn't an ordinary man. Assassins rarely were.

"You need to listen to me, Sara." That soft seductive tone was gone and the familiar command was back. "This isn't how I wanted to have you find out—"

She laughed then, a wild incredulous sound. "No, I'll bet not. I'm sure I was supposed to be the one staring down this barrel."

He ignored her words, his dark gaze holding hers captive. "You picked up the phone, didn't you? Hit Redial and got Mannen's office. I don't blame you for thinking the worst, but I'm not working for him, Sara. Not the way you think."

"Who are you working for then?"

"The Department of Justice."

Her hand tightened on the gun. He tracked the minute adjustment with his gaze. "You've got about sixty seconds to convince me why I shouldn't blow you away."

He seemed to choose his words carefully. "I told you I was in Special Ops. That was the truth."

"Careful, Nick. That word isn't exactly one you're an expert on. It's what you do now that has me interested at the moment."

"I'm an independent operative."

Ice blistered her skin. "Is that the current term for hit man?"

It wasn't lost on her that he failed to answer her question. "I hire out for various jobs, Sara, but not to individuals. To governments mostly—internationally as well as various government agencies in the U.S."

"Illegal activities," she assumed flatly.

He shrugged. "Definitions don't matter. The services of my team are in high demand."

He couldn't realize that his supposed affiliation with Justice was almost as terrifying as admitting to working for Mannen. She'd figured out six years ago that the department couldn't protect her from him. Justice and Mannen were equally dangerous for her.

"How long have you known who I am?" she asked flatly.

He seemed to hesitate then, his gaze dropping to the gun and then moving back to her face. "Since New Orleans."

"In the precinct house?" she guessed.

After a moment, he nodded. "Chatfield's inquiries got some pretty rapid responses. Your name's been flagged on all the databases. As soon as Justice heard someone was inquiring about you, things started to happen. When I saw the excitement your name was generating, I made a few inquiries. Paul Whitmore enlisted my services on the spot."

Whitmore.

She remembered him from that awful time six years ago, and the memory still had the power to shake her. "Your services for what, exactly?"

"For one thing, to verify your identity and deliver you safely back to Justice for safekeeping."

His words seemed to come from a distance. There was a roaring in her ears, terror in her heart. "I'm not going back."

"They've been after Mannen since you disappeared. Piece by piece they're developing evidence to nail him for good. A couple recent cases have brought them closer, but they won't be satisfied until they have enough to keep him locked up for life."

"Let me guess." Her words were brittle. "That's where I come in."

He inclined his head. "Partially."

"I'm not going to let them play at witness protection again." She stated the words baldly, and maddeningly, her hand began to shake. She saw the way Nick's eyes traced the movement, and she rose, the chair clattering behind her. "If I have to shoot you to guarantee that, I will." An ironic smile pulled at her mouth. "I learned from an expert, remember. Don't aim the gun, just point it. And the chest offers the biggest target. Remember, Nick?"

"I remember. But use your head. Your luck is going to run out sometime. Do you really want to take your chances with Mannen's men catching up with you?"

"I've eluded them twice now." She ignored the fact that she couldn't continue to do so forever. When it came to weighing risks, what he was offering, even if she could believe him, was a no-brainer. If she had to take her chances with Justice, where Mannen seemed to have informants, or to be on the run from Mannen's hired killers, she'd rely on her own devices every time.

A slice of memory flashed across her mind—the crumpled bodies in the safe house; the blood. And Sean's surprised expression, his eyes empty and lifeless.

The brief visual snippet had her throat clogging. "I want you to walk, slowly, to that closet." With a jerk of her head she indicated a door in the corner of the room.

He didn't move. "Sara, think—"

"I am thinking, unfortunately for you. I'm thinking your story doesn't hold up. It wasn't Justice on the other end of that phone call, it was Victor Mannen." A sense of urgency seized her when she considered that either Mannen or the government could have someone on their way down here at this very moment. She didn't know which of the options was more frightening. "Start moving, Nick, or I'll shoot you where you stand."

He remained still. "Use your head." His voice took on

an edge of impatience. "If I was working for Mannen you'd be dead already."

"And if you were working for Justice I'd be in custody right now. Nothing about your story makes sense, and I'm not going to stand here and debate it with you. Now move!"

He did as he was bade, but something in his catlike movements alarmed her. She's seen this man demonstrate defense tactics. Seen that lethally intent look on his face before he struck. She followed his path with the gun, never taking her eyes off of him. Her mind was muddled by questions, but her survival instincts were well developed and they were screaming at her now.

"There's an explanation for the call to Mannen. If you don't believe me, all you have to do is call Paul Whitmore. You dealt with him before in the agency and he's—"

"You don't get it, do you?" Her smile was humorless. "Mannen or Justice—it doesn't matter. I'll be dead either way. Mannen will find a way to make that happen. He always does."

Nick was halfway across the room by this time, but closer than she liked. "Back up," she ordered, but it was she who took an involuntary step away.

"You wanted me to go to the closet. That's what I'm doing."

The hand holding the gun began to tremble. She steadied it by propping her free hand beneath it.

He loomed nearer and her finger tightened on the trigger. "Get back."

"Let me explain, Sara."

"Back off or…"

He came a step closer, raised his hand toward her, and his voice dropped persuasively. "Or what?"

The sound of the shot shattered the room. The smell of cordite filled the air, as horror seized her heart. Nick stag-

gered a little, his hand going to his side. She stared, transfixed by the blood seeping between his fingers.

Even now his voice was steady. "Sara, let me…"

She never heard the rest of his words. Dropping the
weapon, she ran from the room, shoving past Marta, who
was standing in the doorway with horror stamped on her
face. Flinging open the front door, Sara dashed down the
steps and raced away from the house. There was no room
in her mind for planning strategy. She was too busy fighting the nausea, the memories. Nick's eyes when the bullet
hit him—not filled with the shocked wonder Sean's had
held, but rather a grim sort of acceptance.

Her heart was hammering loudly in her ears, her breath
sawing in and out of her lungs like a blade. When she
finally noticed she was taking a route she and Nick fre-
quently ran, she veered across the street in another direction. Throwing a look over her shoulder, she took little
satisfaction in the fact that no one was trailing her.

She had to find a place to hide. The knowledge pounded
in her temples. Slowly panic receded, replaced by cold
logic. She'd been planning this moment since her first
night on the island. She'd wait for darkness to fall, then
creep to one of the cars she'd found that usually had the
keys left in it. She'd drive it to the ferry, abandon it once
she was on the other side.

The strategy calmed her, helped keep the shock and terror at bay. She pushed aside the questions about how she
would get away with no money or clothes. She thought of
Nick, the blood on his shirt, on his hands.

Nothing else seemed to matter.

Sara wrapped her arms more tightly around her upraised
knees, her body rocking slightly, and struggled with a suffocating sense of déjà vu. She had no idea how long she'd
spent in the toolshed she'd taken shelter in. Long enough

for the dim interior to gradually fall into complete darkness. Long enough for the cushion of years to melt, and memories, old and new, to mingle.

Chicago. Blood. Danger. Lives threatened, secrets betrayed. Her forehead resting against her knees, she squeezed her eyes shut more tightly, struggled to throw off the weight of the past. When she'd fled the U.S. Marshals, she hadn't taken shelter in a tidy toolshed, but in an abandoned warehouse. It was only the darkness and the insidious memories that made past and present seem to entwine. This time was different. Although still fleeing for her life, she wouldn't be driven by terror and ignorance. This time she had a plan for escape.

It was only the bitter sense of betrayal that was familiar.

Pushing the thought from her mind, she unfolded her body and stood, gave aching joints a chance to adjust. Carefully, she slipped from the shed, ran lightly across the darkened lawn of the stranger's house. She had a couple of miles to run to get to the houses she'd discovered where the owners left keys in the ignition of their cars. She was going to have to hope that the error hadn't been by chance, but by habit. Because whether she stole a car or hitched a ride, she was getting off the island and as quickly as she was able. Away from Mannen's reach.

And far, far away from Nick Doucet.

A lone figure on the deserted beach raised night-vision binoculars, scanned the row of houses. There was no sign of movement in front of any of them. Which could mean that Sara hadn't made it here yet, or that he'd completely misjudged her and she was already on her way off the island.

Nick lowered the glasses, ignoring the burning in his side. The wound should serve as a reminder of what happened when objectivity was allowed to slide. And it was just the start of the mistakes he'd made so far with Sara.

She'd actually shot him.

He felt a glimmer of amusement at the thought, then just as quickly sobered. Given her obvious distaste for guns, he'd have bet that she would have been unable to use one on anyone. For a man not given to making mistakes, this error had been unforgivable. It hadn't been the first time he'd misjudged her, just the most crucial.

It wouldn't happen again.

He'd have done well to deliver her to his employer as ordered as soon as they'd left New Orleans. Nick wouldn't let emotions dictate his actions again. And if he had trouble remembering that vow, he had only to check the wound in his side for a vivid reminder.

Raising the binoculars again, he scanned the area once more, then stopped. The shadow of a palm tree in the distance couldn't quite hide the slim figure that paused in it, before making a dash across the lawn to the driveway.

Allowing the glasses to drop against his chest, Nick ran, too, a swift silent silhouette. Jumping the restraining wall separating the beach from the private lawn, he sped toward Sara, cutting between her and the car parked in front of the house.

He noted the exact moment she saw him. Fear gave her impetus, and he was slowed by the pain in his side. She veered away, running in a semicircle that would still give her a chance to get at it from the other side.

The silence of the night seemed to thrum with the vital battle they were engaged in. Ignoring the physical pain, he ran swiftly, his longer strides outpacing hers. She threw a quick glance over her shoulder, saw him again. He could almost feel her thought process as she headed away from the car and ran all-out across the lawns to escape him.

Grimly he followed, away from the residential area, over

the retaining wall toward a tangled mass of vegetation behind a motel complex. Had the outcome not been so important, he would have applauded her choice. She was much better off trying to lose him by hiding than by attempting to outrun him.

He was less than a dozen yards away from her now. Nick could hear her breath heaving out of her lungs, feel the slap of the pavement under his feet. With a burst of speed, he closed the gap between them as she rounded a group of trees, out of sight.

Only seconds behind her, he took the turn, and his side exploded in pain for the second time that day. Gritting his teeth against the excruciating sensation, he had the forethought to reach out and grab the branch Sara had used on him. With a mighty yank he pulled her off balance. She stumbled, but fought her way out of the vegetation and onto the beach, where her escape would be clear.

With a flying tackle Nick caught her, took her down. They crashed heavily to the sand, driving the breath from them both.

Perhaps it was the tearing pain that helped Nick recover first. His side felt warm and wet. The damn wound had opened up again. The knowledge had him lifting his weight off her and rolling her over, his actions ungentle. If he'd thought to find Sara cowed, he'd been disappointed. Her eyes were bright and defiant as they stared up into his, and he barely caught her up-thrust palm before she rammed it into the bridge of his nose. With more difficulty than he expected, he was able to capture both of her wrists in one of his hands.

For a moment there was nothing but the battling gazes they exchanged. He felt the quick rise and fall of her chest under his, felt her breath mingling with his own. And experienced, once more, the treacherous attraction that had threatened his better judgment since the start.

"What are you waiting for, Nick?" Sara's tone was taunting, a match to her rebellious gaze. "You may as well kill me now, you know. Whoever you plan on delivering me to, Justice or Mannen, it doesn't matter. I'm dead anyway."

"A word of advice, *chérie*. Don't issue such a tempting invitation to a man you shot only hours ago. Not everyone would have my tolerance." Trying to hide the effort it took, he rose, hauling her with him. He had to give her credit; she no sooner got to her feet than he found her poised again—whether to run or to knock him on his ass, he didn't know. Before she could do either, he whipped out a pair of cuffs he had dangling from a belt loop and efficiently locked one bracelet around her wrist.

She gave her arm a yank. "What are you doing?"

Fitting the other bracelet around his own wrist, he snapped it closed with a final click. The moonlight glinted off the silver links connecting them. He raised his gaze from the sight to contemplate her grimly. "I'm limiting your options. Like it or not, the only way you're leaving this island is with me."

Since it was damned tricky to drive left-handed, and his right hand was linked to Sara's, Nick gave the task his complete attention. It wasn't until they were downtown that he asked, "Where to?"

"What?"

Ignoring the wariness in her voice, he said, "You don't trust me. No reason why you should." He didn't allow the fact that the words burned to shade his tone. "You've got questions and you aren't going to believe anything I tell you. So pick a pay phone, *chérie*." He nodded out the window at the phones that dotted the street corners every few blocks. "You can call Justice yourself and get the answers you want."

From her silence he figured he'd surprised her. He'd managed to surprise himself. He'd assumed that she wouldn't accept making the call from his home. But even she couldn't believe that he could tamper with every public phone on the island.

"Who would be available to speak to me at this hour?" There was hostility in her tone, but there was something else, as well. Uncertainty.

He gave a humorless laugh and pulled up next to an all-night drugstore. "Just mention your name. You may have to wait, but I can guarantee that Whitmore will get back to you."

They sat in the darkness, silence stretching between them as she considered her choices. "Go around the block," she finally said.

Nick turned to face her. Her profile could have been etched from glass.

"There's a phone on the corner by the gas station. I'll use that one."

Without a word he did as she asked. Parking the car, he opened his door, carefully got out, and she had no choice but to follow him closely. His muscles were getting stiff around the wound, and he knew he'd pay tomorrow for the excesses of tonight. Walking to the phone, he stood back and allowed her to enter the booth before crowding in behind her.

A car went by slowly, its headlights catching them in their glare for a moment. He could imagine the picture they made. His clothes were soaked in blood, and Sara's legs bore long scrapes from her impact on the sand when he'd tackled her. With the handcuffs linking them, they made an odd enough sight to alarm the most jaded driver. As the car passed by, Nick could only hope their strange appearance wasn't reported to the police. Concocting a believable explanation for the local police would tax his dangerously thinned patience.

He reached into his trouser pocket and pulled out a handful of change. Sara eyed him with familiar wariness in her eyes before picking through it for the proper amount. Then she turned her back on him and fed the coins into the slots. He listened silently as she called information, requesting the number for the Justice Department. He could have given her the number, could have, in fact, had the deputy chief on the phone in less than two minutes. But Nick remained silent. After what had gone down, she wasn't going to trust any information that came from him.

She turned to look at him as she dialed the emergency number she'd been given. "Just give them your name and this number," he directed her. "Tell them you want to speak to whoever is in charge of the Mannen case. Then hang up."

She complied, and when she hung up the phone he opened the booth and stepped out.

"Now what do we do?"

"We're going to sit here—" he led her to a nearby bench "—and wait for the call that will be coming in." With a bit more gratitude than he'd like to admit, he eased down on the bench, pulling her down beside him. He wedged their hands behind them so the cuffs wouldn't show.

"You're bleeding."

Because there was an odd note in her voice, he looked at her. "The wound reopened on the beach. It's nothing to worry about. Just a scratch. Lucky for me you closed your eyes as you pulled the trigger."

Her gaze narrowed. "I guess I'll know better next time, won't I?"

He gave a short, humorless laugh. "There won't be a next time, *chérie*. I don't make the same mistake twice."

"Neither do I," she said grimly.

He studied her, noted the shadows of fatigue under her eyes. No, he was certain she didn't need to review the same lesson more than once. Was equally certain that whatever lessons she'd learned had been hard ones. But the realization wouldn't be allowed to move him. He'd been selected for this job based at least in part on his renown for staying detached from the subject at hand. It was jarring, and not a little humbling, to find his famed objectivity less solid than usual around her.

Deliberately, he looked away. And willed the phone to ring.

When it did, fifteen excruciating minutes later, it interrupted a silence between them so thick it was suffocating. He trailed her to the booth, gestured for her to answer. And then watched her face as she spoke to the person on the other end. Nick could only hear her side of the conversation, but he thought he could imagine the gist of it.

"Yes," she said. Her gaze went to him. "You sent him? Why?" Her face grew paler, although he hadn't thought it possible. "You'll have to excuse me for wanting to take my chances on my own. Your department doesn't exactly fill me with confidence. I happen to know he's been in contact with Mannen." Whatever the man said to her then had her face losing what remained of its color. By the time she held the receiver out to Nick, her hand was visibly trembling.

"Whitmore?" As he spoke into the receiver, he kept his eyes on Sara. Although she was desperately trying to keep her reaction from showing, she was visibly shaken from her conversation.

"Congratulations on finding Parker." Paul Whitmore's voice was hearty. "I was beginning to worry when I didn't hear from you. Tell me where you want to meet and I'll send an agent to collect her."

Nick kept his eyes trained on Sara's face. She had her chin angled, her lips tightly pressed together. He was reminded of the way she'd looked last night, when she'd tried to kick him out of her room by putting a brave front on the nightmares that had so obviously shredded her control. The way she'd looked the first moment he'd hauled her out of the bed and into his arms.

"What do you have in mind for protection?"

There was a moment of silence. Then Whitmore said, "Don't worry. She'll be safe."

"I don't think she's convinced of that." Nick kept his voice mild.

"Well, convince her. We don't have to worry about the leak in the department anymore."

"Why is that?"

"He was found dead on the street outside his apartment today. Victim of a drive-by." Nick could picture Whitmore shrugging. "May be a little convenient, but it solves a problem of ours."

Nick went still, his mind racing. "Do you think so?"

"Listen, you still have another job to do. Tell us where she's at and let us do ours."

Sara raised her gaze to his and he couldn't look away. There wasn't pleading in her eyes—no, never that. But the go-to-hell expression she wore was its own kind of entreaty. One he was having difficulty resisting.

"I'll call later."

"Dammit, don't hang up—"

With a curiously gentle movement Nick replaced the receiver. But he made no move to leave the phone booth. It seemed fitting somehow that the small space encapsulated them from the rest of the world.

"Whitmore is sending someone after me, isn't he?"

"Is that what you want?"

Her jaw tightened. "None of this is what I want. It never has been."

"It seems to me that you have a choice then." Her attention jerked to his, held. "You're afraid to take your chances with Justice. I can understand that. It was a leak in the department that led to your friends being killed."

She squared her shoulders. "And my choice?"

He considered the words before he said them, so he couldn't claim impulsivity. He'd never engaged in an impulsive act in his life. "Simple. You can trust Justice to keep you safe. Or…" He watched the way understanding flooded her face, even before he finished the sentence.

"…you can trust me."

Chapter 6

"Trust you." Sara's laugh was bitter as she elbowed past him. She was in desperate need of the balmy fresh air outside the phone booth, and filled her lungs in a quick, greedy gulp. "You're the last person I'd trust. Whitmore was a bit more forthcoming than you've been, you deceitful son of a bitch. You didn't just happen to go to New Orleans for a family visit. You were *trailing* me."

"Yes."

The quietly spoken word hit her with the force of a punch. It wasn't betrayal she felt. No, never that. The word implied trust broken, and trust had long been a luxury she couldn't afford. But there was no denying the shock, the anger and resentment that welled up violently enough to choke her. He'd played her for a fool. The knowledge roared through her veins, demanded release. "For how long?"

He didn't pretend to misunderstand her. "Seven months."

She stared at him, trying to put times and places in order. "Since Atlanta."

Nick inclined his head. "Justice wanted you brought in. They'd tried before, but couldn't find you. They knew Mannen had someone contracted on you, and that he'd come close a few years ago."

Her gaze jerked to his. "I managed to get away, though, didn't I? I don't need you, I don't need Justice. I'm safer on my own."

"Mannen wants you dead, and it's only a matter of time until he succeeds." Nick's words were no more than the truth, so his stark pronouncement shouldn't have had the power to chill her skin. "Want to know how he got so close, Sara? How I managed to track you after seven months? You were good, *chérie*. Better than I imagined you could be, a kid frightened out of her wits. But you didn't cut all your ties to your old life. And that ended up almost getting you killed."

"You're wrong." The statement sounded as though it was pulled from somewhere deep inside her. "I don't have any ties."

"Not even to an old lady living in an Illinois nursing home?"

When he placed his hand on her back, tried to guide her to the car, she yanked away from his touch, putting as much distance between them as the cuffs would allow. "I was careful. I only sent Sean's grandmother the flowers by FTD, and always right before I left a town. There was no way…" Realization flooded through her; tension spiked into her limbs. "That time in Arizona…I'd gotten sick." She stopped, suddenly remembering who she was talking to. She didn't owe Nick Doucet anything, least of all an explanation. But she was certain he had already guessed the rest. She'd stayed a couple days longer than she should have, and Mannen's hired gun had tracked her through the flower order.

The way Nick himself had done.

Her voice was nearly inaudible. "I never made that mistake again."

"You didn't need to." He started toward the car, and she had no choice but to follow. "This time they hired *me*."

"But you weren't the only one to track me down, were you?" Now that she knew how she'd given her location away, she would never make that mistake again. Which meant, of course, that she really would have to cut that one final tie. The wave of desolation that swept over her then was as sudden as it was surprising. Ridiculous, really, that the token gesture had come to mean so much.

"Actually, I *was* the only one to track you to New Orleans."

Something in Nick's tone drew her attention. He'd inserted the key in the ignition, but he hadn't turned it on. Not yet.

"I'm not so sure you didn't lead the hit man right to me. He may have…" Comprehension slammed into her then, leaving her speechless as the awful realization bloomed. Her gaze swung to his, and she saw the truth on his face.

"You were never really in danger…."

That's all he got out, because in the next instant she launched herself at him. Using her free hand, she raked at his eyes, balled her other fist and swung at him. "You set it up! The whole thing!" His arm went around her, the simplest way to subdue her. But that didn't stop her from slamming her head back, connecting with his chin. She felt no measure of satisfaction at the contact. There was room inside her for nothing but the bubbling fury.

"Just listen—"

She wouldn't stay still, maintaining her struggle until Nick used his weight to push her down to the seat, pin her there. "Listen to me, Sara!"

She glared murderously up at him. "Listen to more of your lies? I don't need to. I'm getting a good idea how your evil mind works. The gunman was yours, wasn't he?"

"I know the experience terrified you." His face was close, too close, to hers. "I'm sorry for that. But I needed to gain your trust quickly."

"And since I didn't fall right into bed with you, getting someone to pretend to kill me seemed the next logical step." She tried to wedge her elbows between them, but he was unmovable.

"My gun was firing blanks." He delivered the explanation dispassionately. "My associate had a device rigged under the slicker, complete with a fake blood packet to make it look realistic. I know it was frightening for you, but you'll never have to see the man again. He left the country, for good."

"Whose idea was this elaborate ruse, Whitmore's?"

"No." Nick gave a short laugh, one devoid of amusement. "His idea was to snatch you off the street and keep you drugged until you were delivered to Justice."

Anger, frustration at her sheer helplessness, clogged her throat. She'd sworn long ago to never be helpless again. But it had been an empty vow. That was never clearer than at this moment. A sudden thought struck her. "What about Chatfield? Was he working with you?"

Nick shook his head. "I couldn't afford to involve anyone else."

Bitterness sounded in her words. "So I'm not the only one you lied to."

"Not everything was a lie." Temper snapped in his voice as he shoved his face closer to hers. "I had no way of summoning that storm, did I? No way of knowing we'd take shelter in that doorway.''

Futilely, she heaved beneath him, attempting to dislodge him and the insidious memories his words had summoned. ''That only makes me hate you more.''

His smile was humorless. ''Hate me all you want. But just remember, I'm at least offering you a choice about your immediate future. That's a lot more than Justice wanted to give you.''

The ride back to his house was accomplished in silence. Her mind was reeling with plans for escape, half formed, only to be discarded as she seized on another. Nick caught her gaze as he parked the vehicle in the driveway in front of his house. ''You don't have much time to make your decision. I'm sure Whitmore already has a locator trace on that number. He won't wait long. If he doesn't hear from me he'll just dispatch a couple agents to come after you.''

Although his tone was dispassionate, or maybe because of it, her temper fired. ''You'll have to excuse me if the decision takes some thought. It's only my life at stake.''

''Yes. The question is, who do you trust to keep you alive?''

Under the circumstances, his words were unfortunate. ''I don't trust anyone.''

''Good. You're less likely to be unpleasantly surprised that way.''

He opened the car door, and she had no choice but to slide across the seat to follow him out, and up to the house. The night air was warm, but didn't chase away the chill caused by his words. He couldn't have told her more plainly how foolish she'd be to trust him. As if she needed the reminder.

Because the cuffs gave her no choice, she trailed beside him as he entered his office, picked up the phone. A frigid block of ice settled in her chest, but it didn't prevent her from observing how he kept his body between her and the desk. The distrust wasn't all one-sided, though she couldn't bring herself to care. In light of his recent revelations, she'd shoot the man again, given a chance.

But shock jerked her attention away from her hopeless situation when he spoke into the phone. "It's me. Get the plane ready. I'm not sure when I'll be there."

As she watched, he placed the receiver in its cradle before heading out of the room and up the stairs, dragging her with him.

"So much for leaving the choice to me," she muttered.

He slid a glance at her. "I leave tonight, with or without you. The first part of my job is over." From his tone it sounded as though he didn't care which decision she arrived at. Striding through his bedroom, he pulled her past the huge bed that dominated the room, and into the adjoining bathroom. Flipping on the light switch, he began unbuttoning his shirt.

Her gaze arrowed to his side. He'd bandaged the wound earlier that day, but the dressing was soaked with a rapidly spreading scarlet stain. "Wet that washcloth, will you?"

With effort, she pulled her gaze away and focused on the dark green washcloth he indicated. Removing it from the towel bar, she focused her attention on soaking it thoroughly. She could hear him releasing the tape securing the bandage, and damned her stomach, which was swimming with rising nausea. It certainly wasn't caused by regrets. She'd done what she had to do. Given what she'd just found out about him, he was lucky she didn't have a gun right now.

Handing the wet cloth to him, she was unable to prevent herself from staring, transfixed, as he used it to staunch the sullen ooze of blood.

"Not feeling remorseful, are you?"

She firmed her lips, looked away. "No."

"Good." Her attention snapped back to him at the blunt pronouncement, and his dark gaze met her own. "You thought you were fighting for your life. At times like those you can't afford to be distracted by worrying about your adversary." A corner of his mouth lifted. "Your instincts were right. Someone with less training might have gone down. You should have moved away after delivering the blow, though. You lost your advantage by allowing me to grab your weapon."

"I'll remember that next time."

Her tart tone seemed wasted on him. "See that you do."

At his direction, she helped fashion a fresh dressing, and they worked in awkward tandem fixing it over the wound. Almost immediately a small red stain appeared on it. Nick didn't seem to notice. He pulled her into the bedroom, fishing in his pants pocket and withdrawing the key to the handcuffs. He freed himself, then handed the key to her. While she worked at unlocking the cuff, he swiftly changed shirts.

She let the bracelets drop to the floor, but oddly, her release brought no sense of freedom. She was caught like a rabbit in a snare, and her hopes for escape were dissipating by the minute.

She wondered how much time had passed since her phone call with Justice. She had no idea how long she had to make her choice, but intuition told her that time was running out.

"Whitmore told me they'd hired you to help bring Mannen down." She shifted a bit away from Nick. This proximity to him was growing unbearable. "From the part of the conversation I overheard between the two of you this afternoon, I figure you're going to pretend to work with him."

"Something like that. Did Whitmore also tell you that

the man Justice believed responsible for leaking your location to Mannen six years ago is dead? Someone shot him on the street yesterday.''

Sara hugged herself, rubbing the sudden chill from her arms. ''Not exactly the government's style, is it?''

The shadows in the room kept Nick's face in darkness. She wanted, quite desperately, to see his expression when he answered. ''No. But it may not have been connected to the man's link with Mannen.''

She gave a humorless laugh. ''Coincidences make me nervous.'' If Whitmore had suspected the agent, they might have kept him under surveillance for a while. Might even have used him to feed misinformation to Mannen. But they wouldn't gun him down in the street. That style was all too reminiscent of her experience six years ago.

On the heels of that thought came one even more chilling. Mannen wouldn't cut the agent loose if that left him without an informant in the department. No, it was far more likely that he'd had no further use for the agent because he'd already picked out his replacement.

Her options were growing increasingly bleak. And as a feeling of hopelessness filled her, she knew she really didn't have a choice at all. Sliding a glance toward the man beside her, she suppressed an involuntary shiver. She knew the danger associated with putting her welfare in the hands of the Justice Department again.

She could only guess at the danger involved in ever trusting Nick Doucet, even a little.

Nick had promised himself that he would discover all of Sara's secrets before they left the Keys. They'd been in Paris for eight hours before he'd discovered the first.

''Your eyes are green.''

Plainly uncomfortable, she tried to jerk her chin from his grasp. ''Yeah, so?''

Without releasing his hold, he continued to study her. He'd known the basic identifiers, of course. But there were endless variations of color, and he hadn't expected the shade of hers—the palest jade. He was reminded yet again of a sleek feline. And if the look in them was any indication, he could expect her to start hissing any minute. The thought brought a smile to his lips, and he dropped his hand.

"You said to leave out the contacts," she reminded him, with a slight edge to her voice. "And you seem to be the one calling all the shots."

He preferred to ignore the sarcasm in her voice. "They aren't prescription, are they?" She shook her head. He hadn't thought so. At least he knew she'd had no restrictions on her driver's license six years ago. He raked his fingers through the strands of her hair. "What's your natural color?"

She moved away from him—whether from annoyance or for a reason more personal, he couldn't tell. He had a moment's regret for having dispensed with the handcuffs. "Brown."

"Light brown? Brunette?"

She lifted a shoulder in what he could have sworn was embarrassment. "Medium brown, all right? What difference does it make?"

"Your natural coloring makes all the difference in the world when we select your next disguise."

The look she threw him was cool. "I've been managing that effectively on my own for the last six years."

"Actually, you have. The reddish cast you chose this time, the hazel contacts—both match your skin tone. They look natural, but I think we can still improve on it." Paying no attention to her narrowed gaze, he cocked his head to consider her. "We'll darken the hair to a deep brunette, I think. Brown contacts to match." He squelched a pang at the thought of concealing the color of those arresting eyes yet again, and focused on the matter at hand. "You're too thin, but with the fashions these days that's an advantage." They'd stick to sophisticated clothes for her, he thought. Casual chic would suit her best.

"Why is it necessary to disguise me at all when you're planning to hide me away until this is over?"

"I don't intend to hide you away. Not in the way you think." From the flicker of disappointment on her face he knew he'd guessed correctly. She'd merely hedged her bets when she'd chosen to accompany him. No doubt she'd considered it easier to escape from one man than from several U.S. Marshals. Although he would have liked to believe her motives were more personal, he was nothing if not realistic. Sara still had every intention of fleeing given the opportunity.

He was going to make sure that opportunity never arose.

He'd realized he was taking a huge step away from his famed impartiality when he hadn't delivered her to Justice as ordered. If he were honest, he'd admit he'd known what he was going to do long before he'd offered her this choice. The realization made him uncomfortable. He could hardly have delivered her to Justice, and certain death. It was a sense of responsibility, nothing more, that had fueled his offer.

But he was very familiar with the mantle of responsibility. This felt like something completely different.

A discreet bell sounded, and he crossed the penthouse to the intercom by the door. Stabbing a finger at the button, he said, "Yes."

The disembodied voice of the doorman filtered through the system. "Your guests have arrived, sir."

"Send them up." He turned back to find Sara regarding him warily.

"What guests?"

"Just some people I hired to help with your new look." His words didn't wipe the caution from her expression. It was telling that her continued distrust had the power to wound. And ironic, given the fact that she had all too much reason for the emotion. "I can assure you there won't be a U.S. Marshal in the bunch."

A fraction of the tension seeped from her limbs. "You told Whitmore you'd call him."

"And I will. Later. But not to reveal your location." He slipped his hands in his pockets and took a moment to consider the scene that had undoubtedly taken place at his beach house within hours of their departure. Whitmore would be infuriated when his agents failed to return with Sara, but Nick wasn't concerned. This job would be completed on his terms. It was his life on the line. His and Sara's.

When the buzzer rang he opened the door to four females, and amid introductions, ushered them all inside. "Ladies. Set your packages down anywhere. I'd like you to get started right away. Your subject is right over there."

They turned as one to regard Sara, whose apprehension was written clearly on her face.

"Mon Dieu!" exclaimed Rose Marie. The tall willowy blonde had her short hair fashioned into pink spikes. She crossed the thick carpeting and threaded her hands into Sara's hair, holding it away from her head. "What did you use to cut this, *chérie,* a lawnmower?"

Half-amused, Nick watched carefully to be sure he didn't have to intercede on the Frenchwoman's behalf. But Sara was behaving herself for the moment. At least she hadn't thrown a punch yet, although her hands were curled into fists. Seeming unaware of her danger, Rose Marie turned to look back at Nick. "I'll have to go shorter, get rid of the damage. Punk is big these days, and she could carry it off. She's got the bone structure."

"Something a bit more subdued, I think." He strolled toward the two women and pretended not to notice the daggers Sara was glaring at him. "A dark brunette, layered cut, but don't lose all the length."

The tone of Sara's voice was quietly lethal. "I'm perfectly capable of choosing—"

"Shasta, we'll want a full wardrobe, fashionable but not faddish. Clean lines, casual elegance." The short round woman he was addressing nodded furiously as she pulled a measuring tape out of her bags.

"Clair," he continued, turning toward another woman, "the makeup needs to complement the new look. See what you can do to narrow the shape of the eyes."

"Really? Seems a shame."

He couldn't have agreed more. He crooked a finger at the last woman and they moved away from the bustle in the room. When they were out of hearing of the others he murmured, "Nice work on such short order, Kim. Can we trust them to be discreet?"

The striking redhead's cool blue eyes were almost level with his own. "Of course, Nick. Have I ever failed you?"

Real affection tinged his voice. "Never." He'd worked with Kim Baxter for a number of years, and she was nothing if not resourceful. "Just be careful. I don't know how long I'll be gone, and she'll take the first opportunity to run."

Kim sent a measuring glance Sara's way. "She doesn't look like much of a challenge."

He followed the direction of the woman's gaze and watched as Sara battled all the pairs of hands reaching for her. "Don't underestimate her. I'd hate for her to shoot you, too."

Shock showed in the woman's expression, to be replaced by speculation. "Care to explain that?"

He didn't. "Don't leave her alone. I want her here when I get back."

Kim nodded. "She will be." Moving away, she approached the other women, and Nick went to the door, opened it. Before pulling it shut behind him, he glanced one more time at the small group of women surrounding Sara. For the first time since he'd met her he caught a look of sheer panic on her face. Obviously being the recipient of all that personal attention was even more alarming than being faced with an assassin.

She wouldn't welcome the unexpected surge of sympathy he felt for her, so he pushed it aside and closed the door.

"Everything's on schedule." Holding the phone to his ear, Nick stood before the huge window in the offices he'd rented months ago, and contemplated the bustle of the Parisian streets below.

Victor Mannen's voice sounded pleased. "Excellent. When can I expect the first shipment?"

"Four weeks. I have half your order filled, and foresee no problem with the rest of it."

There was a long silence on the line. Then Mannen said, "Perhaps you could speed up the timeline. I'd make it worth your while, of course."

"I'm afraid that won't be possible." Nick turned away from the bright, summery scene below. "It's best to procure our items from various countries. There's less chance of leaving a trail that way. The Indonesian market, especially, requires finesse."

"Other suppliers have produced faster results."

"Other suppliers could never handle a shipment of this size." Nick let the truth of his answer hang between them. "We're talking four times your usual numbers, with quadruple the profits, for half the overhead. I think it's worth the wait.''

''Given your reputation, I suppose I'll be satisfied with that.''

Since Nick had spent years establishing that reputation, he accepted the compliment as his due. ''I have associates who can handle the rest of the labor on this end for now. I need to focus on the receiving end.''

''Of course. When will you arrive in Chicago?''

He deliberately kept his answer vague. ''Soon. I'll let you know. I have a few details to clear up first.''

''I can appreciate a man who tends to details. I'm not one to forgive loose ends.''

His mind flashing to Sara, Nick said only, ''No. Neither am I.''

Moments later he cut the connection, and sent an inquiring glance at the other man in the room. ''Anything?''

Luc LeNoue never looked up from the computer monitor. ''Are you kidding? Trace attempts started within five seconds of his answering the line. So far I've bounced them off of Tampa, London, Tokyo, and—my personal favorite—Reykjavik. Had enough yet?'' he crooned to the machine, his gray gaze avid. ''No? How about some Moscow?'' He pressed another command on the keyboard, and another red light glowed on the map taking shape on the screen.

''Quit showing off and put an end to it.''

With a noticeable show of reluctance, Luc pressed another command and the screen went blank. Whoever was on the other end of the trace would, within milliseconds, hit a figurative brick wall.

''You're a fun hater, you know that?'' The question was voiced pleasantly enough. Luc clasped his hands behind his head and leaned back in his chair. ''I was going to goose chase the locator to the Vatican. That always freaks people out.''

"You really have a criminal mind," Nick said, amused despite himself. He'd employed the other man for almost three years now. While Luc still had a few lessons to learn about following directives, his enthusiasm for his job could be refreshing.

"So." The other man regarded him fixedly. "Want to lay bets on who ordered the trace?"

Nick lifted a shoulder negligibly. "It could have been Justice, I suppose. I'd be surprised if they didn't have Mannen's lines tapped. But I'm also certain he'd give me the number to a secure line. He hasn't escaped arrest this long by being stupid."

Luc raked a hand through his short, sandy-colored hair. He hadn't bothered to dye it back after the last task he'd completed. With his battered, pugilistic features, he resembled a boxer who'd spent too many years in the ring. "So you figure Mannen's behind it."

"He'd be a fool to hire me for a job like this and not take some precautions. If he were a fool, I wouldn't be working with him."

"So he's not stupid, just crooked and rich."

"Exactly."

"Well, speaking of stupid and crooked..." Luc's face sobered. "I understand Hinrich and Roven have been asking around for Michel Falcol. Discreetly, of course."

Raising a brow, Nick considered the information. Falcol was one of a half-dozen international identities he had established for himself, and the one he was using in his dealings with Mannen. The two men had been Mannen's suppliers in the past, and no doubt were unhappy about being replaced.

"Keep listening. Let me know if the inquiries continue."

"Sure. I've been thinking, though…"

Nick folded his arms and sighed. In his experience, it never boded well when Luc thought too much.

"…maybe I ought to accompany you to the States. Sounds like you might have your hands full."

"We discussed this. Martin and Kwilisz will come with me. I need you at this end to keep me apprised of developments here."

"Is Kim going?" Though the man's tone was studiedly nonchalant, it was plain to discern the source of his sudden interest in accompanying Nick.

"She'll have to. But I'm counting on you to let me know if our arrangements begin to raise any interest here."

Luc nodded, although it was plain to see he wasn't happy about the situation.

Nick gestured to the computer. "I need to make another call. Think you can work your magic again?"

With a spark of his earlier enthusiasm, the other man turned back to the computer and started the necessary program. "United States again?"

"Yes." There was a spurt of emotion in Nick's veins, one he was surprised to identify as adrenaline. "It's time I contacted Whitmore. I'm sure he's been expecting my call." The thought of the man's certain fury at what he would consider Nick's renegade actions wasn't a concern. It was time the agent learned that he wasn't making all the decisions in this case. Governments only employed independent operatives to do what they couldn't legally do themselves. Were Nick to be caught up in the web he was weaving for Mannen, Justice would disavow any knowledge of his activities. He was assuming all the risks, and Whitmore needed to learn that Nick played by only one set of rules.

His own.

* * *

Darkness had fallen before Sara heard a noise at the door of the penthouse. Kim, the woman Nick had obviously left to stand guard over her, rose and checked the security hole. A card rattled in the lock, and she moved away as Nick opened the door and stepped inside.

From her stance near the windows Sara watched him freeze and sweep the room with that all-encompassing gaze of his. When his eyes landed on her, he relaxed imperceptibly.

"Did the two of you eat?"

"She wasn't hungry." It was Kim who answered. Sara had turned back to the window to stare sightlessly at the glittering skyline and grapple with the emotions tangling in her chest.

He'd come back. Ridiculous, perhaps, but she hadn't been all that certain that he would. She didn't know what to expect from Nick Doucet. And she was becoming increasingly concerned about her own state of mind. It would have been simpler, far simpler, if he'd stayed away. Gone about his mysterious business and left her to construct a plan to get back to the States. Alone. It was certain that she couldn't expect to disappear in Europe with the same ease afforded in her own country. An American woman would stand out, and establishing new identities would be much more difficult, not to mention expensive.

That thought triggered another, and she turned to see Nick closing the door as Kim left. "How'd you get us into this country?"

Taking his time answering, he turned on some more lamps. "I'm assuming you remember the plane ride."

"You know what I'm talking about." Since he didn't seem inclined to discuss it, she moved toward him, intent on pressing the issue. "People need passports and probably all kinds of papers to cross borders. I don't have a passport."

"Perhaps not. But Amber Jennings does."

As she gaped at him, he slipped out of the fawn-colored jacket he'd worn over his black slacks and shirt, and rolled his shoulders tiredly. "Has your appetite returned? I haven't eaten."

She reached out, tugged at his sleeve when he would have reached for the phone to dial room service. "How'd you do it, Nick?"

His enigmatic dark gaze surveyed her calmly. "I have a certain expertise in these matters." He must have decided that his cryptic answer wasn't going to satisfy her because he went on. "You remember the plane stopping to refuel in Brussels? One of the mechanics there is very obliging. For a fee he smuggles an envelope to the pilot, who takes the opportunity for a quick outside visual check of the aircraft." He shrugged. "The documents won't do you any good now, I'm afraid. I've already destroyed them."

Ignoring the direct hit those words made, Sara stepped nearer. It was anger, rather than logic, dictating her actions, or else she never would have allowed herself to get so close. "You needed a picture for them, didn't you, Nick? Want to tell me where you got it, or should I guess?"

He looked amused, damn him. "Your phony driver's license photo doesn't do you justice. And if your weight on there is accurate, you really are too thin."

Although she'd half expected the admission, it didn't lessen her fury. "You went through my things!"

His fingers curled around her wrist, and too late she let go of his shirt, tried to step away. He didn't allow it. They remained close, their gazes locked, and then his grip on her wrist loosened, turned caressing. "I scanned the photo and sent it to my contact in Brussels. He's adept at doctoring documents. I'm equally adept at picking pockets, but it wasn't necessary. You were sleeping. Your purse was right there.''

His thumb rubbed over the sensitive skin of her wrist, lingered on the pulse pounding madly beneath the surface. ''It was a bit impolite, perhaps, but hardly on the same level as shooting your host.''

She yanked at her arm, but he didn't release her. ''Where's this interest come from, Sara, hmm?'' His free hand went to her hair, toyed with the ends of the newly cut and colored strands. ''Righteous indignation, or something deeper? You weren't by any chance hoping to get your hands on those papers and take off, were you?''

Since the thought had crossed her mind, it took some acting to look disinterested. ''What? And leave my gilded cage here? Why would I do that?'' The heat radiating from his clasp on her wrist was distracting, his proximity more so. His gaze dropped to her lips and her throat abruptly went dry.

''Because you don't trust me any more than you do Justice.'' The words were uttered absently. He cupped her jaw in his hands and rubbed a thumb across her lips. Lightly. Seductively. Her senses began to thrum with heightened awareness, drawing her body taut with shimmering tension.

Alarms shrilled dimly in the corners of her mind. It was his words she should be attending to. For some reason they seemed important, but her concentration was splintered by the intensity in his eyes, the warmth of his touch.

He wanted her.

There had been a time not too many hours ago when she'd almost forgotten that fact. Shooting a man should have discouraged even the most blatant interest. And it had been easy to convince herself that Nick's pursuit of her had been irrevocably linked to his connection with Justice. But there was no mistaking the primal emotion gleaming in his ebony eyes. The raw carnal need she saw there summoned an answering flame low in the pit of her belly, one that sheer will alone couldn't banish.

The hand holding her wrist loosened to slide up her arm before resting on her bare shoulder. "If this is a sample of your new wardrobe, I approve."

It was difficult to concentrate with his breath stirring her hair, his hand toying with the edge of her skimpy top. It would barely qualify as a shirt. It was little more than a shiny handkerchief held in place by some strategically placed straps across her back. It didn't allow for a bra, and all Nick would have to do was slip his hands under the loose bottom, glide them over her ribs and cup her bare breasts.

And she found that she wanted him to. Quite desperately.

The strength of her longing was staggering. He had one hand placed lightly on her back, his fingers grazing her vertebra. His eyes had gone slumberous, and his head slowly lowered toward hers. When she felt him take one earlobe in his teeth to score it gently, desire rocketed through her system. And the alarms in her mind sounded even more loudly.

His mouth cruised along her jawline before sampling the sensitive cord of her throat, and a gasp shuddered out of her. It occurred to her, belatedly, that desire this strong, this overwhelming, was its own kind of trap. It could soothe fears, dull instincts and jumble the senses.

And it could tempt her to lower her guard with the wrong man, for all the wrong reasons.

She tensed at the realization. She knew, better than most, that some men didn't hesitate to wield sex as a weapon. Given her reaction to Nick Doucet, sex would be a potent weapon indeed.

The thought evoked a glimmer from the past, one she

usually took pains to avoid. Images scraped across her memory, trailing a chill in their wake. She shuddered.

"What is it?" His words rasped in her ear, sharp with need. With one deft hand he rubbed her back, as if he could smooth the sudden rigidity from her bones. Rearing back a bit, he studied her, and what he saw in her face had his mouth flattening, his eyes becoming abruptly shuttered.

She leaned back against the arm that was still holding her closely. "I was thinking how effective a weapon sex could be, in the right hands. I'll bet you're a master at those kinds of games, aren't you, Nick?"

There was stunned disbelief on his face, quickly replaced by a savage temper, all the more frightening for being controlled. "You think I'd bind you to me with sex, Sara? Is that it? Believe me, if I thought that was possible I'd have been on you, inside you, before we left New Orleans."

Despite his words, or perhaps because of them, he let her go, turned toward the phone. But not before she recognized the stamp of arousal on his face, its lean lines still carved with frustration.

She listened to him place an order with room service and knew the tight clipped tone he was using was evidence of temper. But she couldn't regret her words, even if they'd wounded him. Because they'd caused him to release her, let her put some much needed distance between them.

And one thing was becoming increasingly certain—she needed that distance to protect herself. Regardless of Nick's intentions, she couldn't afford to lower her defenses with him. The man had a way of slipping through her guard as no other ever had.

She heard him replacing the phone in its cradle, then silence stretched, thrumming with tension. "So is Kim to be my permanent keeper?" The question had been nagging

at her the entire afternoon. When he didn't answer, Sara
turned, waved an arm to encompass the room. "Is this my
new jail?"

"You'll stay with me."

The words, although not altogether unexpected, weren't
the ones she'd hoped for. "But you said before that Justice
had hired you to bring down Mannen."

"That's right."

"How do you intend to do that from here?"

He looked up, and there was an indefinable glimmer in
his eye. "I don't."

The two words hung suspended in the air between them.
She stared at him, questions churning inside her, along
with a looming sense of foreboding.

"Mannen's in Chicago, so that's where I have to go."

His meaning was all too clear, but she backed away
from it, and him. It was too horrible to even contemplate.
"You mean…you'll have to go there sometime. You'll
have to…"

The signs of his earlier temper had vanished. He was
watching her with an impassive expression that lent his
words a cold, dead weight.

"I promised I'd protect you—hide you—and I will. I
figure the best place for that is in Chicago. Right under
Victor Mannen's nose."

Chapter 7

Sara stared at Nick, shock and terror sprinting down her spine. "You're crazy!"

"It's the best way. It's the last place Mannen would expect to find you…hell, it's the last place *Justice* would expect to find you."

"I'm sure the genius of your plan will be of great comfort to me when I'm dead!"

In response to the rising emotion in her voice, his went lower, became more soothing. "That's not going to happen. We're changing your identity again as well as your appearance. Neither Mannen nor Whitmore will suspect a thing."

She could feel sheets of ice glazing her insides. It was a measure of her fear that a hint of pleading entered her tone. "I could stay here. With that woman, or someone else. Or with lots of guards. As many as you want—" She broke off because he was already shaking his head.

"You had two choices when you came with me. That remains unchanged."

Justice or Nick. She didn't need for him to verbalize the words to remember the impossibility of the decision. For the first time she actually gave serious thought to changing her mind. Certainly the government would never take such a risk with a prize witness as to dangle her before Mannen.

But that thought was swiftly followed by another. The danger of putting her trust in Justice was just as real, if perhaps more removed than what Nick was proposing. Mannen would still have someone cultivated in the department. Someone who would report any information on her directly to him.

Turning her back on Nick, Sara walked to the window once more. Gazing sightlessly at the warm glow of lights, she hugged her arms around herself and chose to blame the river of cold coursing through her body on the hare-brained designer who'd dressed her. She'd have given anything for a sweatshirt.

"Would I have to see him?"

"There's no point if you don't."

A shudder worked through her. She heard Nick approaching, but willed him not to touch her. She felt like she would shatter in a million pieces if he did.

"I thought on some level that might appeal to you."

She whirled to look at him, her jaw agape.

"What is it you feel for him, Sara, besides the fear? Any lingering feelings of hate? Desire for revenge?"

An image of Sean's surprised eyes, his lifeless body, flashed across her mind. She pressed together lips suddenly inclined to tremble, and refused to reply. But that didn't stop Nick from continuing, his shaman's voice drifting through her system. "I'm offering you a chance to stop running. A chance to stand up to the man, and help make him pay for everything he did to you...to your friends. How much longer are you going to take the easy way out, Sara?" A note of something indefinable entered his voice.

"I can tell you from personal experience that you can't outpace the guilt. If you could, half the people on earth would be on the move."

The impact of his words was like a sucker punch to the solar plexus. She knew only too well that he spoke the truth. Six years was a long time, but she had yet to escape the memories. She'd never managed to run fast enough, far enough, to do so.

In that moment she found herself hating him. Feeling raw and exposed, she lashed out. "What do you know about it? Do you know what it's like to have six deaths on your conscience, hmm? Can you imagine being responsible for the murders of innocent people?"

"Yes." His expression became blank, and his voice was oddly impassive. "I know exactly how that feels."

She had no idea how long it was before Nick entered the room to contemplate her sitting alone in the dark.

"Sara."

That was all he said, but she couldn't summon the will to fight anymore right now. She was weary, with a bone-deep exhaustion that went far beyond the physical. "I was the one to involve the rest with Mannen." Her gaze lifted to his. "You knew that, didn't you?"

He came farther into the room. "No."

"There were five of us. An odd collection of kids who sort of found each other one by one and clung. We were all runaways—no diplomas, no skills. We took what jobs we could get, but when we pooled our money we could at least find a place to stay where the rats wouldn't keep us awake all night. I'm the one who answered the ad in the paper. It was an upscale restaurant, not snooty, but nice. They needed a hostess. I used the ad as a reason to get inside one afternoon, hoping at least for a job as dishwasher."

She could still remember her first sight of the gleaming hardwood floors, the vaulted ceilings and brass-plated bar. She'd never seen anything like it in her life. The woman she'd spoken to had probably been only a half-dozen years older, but it had been glaringly apparent that there were miles between them when it came to background.

"The lady there wouldn't even let me talk to the manager. She was showing me out when a man walked in the door. I knew from the change in her attitude that he must be someone important. He was the owner, though he apparently didn't spend much time there." And his name, she'd later learned, was Victor Mannen. He'd stood in the doorway, elegant and tailored in his custom-made clothes and immaculately groomed silver hair, and taken in the scene in seconds. "For some reason he stopped her. I didn't understand why. Not then. But he invited me back to the offices, and after talking to me for a few minutes, he offered me a job. Just cleaning up and the like, but I was thrilled.

"I suppose he could smell my desperation." She realized now that he'd been a man to sense that kind of thing, to feed on it. "I figured he might expect some kind of payback, so I was careful around him. But he wasn't there that much, and when he was, he seemed okay. After a few months I finally screwed up enough courage to ask about jobs for my friends. It wasn't long before we were all working for him, in one manner or another."

They'd been, she remembered, stunned by their good fortune. So when they'd gradually come to experience doubts regarding some of the associates who occasionally met Mannen there, or about the nature of the errands they were assigned, those doubts were quieted by the steady pay and the dependable source of meals. Survival on the streets hadn't allowed for ethical niceties.

"How long did you work for him?"

Nick's voice was a velvet link in the darkness, one she seized gratefully to prevent the recollections from sucking her under. "About a year for me. More than half that for the others. It all changed when we lost the place where we were living. Our landlord threw us out when he found there were five of us in a studio apartment. It was my idea for us to sleep at the restaurant."

The sick feeling of responsibility swam in her stomach, a familiar companion. "It was easy enough to lift the keys, get copies made. We'd wait until all the help had gone home, sneak in the back and crash in the office area. They were doing some construction there, taking out some walls, making Mannen's office larger. We would just move the tarps off the furniture and stretch out for the night, put everything back in the morning. No one showed up around there before 10:00 a.m. It should have been okay."

"Until Mannen came in unexpectedly." There was a grim note in Nick's tone, but she didn't have time to reflect on it. She pulled up her knees and hugged them to her chest, as if to protect herself from the sting of the memories. They swarmed anyway, like vicious bees.

"We were sleeping. I think it was Sean who heard people moving around. He went to the office door and recognized Mannen's voice. We barely had time to drag the tarps back over the stuff and hide before they entered the office." With a grim sense of irony she remembered how their greatest fear then had been that they'd be fired for the liberties they'd taken. Instead, they'd embarked on a nightmare.

"Three of them dived behind a couch. Jason had wedged himself in a corner between a bookcase and the wall, and I was still rushing around looking for a hiding place. The door started to open and I crawled into the closet. It was the worst place to choose. The door had been taken off in the remodeling, and if Mannen had been in the right position, and looked up at the right time, he'd have seen me easily.''

''But he didn't.''

She shook her head, forgetting the gesture would be indiscernible in the darkness. ''He had two men with him. One we'd seen around before, and one was a stranger. It was late, around 2:00 a.m., and from the sound of their conversation, they were discussing drugs. The other man was telling Mannen the price of the next shipment was going to double, and Mannen's voice got really cold as they argued. Finally, though, he agreed and had the guy make a call to set the plan in motion. Then, when the call was over, he looked over at his associate…'' She stopped, swallowing. Just the mental image of the scene still had the power to make her throat go dry ''…and told him to shoot him.''

I think we're done here, Peter. Kill him.

A chill eddied through her at the eerie memory. ''There were three shots, and then the sound of something hitting the floor. The other man, Peter, asked if this was going to mess things up, and Mannen said that the shipment would arrive anyway, he'd just eliminated the middleman. He told him to get rid of the body and clean up the mess, then walked out.''

She rested her forehead against her raised knees. She'd recited this scene endlessly for the Justice agents, but it never lost the luster of terror. That emotion had merely been a prelude for what was to come.

When she raised her head again she was disconcerted to find Nick squatted down in front of her. Close. All too close. The shadows blended with his inky hair, left his eyes unreadable.

''So you were right, of course,'' Sara murmured. ''A while ago. It *was* my fault—all of it. They wouldn't have met Mannen if not for me, wouldn't have been in the restaurant that night if I hadn't suggested it." *Wouldn't be dead.* The words she couldn't bear to speak hung in the air between them.

"Feeling guilty isn't the same as being guilty. And it's a natural reaction for a lone survivor in a situation like the one you were involved in."

The bleak certainty in his voice had her watching him carefully. "Do *you* feel guilty?" He was close enough that she saw the flicker in his eyes, although he didn't answer. "You said you knew what it was like to be responsible for the murders of others."

His countenance, usually so inscrutable, grew fierce, but she was strangely unafraid. She had a feeling the emotion was directed inward.

"Yes." His voice was clipped. "I feel guilty." He rose abruptly, turned away. "But there's a difference between your situation and mine. You didn't cause your predicament, it rose up and enveloped you. People died on my watch because I made a mistake."

It was telling that in that brief exchange she learned more about Nick Doucet than in all the days she'd known him. She recognized the ghosts in his eyes, knew how cruelly the demons could haunt. The tiny chink in his armor opened a corresponding crack in her own. Curiosity, and something more, had her asking, "What happened?"

There was no reason for him to tell her, so she didn't know which of them was more surprised when he started to speak. "I was still in the Green Berets, on assignment in Bosnia. I was wounded, and some villagers hid me from the faction hunting me, nursed me back to health." His voice was all the more compelling for its complete lack of expression. "They lived in terrible conditions. No sanitation, no medicine, no money. I wanted to repay them, so when I was well enough to leave, I made sure regular shipments of supplies got back to them. Medicine, food, clothes.''

Her throat dried. She could already imagine the rest. His next words confirmed her fears.

''The rebels discovered the regular line of supplies and got suspicious. They tortured one of the village elders until he confessed they'd helped me. Then they torched the village.''

A small gasp escaped her, but Nick didn't appear to hear it. He was lost in a hellish past from which there was no escape. ''Sixty-six people died in the fire.''

She searched for some way to comfort him. ''You were trying to help them. You couldn't know—''

He turned to look at her then, and his face was fierce. ''You're wrong, it was my *job* to know. And I learned the lesson well. Emotion, no matter how noble, has no place in an assignment. It only clouds thoughts, dulls instincts. It's a lesson I'll never forget.''

His words, the message behind them, silenced her. He couldn't have made it any clearer that feelings wouldn't be allowed to sway him on this mission. There was no reason for the realization to wound her, since she harbored the same vow. It had been a long, long time since anyone had been allowed to get close to her. There was no reason for the fact to pick this moment to hurt.

Suddenly sorry she'd ever introduced the topic, she ran a hand through her hair, a bit disconcerted at the tactile reminder of its new length. ''It's been a long day,'' she said abruptly. ''I'm going to bed.''

He rose, put out a hand to help her from the chair. ''The bathrooms should all be stocked with whatever supplies you might need. Help yourself.''

It was a relief when he let himself out of the room, as quietly as he'd entered it. A relief to be alone and to focus on rituals that were soothing in their routine.

FREE GIFTS!

NO COST! NO OBLIGATION TO BUY!
NO PURCHASE NECESSARY!

PLAY THE
Lucky Key Game

Scratch gold area with a coin.
Then check below to see the books and gift you get!

345 SDL DH27
245 SDL DH23

YES! I have scratched off the gold area. Please send me the 2 Free books and gift for which I qualify. I understand I am under no obligation to purchase any books, as explained on the back and on the opposite page.

NAME   (PLEASE PRINT CLEARLY)

ADDRESS

APT.#   CITY

STATE/PROV.   ZIP/POSTAL CODE

2 free books plus a gift	1 free book
2 free books	Try Again!

(S-IM-OS-01/02)

The Silhouette Reader Service™ — Here's how it works:

Accepting your 2 free books and gift places you under no obligation to buy anything. You may keep the books and gift and return the shipping statement marked "cancel." If you do not cancel, about a month later we'll send you 6 additional books and bill you just $3.80 each in the U.S., or $4.21 each in Canada, plus 25¢ shipping & handling per book and applicable taxes if any.* That's the complete price and — compared to cover prices of $4.50 each in the U.S. and $5.25 each in Canada — it's quite a bargain! You may cancel at any time, but if you choose to continue, every month we'll send you 6 more books, which you may either purchase at the discount price or return to us and cancel your subscription.

*Terms and prices subject to change without notice. Sales tax applicable in N.Y. Canadian residents will be charged applicable provincial taxes and GST.

If offer card is missing write to: Silhouette Reader Service, 3010 Walden Ave., P.O. Box 1867, Buffalo, NY 14240-1867

BUSINESS REPLY MAIL

FIRST-CLASS MAIL   PERMIT NO. 717-003   BUFFALO, NY

POSTAGE WILL BE PAID BY ADDRESSEE

SILHOUETTE READER SERVICE
3010 WALDEN AVE
PO BOX 1867
BUFFALO NY 14240-9952

NO POSTAGE
NECESSARY
IF MAILED
IN THE
UNITED STATES

Returning to the adjoining room, she dug through the small pile of clothes Claire had left and found a thin satiny shift. She was unable to tell if it was an undergarment or sleepwear, but it would serve as the latter tonight. She put it on, then crossed to the sliding glass door to the balcony. Opening it wide, she turned and slipped into bed, settled her head on the pillow. The door to the bedroom was pushed open and she could make out Nick's form moving toward her, the bandage on his side standing out starkly in the shadows.

She sat up, yanking the covers to her chest. "I don't want to discuss anything else tonight."

"Neither do I."

Disbelief leadened her limbs, left her incapable of movement when he lifted the other side of the bedcovers and slid in beside her.

"You can't believe—"

"That I trust you? No, as a matter of fact, I don't." He reached over, clasped one of her hands, laced their fingers. "But I thought you might find this method preferable to being handcuffed every night to the bed frame."

He was, she noted, wearing some sort of low-riding boxers. She made the observation with a sense of relief, but the thought of lying next to him all night wasn't a way to guarantee restfulness. "What are you afraid of?" Desperation made her voice caustic. "We're thirteen stories in the air. Do you think I'm going to jump or attach myself to the outside of the building and climb down?"

Her sarcasm had no effect on him. "All I'm sure of is that you'll be looking for some way out, and this is the only way I can keep track of you and sleep, too."

Unceremoniously he reached over, grasped her waist and slid her down into the bed. Ignoring her rigid limbs and sputtered protests, he lay close beside her and threw his free arm across her middle, anchoring her in place.

"I don't...I can't sleep with any...with you here."

His response failed to reassure her. "You'd better get used to it. For the rest of our time together, this is the way it has to be."

Sara lay there, tense and all too aware of the heat emanating from the man lying too close beside her. The situation got more intolerable by the minute, and increasingly perilous. Nick was still, his breathing growing steadily deeper. While she...she was having difficulty drawing in a breath at all.

The only person she'd ever slept with—really slept with—was Sean. They'd been children, snuggled up like puppies as much for warmth and comfort as anything else.

There was nothing in the least bit childlike in the feelings induced by Nick Doucet.

Her lips parted; she couldn't seem to get enough oxygen. He wasn't pressed against her, was only touching her with his arm, and its position was far from loverlike. But that didn't stop her from imagining the tiny amount of space between them, didn't prevent her from thinking about the test to her willpower if his touch turned more intimate.

She squeezed her eyes shut tightly and willed her wayward imagination to halt. As if realizing the silent struggle going on inside her, Nick spoke, his breath stirring her hair. "You've been awake eighteen hours. Sleep, *mon ange.*"

And despite the turmoil of events that had transpired in the last few days, miraculously, she did just that.

"You need to affect a Southern accent for your new identity, but don't worry. We'll practice until you master it." He'd had breakfast served on the small terrace outside the living room. Sara looked up, shot him a cool glance across the table.

"Well, if that's not just the kindest offah Ah've evah had."

He lifted a brow, impressed despite himself at the deliberately accurate drawl. "Good job. I forgot about your stint in Atlanta."

"And Biloxi before that. Picking up a drawl when you're surrounded by Southerners isn't all that difficult."

He gave a nod. "You'll need to tone it down a bit so it's more subtle. As Raeanne Backstrom, you've had the benefit of finishing schools that would eliminate all but the Southern belle flavor of the dialect." His smile was slight. "As a matter of fact, right now you're on a trip across Europe, compliments of your parents, after just completing your second year at Wellesley."

Abruptly her face smoothed, became that impassive mask he was becoming all too familiar with. "The drawl is child's play. But don't you think it's a bit much to expect a tenth-grade dropout to play the part of a college student?"

It was the emotion behind the question that he was most interested in, and so his answer was absent as he considered it. "You'll be well rehearsed in every aspect of the identity before we leave here." Something was clearly bothering her, but she didn't respond, and he felt a flicker of impatience. It was becoming more and more difficult to watch her don that blank expression. Although it would be an effective tool in the charade they were about to embark in, he was all too aware that she used it with him as a way to keep him at a distance.

It shouldn't matter. He'd waited patiently for days in rotting jungles halfway across the world, or under the searing desert sun, to complete a mission. He'd taught his body how to ignore pain and hunger until an assignment was concluded, his quarry terminated. So it was both humbling and infuriating to constantly fight to control other, more primal physical responses when it came to Sara.

He could, he supposed, blame part of his tension on the night he'd spent beside her, listening to her breathing. Inhaling her scent. And yet not touching her in any way that mattered. His gaze narrowed as he watched her move her breakfast around on her plate without tasting much of it. Too many hours of the night had been spent reminding himself of all the reasons for not making love to her the way his body had demanded.

With effort, he forced his mind back to the task at hand. "We'll have to shave four years off your age to make the identity fit, but I don't think that will be a problem."

Pushing her chair back, she rose, went to the wrought-iron railing surrounding the terrace. "What will happen if Mannen starts looking into my background? Won't he be able to discover that this Raeanne person shouldn't be in America?"

Nick didn't think it was a question of whether Mannen would check her background; he was counting on the man doing just that. "The identity will hold up to scrutiny. You and I will have met while you traveled across Europe. In order to be with me, you made an excuse to switch tour groups and paid someone who bears a resemblance to you to take your place, thus keeping your parents unaware of your real whereabouts."

"I went to a lot of trouble to be with you," Sara said, her tone openly mocking.

"Yes, and your parents wouldn't approve of your new lover." He saw her spine stiffen, but she didn't turn to look at him. He wondered for a moment if his words had managed to pierce her stoic demeanor. Certainly they'd infused him with a warmth that was as immediate as it was undeniable. "It's the most believable story, and one that will allow us to appear together in public while we're in Chicago.''

Although the morning air was balmy, she hugged her middle, rubbing her hands up and down her arms. ''And that's important—why?''

''Mannen hasn't stayed out of prison this long by being careless. He'll have checked me out thoroughly, and I expect him to do a run on you, too. When he finds exactly what he's supposed to, his suspicions will be allayed.''

The last place the man would expect her to show up would be on his doorstep. By providing Sara with a new look, a drawl and a foolproof identity, Nick would assure her the boldest, most impenetrable cover imaginable. He couldn't blame her for the nerves, but he didn't like to think of her being afraid. Didn't like to consider the very real fear she'd experienced because of him already.

He rose and crossed to her, caging her body by propping his hands on the railing beside hers. She tensed against him, and her delicate profile could have been etched from marble. ''I know it's frightening to contemplate, but I really do think this is the best way to keep you safe. And there's nothing I wouldn't do to protect you.'' The words were no less than the truth. She wouldn't be the first innocent placed in his safekeeping. He'd learned in the most tragic way the importance of maintaining his objectivity in a job like this. But objectivity faded the moment she turned to look at him, her expression uncertain.

It was the most natural thing in the world to lower his head toward hers, to brush his lips over the curve of her cheek. When he heard the tiny explosion of her breath he felt a savage desire to do even more. To turn her around fully in his arms and crush her mouth under his, to force her, finally and completely, to acknowledge the primal sexual awareness that burned between them.

The pretense they'd be engaged in would be dangerous

on more than just the obvious level. Pretending to be
Sara's lover would be a charade that would be only too
easy to play, only too easy to imagine. He'd quickly become fascinated by her, and fascination could ignite all too
easily to more. Much more.

He was too well versed in control to allow that to happen. He took a step back, and then another.

"If we were supposed to have met in Paris, I should
probably know more about it," she said.

The slight unsteadiness in her voice pleased him. "We
have three days before we leave for Chicago. Between now
and then I should have some time to show you around the
city." He'd have to steal time away from days already
filled with handling last minute details, but already he was
planning on how to do just that. The thought of spending
a few stolen hours with Sara in the city of lovers was just
too tempting to pass up.

Victor Mannen waited for Franklin to leave his office
before tearing open the long-awaited package. He
skimmed the dossier inside quickly, then, pleased, read it
again more thoroughly.

His new contact at Justice was earning his keep. He'd
been able to access international law enforcement databases, and the resulting information was interesting indeed.

Interpol had a file on Michel Falcol. So did Scotland
Yard and the FBI. Pieced together with the information
he'd already compiled, it provided Mannen with a better
picture of his new business associate.

Picking up his gold pen, he circled some facts as he
read. Escaped custody for arms smuggling in Italy, 1994.
Wanted for questioning in relation to a hijacked munitions
truck near Fort Bragg. Known associate of DELGAN, an
international band of mercenary terrorists with no known
allegiances.

A man with no loyalty except to the highest bidder. Given his deep pockets, it was a quality Mannen could appreciate.

In all, Falcol was wanted for questioning in relation to a dozen separate incidents. And it was clear from the interest he'd generated in the different agencies that he hadn't overestimated his abilities when he'd spoken to Victor.

He flipped a page. There wasn't a picture included, and the physical information was sketchy at best. Michel Falcol: birthplace unknown. First identified in Belfast, 1992. Dark hair, dark eyes. Identifying marks: a one-inch scar below left eye. Wound believed to be received in a knife fight with a Turkish colonel involved in the black market. It was interesting to note that Falcol was wanted for questioning in that man's disappearance, along with his other crimes.

Satisfied, Mannen closed the file folder and rose, walked across to the Renoir on his wall. Moving it aside, he opened the wall safe behind it, set the file inside. Locking the safe and replacing the picture, he strolled across the plush carpeting to the cut crystal decanter of ice water he kept there.

It was soothing to the ego to find he'd chosen wisely when he'd settled upon Falcol. He was comfortable with men without scruples. Most could be easily controlled by money, but this man might prove to be a cut above the brainless robots he usually employed.

Raising the glass to his lips, Victor smiled. He found he was quite looking forward to the experience.

"I still can't get over how different you look," Sara murmured.

Nick and she were walking down a narrow sidewalk after their dinner. He held her hand, the gesture making them blend in with the young lovers and honeymooners strolling nearby. If he were a less wary man, it would be easy to forget at times like these that the contact was primarily for security.

He looked down into her eyes, and had an instant's regret that he'd taken the precaution of having her wear the new brown contacts. "My coloring is too dark to change easily. I've found it more convenient to use subtle alterations to modify my appearance." Altering his hairline was one such measure; the addition of the half-moon scar beneath his eye was another. Small rolls of padding inside his jaw changed the shape of his face. Taken separately, they were inconsequential details, but together they gave him a totally different look.

He wouldn't be using the Falcol identity after this assignment. It would be too risky after playing it publicly in Chicago. No, when that job was over, Michel Falcol would cease to exist, and Nick would become somebody else, with yet another manufactured background to match his new identity. The fact reminded him, not for the first time, of the similarity between Sara and him.

"What did you enjoy the most today?" He wasn't making idle conversation; he was genuinely interested.

"I think…Place de la Bastille." She must have read his surprise, because she gave a self-conscious shrug. "So much suffering went on there. It's inspiring to consider the bravery it took for the people to storm the place, and bring liberty in the process. It's hard to imagine that kind of courage."

He guided her closer to the storefront to avoid a group of giggling young girls headed their way. "I wouldn't think it would be so difficult for you to understand that kind of bravery. Not after what you've been through."

Her laugh was devoid of humor. "Believe me, courage is the last quality I can claim."

Frowning, he halted her when she would have started walking again, and crooked a finger beneath her chin, forced her to look at him. "Why do you say that?" He was honestly puzzled. He knew hardened soldiers who wouldn't have survived what she had. Who would have lacked the will and the cunning to elude Mannen for half a dozen years.

"Given my history, if I'd been in Paris in 1789 I wouldn't have been part of the group storming the Bastille, I'd have been running in the opposite direction." Her gaze clashed with his. Self-mockery made her voice sound brittle. "Because that's what I do, Nick. Hardly the stuff heroes are made of."

He thought there was a warning in her words for him, one he'd be wise to heed. Sara had made a habit of running from Mannen, and there was no reason to believe that had changed. She wouldn't willingly confront the murderer who'd ordered her own death more than once. Getting her to cooperate might turn out to be one of the toughest tasks Nick had ever undertaken. A cautious man would be prepared.

There was a nightclub nearby he thought she'd enjoy, and he was about to suggest that they head that way when his cell phone rang. He answered it as they waited to cross at a corner, and heard Luc's voice on the line.

"Wanted to let you know, I got the documents this afternoon. Everything looks in order."

Their new passports and identification had arrived. The light changed and Nick led Sara across the street, keeping an eye on the oncoming traffic. Pedestrians definitely did not have the right of way in Paris. "I assume they're satisfactory?"

"As always. Do you have plans this evening?"

Nick looked at Sara from the corner of his eye and saw

that she was openly listening to his side of the conversation. "Why do you ask?"

"Our two friends are in town. I understand they're looking for you."

Hinrich and Roven. Luc's grim tone tipped Nick off. The fact that the two smugglers had come hunting for Falcol could mean serious trouble. Losing what most certainly had been a lucrative contract with Mannen, they'd be looking to screw this job up for Nick in any number of ways. And he had a feeling that Mannen would spook easily if it appeared there were complications.

Nick's gaze narrowed as he mentally sifted through his options.

"You heard me, didn't you?"

"Yes." Helping Sara up the curb, he regretfully turned away from the direction of the nightclub he'd planned to visit and looked down the street.

"What do you propose to do about it?"

Raising a hand to hail a passing taxi, Nick replied, "I propose to let them find me."

Every major city in the world, regardless of its beauty or history, had an underbelly. It was, perhaps, nature's most consistent equalizer. Nick had spent more time than he'd like to consider lurking in alleys much like this one, in locales scattered across the globe. In his line of work it was a given, something to be accepted without reflection.

He waited for Luc's signal. The other man had planted a few well-placed rumors about where Michel Falcol would be tonight, and now Nick waited to see if Hinrich and Roven would take the bait. He had no reason to suspect otherwise. Both men were ruthless about eliminating competition.

The cell phone in Nick's pocket vibrated soundlessly. He reached for it, held it up to his ear. "Yeah."

''South of you, one block, heading your direction.''

Without another word, Nick broke the connection and replaced the phone in his pocket. He slipped from the shadows and approached the alley's entrance, adrenaline spiking in his veins.

A vagrant stumbled into the alley, clutching a prized bottle, but came up short when he saw Nick. Not a word was exchanged, but the man retreated far more quickly, with more coordination, than he'd managed a moment ago. It was for the best. The last thing Nick wanted was a bystander to worry about.

Voices were coming closer, the words guttural and low. German. So that would be Hinrich talking. Although he knew a bit of the language, Nick didn't spend time trying to translate. He simply waited until the men were nearly even with the alley, then slipped out of it, to stand before them.

''Messieurs.'' His French was flawless, his sudden appearance taking the men by surprise. ''I understand that you seek Michel Falcol.''

The pair recovered quickly. They drifted apart so that each would flank Nick if they rushed him. ''What do you know of Falcol?'' It was Roven speaking. French was his native tongue, although from what Nick had heard he'd spent most of the last decade out of the country.

''I know that you have found him.''

There was a quick verbal exchange between the two men, and Hinrich eyed Nick more speculatively. It was clear Roven had interpreted for him.

''You heard correctly,'' Louis Roven told Nick. He smiled, a quick baring of pointed teeth. With his sharp features and slight body, he had a rodentlike quality. ''We have heard of your reputation and wish to discuss business with you.''

''Step into my office.'' Nick waved them into the alley,

and after exchanging a quick look, the men followed him as he backed into its shadows.

"Do you know who we are?" Hinrich's accent was atrocious, but understandable.

"Your reputations precede you."

This reply seemed to give the German some trouble, so Roven took over the conversation again. "As does yours. It appears we have a client in common. The American."

"Correction. He used to be your client. Now he's mine." Nick lifted a shoulder nonchalantly, a gesture guaranteed to infuriate. "Had he been satisfied with your services, *mes amis*, he would not have come searching for me. Your operation is not large enough to meet his requirements."

Hinrich must have picked up at least some of his meaning, because he released a furious spate of German. Roven smiled again, but there was no humor in the expression. "Surely you do not mean to be deliberately offensive. We are reasonable men. We are willing to offer to act as partners in the endeavor. Equal split."

Nick threw his head back and laughed, while both of the men eyed him narrowly. He didn't answer; he didn't need to. His response was insultingly clear. There was a flash of metal as Hinrich slipped a knife from his sleeve, a nearly silent *snick* as the blade opened.

"Given your reputation, I had expected more intelligence." Roven's voice was steady as he and his friend advanced upon Nick. "But rumors have a way of inflating reputations, don't you agree?"

Nick's blood cooled, leaving his mind clear and calculating. "I'll let you be the judge of that yourself." The words had no sooner left his mouth than his left foot kicked out, knocking the knife from the German's hand.

Roven fell back, his hand groping at his leg. Ankle holster, Nick realized, even as he dove with the German toward the dropped knife. The near silent deadly scene took on a sense of increasing urgency. He managed to dodge the hamlike fist Hinrich threw at his chin, catching the blow on his shoulder instead. With a move he'd shown Sara in Florida, he flattened his palm and drove the butt of his hand straight up, splintering the man's nose. From the corner of his eye he detected movement, and grasped the German's shirt, swinging the man around to block the oncoming bullet.

Hinrich jerked as his body absorbed the shot Roven fired just then, and Nick used him as a shield to rush the other man. Roven paused, his eyes widening in horror as he realized his mistake, and in the next moment, Nick had reached across Hinrich's sagging shoulders to grab the other man by the throat.

"Drop it." Something in his face must have convinced Roven, because the gun was allowed to slide from his hand. Nick used his free hand to shove Hinrich's limp body aside.

"Falcol." The man wet his lips, his eyes rolling madly. "This has all been a terrible mistake."

Nick's smile was almost gentle. "That's right. And you made it." He drove a fist into the man's belly, doubling him over, before delivering the blow that sent him crashing to the ground, where he lay still and unconscious.

"And you call me the showoff."

Nick didn't look around at the sound of Luc's voice. "Poor timing, as usual."

"What are you complaining about?" The man strolled closer, kicked Hinrich over. "There were only two of them."

Nick straightened, aware of dampness at his side. The damn wound had opened again. "So you won't complain too much about clean-up detail." He ignored the other man's groan. "Take care of it. At least with them out of the way there's less chance of the job being compromised.''

Expertly, Luc squatted down, felt for a pulse on the big German. ''No,'' he said, his gaze meeting Nick's. ''I have no question about the *job* being compromised.''

The man wasn't known for his subtlety. ''Meaning?''

''Just that it's risky to take the woman to Chicago.''

Nick's jaw tightened. He wasn't used to having his decisions questioned. ''It's a calculated risk, I think.''

''You've changed the game plan for her, and that's not like you. I've never known you to grow obsessed over a woman.''

Voice curt, Nick retorted, ''I know exactly what I'm doing. Make sure you go through Hinrich's and Roven's pockets before you tip off the police to come down for them. If they're carrying anything that can point to us, get rid of it.'' Turning, he strode away, but was unable to forget Luc's words. He was wrong, of course. He'd learned in the most tragic way possible what happened when he was distracted from the assignment at hand. He wouldn't make that mistake with Sara, despite his attraction to her. Because if he did, the consequences would be deadly.

Chapter 8

It was Kim who met Nick at the door, and when he caught sight of Sara in one of the armchairs across the room he looked distinctly annoyed. "You should have gone to bed."

She surveyed him, silently taking inventory. Gone was her urbane date from earlier this evening. The same subtle air of menace that she'd intuitively sensed the first time she'd met him was back. She'd long since found that her first impression had been all too accurate.

Kim gasped as he walked by her. "You're bleeding."

He shrugged off her concern, continued toward Sara. "Just reopened a previous injury."

Sara's stomach went hollow. Her gaze arrowed to the stain spreading on his shirt. He'd never sought a doctor's opinion in Florida when the wound was fresh, and he'd reinjured the area twice now. It was ridiculous, under the circumstances, to feel guilty for that. "What happened?"

"A misunderstanding." He stopped before her chair and

reached for her hand, pulled her up. "With as little as you've eaten and slept in the last several days, you should be dead on your feet."

She kept her voice and her gaze steady. "Something tells me that might be an unfortunate choice of words, given your recent outing." She saw the awareness flicker in his eyes, but didn't expect an explanation. She didn't get one.

He turned his head, spoke to the woman getting ready to leave. "Is everything set?"

Kim halted in the act of slipping into her jacket. "Most of the deliveries have been made."

"The wardrobe?"

"All but the shoes."

"Have them here first thing in the morning."

Her brows rose. "Do you realize—"

His tone was implacable. "First thing."

"All right." With a gesture of surrender, she pulled open the door, let herself out. And then Nick and Sara were alone. He started undoing his shirt, using just enough care that she could tell what the action cost him. And she was hit with the sudden certainty that whoever Nick had had a misunderstanding with had suffered far worse than he had.

She had no idea where the conviction came from. Perhaps from the simmering aura of latent danger that shimmered off the man in waves. He hadn't shaved since that morning, and his jaw was shadowed. With his dark clothes and fierce expression, he looked like a bad man to cross. She didn't doubt that someone else had recently reached a very similar conclusion.

"Here. Let me." Pushing his hands aside, Sara finished unbuttoning his shirt, wincing a little when she saw the blood-soaked bandages. "C'mon. I'll help you clean up."

He followed her wordlessly into the bathroom, where

she rummaged through drawers until she found the necessary supplies. Then, schooling her face to impassivity, she gently removed the soiled bandage and set about cleaning the wound again.

The muscles beneath her fingers tensed when she touched him, and she swallowed. The last thing she needed was a reminder of what it felt like to touch that hard sinewy body, to feel his warmth.

To provide a distraction for them both, she asked, "Who did you have a run-in with tonight?"

He shocked her by answering. "Smugglers. They'd done some business with Mannen in the past and were feeling rather territorial."

Smugglers. She swallowed. "What do they smuggle? Arms? Drugs?"

"People." He waited for her gaze to bounce up to his before continuing. "Mannen has discovered the hottest black market commodity. They find people in various countries willing to pay a fee to be provided passage to the United States. In return they're promised documents and jobs. Instead, they're sold to various buyers as virtual slaves."

Her hands had stilled as he talked, horror blooming. "In this day and age? How is that possible?"

"Some of the buyers allow the immigrants to pay off the cost of their freedom through years of labor. Most are held captive with no end in sight. They're sold for prostitution and free labor. Unfortunately, there doesn't seem to be any shortage of buyers."

She reached for the gauze, surprised to find her hands trembling. "I can't believe that goes on in enlightened countries."

His voice, his face, were sober. "Greed is the lowest common denominator. No country is free of its reach."

Carefully, she taped the edges of the bandage she held

against his side. "So why were the smugglers interested
in you?"

"That's easy." His smile was humorless, sharklike.
"I'm Mannen's new source."

Her fingers stilled, and he pulled back to look over her
handiwork. Obviously satisfied, he shrugged out of his
open shirt, wadded it in his hand. He walked past her, but
she remained motionless. She couldn't have moved if she
tried. It occurred to her that Nick was no stranger to risk,
to the shadowy world of pretense and subterfuge. A world
in which he was, from everything she'd seen, more than
capable of handling himself.

He just might be as deadly as Mannen was. At the
thought, a shudder worked down her spine. He'd be a for-
midable man to cross.

And an impossible one to trust.

The hours spent in the air the next day weren't long
enough to soothe Sara's nerves. If anything, with every
mile they drew closer to O'Hare, the knots in her stomach
drew tighter. Spending much of the time in the plane becoming accustomed to her new identity did little to alle-
viate her anxiety.

"You'll need to show these when we land." Nick finished the conversation he was having with Kim and came
to sit beside Sara, handing her a bundle of documents. She
looked through them with something approaching dread.

"It appears that I'm well traveled." Her passport—
Raeanne's passport—she corrected herself mentally, bore
several stamps, the most recent to London. And yet it was
her own face she saw staring back at her. She'd switched
identities often enough that she didn't experience so much
as a start at the sight of her familiar face with dark hair,
and brown eyes. But she was intrigued by the speed with
which he'd managed to obtain the forgeries. Of course,

with his business contacts, the documents were probably no more difficult to manage than the wardrobe and hairstylist.

Flipping through the rest of the papers, she also found a Georgia driver's license and a social security card. "How much do forgeries like these cost?"

There was a smile in his voice. "Do I detect a note of criminal interest? Quite a bit, actually, although they would have been pricier if we were having a false one produced instead of just copying one on record with a new face."

"So Raeanne Backstrom isn't actually missing hers." When he shook his head, Sara asked, "What happens if she should return to the States early, about the same time Mannen runs a check on me?"

Nick reached over and took her hand, unmindful of her resistance. "That won't happen. I've left some men behind to keep track of Backstrom, along with a few other tasks." His next question almost took her mind off the thumb he sent skating across her knuckles. "Given the cost of good forgeries, I'm assuming you've always used the infant death method to establish your identities."

She shot him a sideways glance. "Actually, I'm quite adept at it by now." She'd often been thankful, especially in moments of black humor, that she lived in the information age. Although she'd had little long-term planning in mind other than survival when she'd first fled the agents, it had quickly become apparent that she would need new identification to get a job. She'd haunted bookstores, libraries, and used the Internet as a tool. It hadn't been long before she'd learned the benefits of cross-referencing counties for birth and death records, and the most reliable companies to use for issuing professional-looking social security cards.

She'd never run into major problems with any of the

identification she'd used. But then, she'd rarely stayed in one place for long.

"Did you memorize the information I put together for you?"

Annoyance momentarily took the place of the nerves. "You know I did."

"Let's go through it once more. Age?"

She sighed, and gave her hand a discreet tug. It was held fast. "Twenty."

"Place of birth?"

"Savannah."

"Parents' names?"

"Margaret and Henry, divorced three years ago, neither remarried." She cut off his next question with a regal lift of her chin. "Give me some credit. I do have a bit of experience with this, you know."

"Yes, you do." His eyes were midnight dark, and as usual, unfathomable. "You'll need to get used to my identity, as well. I'll be using the name Michel Falcol."

Her palm was getting slippery. She preferred to believe it was her destination, and not her reaction to Nick, causing the sensation. "And how is it that our little Georgian peach met and fell for a smuggler?"

"We met at a nightclub in Paris. Le Rouge. The attraction was immediate and mutual." Was it her imagination, or was his voice growing lower, more intimate? "You agreed to accompany me on business because we could not bear to be parted."

"Love at first sight?" She tried for a mocking tone, but the words sounded breathless instead.

"Perhaps not love. But certainly...obsession."

Her pulse tripped, and it was difficult to continue to meet his gaze. "I'm a decent actress, but I think *obsession* might be beyond my capabilities."

He raised her hand to his lips, pressed a kiss to her palm.

"Then I'll have to help you with that as much as I can, won't I?"

The bustle at the airport provided sensory bombardment. Loudspeakers were blaring, a dozen different languages could be heard in the Customs area, and the line for processing moved faster than Sara would have imagined possible.

Or perhaps it only seemed that way because she was so very reluctant to be back in Chicago.

Her entire body seemed encased in ice, and she barely resisted the urge to rub her hands together to generate some heat in her frozen limbs. It was ridiculous, she thought a little wildly, as they stepped closer to the customs and immigration official. She'd never been in O'Hare before. It shouldn't inspire such panic.

But she knew it wasn't the airport that caused her reaction, but its proximity to Victor Mannen.

"Relax," Nick murmured, and her gaze flew to his. He stepped forward, showing his papers to the man behind the counter, and Sara had a sudden thought that perhaps hers wouldn't pass inspection. A wild hope began to bloom at the thought, even as Nick moved on and Sara laid her documents on the counter. What would happen if they suspected hers were forged? They'd have to take her off somewhere and question her, wouldn't they? And she doubted even Nick could arrange it so that he could be in the room with her.

Being separated from him would be the first step toward obtaining her freedom. A freedom that was becoming increasingly crucial with every second she spent in Chicago.

Her documents were stamped and pushed back toward her. Even as she reached for them, Nick casually picked them up. "I'll keep those for you, Raeanne. You know how you are about losing things."

Their eyes met, and she thought for an instant that he'd been able to read her mind a moment ago. His expression was shuttered, and she realized abruptly that it wouldn't be necessary for him to have any paranormal powers.

She'd never made a secret of the fact that Chicago was the last place on earth she wanted to be.

The limo pulled to a stop in a curved drive a full quarter mile from the front gate of the estate. Sara stared through the window in disbelief. Kim, too, was making no secret of her shock.

"Who'd you have to bribe to land this place?"

"The owner is out of the country indefinitely. I was able to sublease it, fully furnished." Nick looked at Sara. "Are you all right?"

"Of course," she replied coolly. Not for a moment would she admit that her heart had been galloping since their plane had landed. They got out and walked up the steps, Nick producing a key and ushering them into the house.

"Some layout." Kim poked her head into rooms, strolling from one to another. "What did you say this guy does?"

"The owner? From his extended stay in Greece, I suspect he spends much of his time evading the Internal Revenue Service."

The limo driver followed them inside, depositing the bags on the marble floor in the front hall. Kim looked at Nick, her brows raised. "Do you suppose this place is as clean as it looks?"

"I'll let you check and see if it meets with your approval."

With a slight frown, Sara wondered at their exchange. Kim nodded, squatted down in front of one of the bags and unzipped it, withdrawing some equipment.

Nick stepped forward, took Sara's arm. "Let's have a look."

The owner's taste ran to the avant-garde, with sparse furnishings highlighting the structure. They walked into a large room that boasted acres of polished parquet flooring, with mirrored octagon-shaped pillars dotting the space. A bar covered by the same mirrored panels was tucked away in one corner, and a fireplace spread across one wall.

Kim walked into the room behind them, with a wand-shaped instrument in her hand, and moved slowly through the room, holding the tool in the air. When she got through the space she gave Nick a quick look and a thumbs-up.

Noting the exchange, Sara asked, "You're afraid this place is bugged?"

"It seems unlikely, but it would be foolish not to check." Nick considered her from where he stood across the room. "If we find anything, most likely it will be the owner's. It's doubtful Mannen knows of my arrival date, much less where I'll be staying."

His words were anything but reassuring. She, better than anyone, knew the length of Mannen's reach. As well as his ability to manipulate lives—or end them—at a whim. A shudder worked down her spine.

Seeing her reaction, Nick moved closer, trailed a finger lightly down her arm. "There's no reason to be afraid. I'll be right by your side every minute."

His words elicited another shiver. Because, of course, that was one of the things she feared the most.

"Tell me again where we're going. And why."

"It's a fund-raiser...for battered women, I think. There's a celebrity auction at the end of the night. Until then it's mostly meet and greet. Cocktail conversation. Nothing to worry about. Stop fidgeting." He reached over, covered the hands that were twisting on her lap.

"I'm not." The denial was a matter of pride. So was pulling away from him and deliberately stilling her fingers' nervous movements. She was more practiced than most in the art of pretense, but Raeanne Backstrom would be expected to be at home gliding from one group of people to another, making small talk and looking bored. In situations like that, Sara had more experience serving drinks and trying not to slug the men who grabbed her butt.

She took a deep breath. It helped when assuming a new identity to visualize the person's life. To think about the places she would have been, the things she would have done, her likes and dislikes. A woman like Raeanne would be used to traveling in limos. She wouldn't have immediately noted that it was the same car and driver who had brought them to the house from the airport. She wouldn't have observed the driver at all. Her eyes, her attention, would be on the man at her side.

Sara turned to look at Nick again. *Michel.* He was dazzling in a tux, wearing a collarless black shirt beneath. His hair was gelled back, emphasizing the difference in his hairline. With the scar curving beneath his eye, all he needed was a deck of cards and a glass of whiskey to complete the picture of dashing riverboat gambler. A charming rogue who was equally adept with the ladies as he was with the six-gun strapped to his side.

Nick was minus the deck of cards, but he wore his customary ankle holster. And she knew that the seductive threat he presented was all too real. "You didn't tell me why we're going to this."

"It'll give you a chance to get used to your role, and provides our first opportunity to be seen together in public." Lazily, he stretched his arm out on the seat behind her, his fingertips brushing her bare shoulder. His gesture made her exquisitely aware of the amount of skin her dress left bare. "The gown suits you."

"It suits Raeanne." Certainly Sara had never worn anything like it before. The royal-blue color was a shade she'd never have chosen. She'd spent too many years trying to avoid attention to be comfortable in bright colors. And its strapless bodice seemed alarmingly skimpy. The dress clung to her figure and ended several inches above her knees. It allowed for only the barest of undergarments. She had pajamas that were less revealing.

To complete her outfit, Nick had presented her with large teardrop diamond earrings, a glittering matching necklace and bracelet, and two rings. The jewelry felt like dead weight against her skin. She imagined its combined worth would keep a large family comfortably for several years. Wearing it only added to the nerves fluttering in her veins.

"We're almost there." He brought her hand to his lips, skimmed his mouth over her knuckles. "Remember, we're besotted with each other."

Heat pooled in her belly at the intimate contact. "That's going to be a reach."

His face drew closer, his lips brushing hers as he whispered, "Not for me."

When the limo pulled to a stop before the brightly lit building, Sara's pulse was still rocketing. She started to get out of the car, remembering at the last moment that she would be expected to wait for her escort to aid her. Nick took her hand, and she was certain he could feel the evidence of his effect on her. She looked at him, saw the smile of anticipation on his face. Leaning toward her, he whispered, "Let the games begin."

Games, Sara thought two hours later, would hardly be the description she would have chosen. Warfare would be more accurate, couched in pleasant tones and highlighted with plastic smiles. Words used as nasty little weapons designed to draw blood. A case in point was the pair of glittering women at her side air kissing each other's cheeks.

"Monique…what a lovely little outfit! Is Isolde still dressing you? Aren't you the most loyal thing! You must be one of the few clients she's managed to hang on to."

When she paused to draw a breath the other woman cooed, "Oh, Lisbet, you look marvelous. You must give me the name of your surgeon. When I'm your age I'll want to look just as stunning as you do."

Sara hid her grin by lifting her wineglass to her lips. Check and mate, she thought, amused. Apparently life could be a battlefield regardless of the surroundings.

Her attention shifted as Nick introduced her to the couple he was chatting with. "This is my very good friend, Raeanne Backstrom." He used the word *friend,* but his tone, the possessive hand on her back, screamed *lover.* She tensed infinitesimally and held out her hand in greeting. "Ah'm delighted to meet you." As she spoke to the couple she was all too aware that Nick was still touching her. His hand rested at the base of her spine. And the weight of it there was doing curious things to her ability to concentrate.

It was more difficult than it should have been to speak to the woman, whose name she'd already forgotten, about the beastly heat in Savannah this time of year. Yes, she agreed, as Nick's fingers turned caressing, Athens had a wonderful university, but her mother had graduated from Wellesley and it had been important to her that her daughter attend there, as well.

Nick's hand lowered, cupped her bottom, and her fingers went numb.

"Careful, *chérie.*" With quick reflexes he managed to keep her wineglass from spilling. His smile encompassed the group as he righted it. "The champagne here flows freely, but we do not want it to flow *that* freely, do we?"

There was polite laughter, and when the couple drifted away after another few minutes of chatter, Sara released a breath.

"Relax, you're doing fine." Did his whisper have to be delivered in that intimate tone, so close to her ear?

"How fond are you of your hands?" A casual smile was on her lips as she delivered the question, while her gaze drifted over the assembled crowd.

"As it happens, I'm attached to both."

She ignored both the laughter in his voice and the bad joke. He didn't need any encouragement. "Unless you want to go home minus one of them, I suggest you keep them to yourself."

He dropped a kiss on one of her bared shoulders. "I've always had a weakness for dangerous women."

It was apparent from the surreptitious looks coming his way that there were plenty of women in the room who also had a weakness for dangerous men. Sara had lost count of the number she'd noticed staring their way. To be the recipient of that avid attention would normally make her uncomfortable, but it was only too easy to recognize the source of their interest. Nick made an attractive package, his imperceptible aura of mystery compelling. He'd muted the dangerous power of his personality for this outing, but she still had to remind herself more than once that his acting ability was superior even to her own. Although his pose was loverlike, his gaze when he lifted it to scan the room was shrewd. Assessing.

"I understand a few local artists will be auctioning off some of their work, as well." With a deft touch, Nick guided her to a semisecluded corner of the room, where various paintings and sculptures were showcased. "Do you see any you like?"

She studied the artwork as an excuse to avoid looking

at him. "I can't say I care for the pieces that don't look like anything."

"Abstract art is an acquired taste. What do you think of this one?"

It was hard to focus on the painting he indicated while he had his arm draped lightly across her shoulders. His index finger traced the skin above her bodice and then dipped beneath it.

Swiftly, her head turned to his, her lips parted. He was gazing at her mouth, his eyes heavy-lidded. She had an instant to be grateful for the privacy of the corner, an instant of mingled anticipation and dread, before his mouth met hers.

This wasn't the featherlight brushing of lips he'd given her in the limo, but a kiss that was possessive and rawly carnal. A man branding his mate until such time as he could make the act that much more intimate. Sara struggled with the emotions crashing and careening inside her as he pulled her into his embrace. Her hands slid around her neck, the memory of the last kiss they shared all too vivid. Thought fled then, to be replaced by sensation.

His taste was darkly sensual, and evoked an answering hunger. And in that instant she knew he'd been holding back from her the other times. He kissed her deeply. Intensely. The way a man kissed a woman he intended to make love to a moment later, his mouth ravaging hers.

Helplessly, she clutched his shoulder with one hand as the other twined more tightly around his neck. And for the first time since she'd met him, she returned his kiss without the inner guard that was usually second nature for her. When his tongue probed her mouth, she welcomed it, played with it. And when he pressed his body closer to hers and she felt the evidence of his arousal, it evoked an answering tumult of desire.

Until he lifted his head, waited for her to open her eyes, try to focus. "Would you like to leave early?"

It wasn't his words that had the passion-induced haze suddenly clearing from her brain. It was the look in his eyes—clear, focused, despite the obvious passion also visible there. She stared at him for a minute, trying to make the adjustment he had, and failing miserably.

A cool, cultivated voice sounded beside them. "The artwork is hardly museum caliber, but it's all for a good cause, isn't it?"

As Nick turned to greet the newcomer, Sara took another moment to calm her raging pulse. So it was delayed comprehension that punched in when she saw the elegantly groomed gentleman speaking to Nick, belatedly recognizing the voice she hadn't heard for six years.

Victor Mannen.

Ice filled her body so suddenly, so completely, she imagined steam should rise as frigidity met what had so recently been heat. There was a roaring in her ears, and she knew she would have swayed if not for Nick's arm wrapped around her waist.

"Darling." His arm tightened. "This is Victor Mannen, the business associate I mentioned."

Somehow, a smile formed on her lips. As if detached from her own body, she watched her hand raise, felt, with a distant horror, him encompass it with his own.

"Miss Backstrom. A pleasure."

Her heart was kicking in triple time and she thought she might hyperventilate. "Mistah Mannen," was all she could manage to say.

"I didn't realize you had arrived in the city, Michel." Mannen's attention had switched back to Nick, and Sara, stunned, was left to battle her other turbulent emotions.

He didn't recognize her.

There hadn't been as much as a flicker of recognition

in his expression before he'd addressed Nick again. Had it been so long? Was she so changed? Or had she been so inconsequential to the man that her looks had never registered with him six years ago?

The answer, she thought, fighting the nausea rising in her stomach, was probably a combination of the three.

With effort, she forced herself to focus on their conversation, and on her role. She pretended to sip from her glass, although she knew better than to try and swallow. Her throat had seized up the first moment she'd recognized the man.

She used his focus on Nick to give herself a bit of time to recover. If she had changed in appearance, he hadn't. His hair was still thick, silver and perfectly groomed. He looked born to a tuxedo, the severe black accentuating his aesthetic looks. Her gaze traveled lower, and fixed on the hand with which he held his glass. The diamond flashing on his little finger was familiar. The brilliant jewel had winked as he'd made a dismissive gesture, ordered the stranger's murder.

I think we're done here, Peter. Kill him.

When her gaze raised again, she saw that Mannen had noticed her interest. Quelling panic, she manufactured a smile. "Ah was just noticing yoah ring. Ah'm afraid Ah've a weakness for jewels."

"Beautiful women deserve flawless gems." Mannen's words were delivered with just the right amount of flattery.

Nick reached over and ran a light finger along her necklace. "My thoughts exactly."

"You'd be dazzling even without adornment," Mannen said.

She gave him a coy look that would have done the confidently rich Raeanne proud. "You're very gallant." She tilted a look up to Nick. "Isn't he gallant, Michel?"

His fingers grazed her hip as he gave her a possessive look. "He only speaks the truth."

She placed her hand on Nick's arm, caressed it a little. "If you two gentlemen would like to discuss business, Ah'll just disappear to the ladies' room to freshen up."

"I wouldn't think of interrupting your evening," Mannen interjected. "I just wanted to take the opportunity to welcome you to Chicago. Falcol." He nodded to Nick. "I'll be talking to you soon. Miss Backstrom—" his pale gray gaze landed on Sara, and ice water splashed through her veins "—it was a pleasure meeting you."

He walked away, joining another group standing some distance away, and Sara felt her knees weaken as reaction set in.

"You were wonderful."

"Tell that to my heart. It's in my throat right now." She started away, glanced at Nick as he accompanied her. "I really am going to the rest room, and I don't need an escort."

His voice was imperturbable. "I don't mind."

Her lips tightened. "Afraid I'll go out the window?"

"It's been known to happen."

Because the words were no less than the truth, she didn't bother to answer. But she was glad the rest room door represented a barrier that even he would have to respect. The space was a haven in which she could take a few precious moments to recover. A haven, she ascertained with a few quick glances, without windows or another exit.

She dampened a paper towel and dabbed at her neck, finding relief in the action. Her body had been jolted from one response to another in the last few hours, and coupled with the jet lag just beginning to make itself known, she was starting to feel the effects.

Two other women entered and came to the counter to

repair their lipstick. One of them, a tall, slender blonde with watchful eyes, looked at Sara. "Are you all right?"

Reaching for her composure, she shifted back into role. "Ah'm fine, thanks. Too much champagne on an empty stomach."

The taller of the two, another blonde with a mass of curls piled atop her head, said, "The waiters with the red sashes have the trays of hors d'oeuvres. You should snag one of them before the auction starts."

Sara studied the woman. "You have something to do with this auction, don't you? Ah've seen you rushing back and forth, answering questions."

The woman shrugged. "I'm on the committee that arranged it."

"Don't let her kid you," her companion interjected. "She's practically pulled this thing off single-handedly. The only thing she refuses to do is emcee the auction and get all the publicity. I'm Addison Jacobs, by the way."

"Meghan Patterson," the other woman said.

"Raeanne Backstrom." Sara tossed the paper towel she'd been using in the trash container, and opened her purse for her lipstick. The act would give her a few more moments before she had to go back and rejoin Nick, and confront that onslaught of emotion once again.

"I saw you speaking with Victor Mannen earlier." Addison blotted her lips and crumpled the tissue. "Do you know him well?"

Pretending to repair her makeup gave Sara a much needed diversion. Peering intently into the mirror, she outlined her lips. "He just came up and introduced himself this evening. Ah'm afraid Ah don't know anyone in the city."

Addison Jacobs opened her purse and dropped in her lipstick. Then she pulled out a card. "Then you probably aren't aware of Mannen's reputation. Just be careful of him. If anything comes up that you'd like to discuss, anything at all, just call the number listed here.''

Slowly Sara reached for the card, her gaze going from one sober-faced woman to the other. After the two had turned to leave, she looked down, read the print:

Addison Jacobs
  Cook County Assistant State Attorney
  239-555-1326 ext. 204

Chapter 9

After some internal debate, Sara gave Nick the card when they got back to the house that evening. He frowned down at it. "Which woman was she?"

"The tall blonde in the red dress."

"You're sure?"

Sara raised her eyebrows, looked at him. "There were only two of them. Do you think I'd get them mixed up?"

"No, but the other woman was with a guy I'm sure was a cop."

It was her turn to frown. "I didn't notice any policemen in there."

"He wasn't in uniform." He didn't say more—he didn't have to. Sometimes she'd been able to pick out cops herself just by looking at their eyes. Although come to think of it, Nick had that same impassive, watchful manner about him. She almost pointed that out to him, but thought he wouldn't appreciate the comparison.

Wandering into the drawing room, she carefully set the

picture Nick had bought for her against the wall. Without lights on, the moonlight streamed in through the open drapes and reflected in brilliant shards off the mirrored pillars. She stopped, transfixed by the sight. It was almost as if the room had been built with this scene, this moment, in mind.

Nick went to the bar in the corner. "Would you like a drink?"

"No, I had enough champagne." Her mind went back to the card she'd given him. "What interest do you think Jacobs has in Mannen?"

"Law enforcement has been bearing down on him recently. From what Whitmore said, the state attorney's office had a hit man ready to flip on Mannen. Even gave up some tapes of conversations he had with Mannen hiring him for jobs. Someone got to him in jail, though—he OD'd on his own heart medicine. Justice has something else in the works—a money laundering operation Mannen was involved in."

Sara went still. "A hit man?"

"As far as I know, he was never hired to hunt you."

There seemed to be a sudden draft in the room. She rubbed her arms. Maybe that particular assassin hadn't been set on her, but others had over the years. Mannen probably had someone trying to pick up her trail right now. "Sounds like they've got enough against him. Why do they need me? Or you?"

"He has a way of slipping out of the tightest of nooses. Matching his voice to the one on the tape will be dicey, and white collar crime can take years to untangle. They want him bad, and they want a pile of charges high enough that he'll never escape them."

She heard the slight clink of ice against crystal. Either Kim had stocked the bar, or Nick had had that taken care of. Just like he'd taken care of renting the house and hiring a driver.

"What did you do with the picture?"

"I set it next to the door." Thoughts of the gift he'd presented her with summoned a welter of emotions. The clothes and jewels were easy to dismiss; they were part of this whole charade. But the picture he'd bid on was harder to disregard. It depicted a coastal village, hazed with fog, with the sun sending splinters of color through the mist. The painter had lent the common scene an almost holy light.

The painting was totally inappropriate for her, of course. She had no illusions about anything in this world. She'd been too busy dodging storm clouds to search for the silver linings. But something about it had drawn her, although she'd never mentioned it aloud. Nick had either noticed the way her eyes had repeatedly returned to this painting, or he'd instinctively known she would find it compelling. She wasn't certain which possibility was more disturbing.

But she did know that it was the first present anyone had given her since her fifteenth birthday. Her mother had sprung for a case of Old Style that day, and urged Sara to invite all her friends over to tie one on. Even a delinquent girl of fifteen knew a mother like that just didn't give a damn. But then, that was hardly the worst example of Janie Parker's parenting. Not even close.

"You did a good job tonight." Focusing on Nick's words was a way to skirt the memories, one she seized gladly. He strolled back toward her, minus his tux jacket, the first button of his shirt undone. "You stayed in character—even when Mannen appeared."

She asked the question that had been bothering her ever since she'd been unexpectedly confronted by the man. "You knew he'd be there, didn't you?"

Nick brought the glass to his lips, drank. Lowering it,

he said, "If you'd known you were going to meet up with him tonight you would have been nervous."

His evasive response made a few other things begin to make sense. Her voice brittle, she said, "Nervous at seeing the man determined to kill me for the last six years?" She made a disbelieving sound. "Why would you think that? You took him by surprise, too, didn't you? He didn't expect to see you there."

"The element of surprise is often an invaluable weapon."

"Well, here's a news flash for you. Don't use me like that again. Not if you still want to be walking upright."

His eyes narrowed. "I thought you understood our cover."

"You established us as lovers with your show of possessiveness all evening. That wasn't your intent with that final scene. You saw him there, didn't you? Knew he'd approach us. So you made a point of enacting that little drama in the corner for my benefit." The memory of the ease with which he'd ignited her desire, while remaining largely unmoved himself, still had the power to humiliate. "Something to distract me so that when I came face-to-face with him I'd be completely blown out of the water."

There was something in Nick's eyes, a dangerous glitter. Then he stepped closer, out of the blade of moonlight, and they were shadowed again. "I thought the meeting would go better if—"

"You thought." Because her voice had risen a bit, she stopped and drew a breath. "Well, I don't appreciate being manhandled for show. To have my feelings manipulated for—"

Two quick steps and he reached her, his face lowered to hers. "If you think you were the only one affected by our kiss, you're not as observant as I thought."

She remained stubbornly silent, unwilling to debase her-

self further by reminding him that he hadn't been the one
left staggering for composure, vulnerable to the next huge
shock when she'd realized who had approached them.

Somehow, without moving, he managed to loom closer.
Sara took a quick look at Nick's face and moistened her
lips. Her retreat was involuntary, and short-lived. The col-
umn was at her back. When he took another step forward,
she was caged between his heat and the coolness of the
pillar.

"If you're saying tonight was all for show, you're kidding yourself." His voice was edged with a measure of
the frustration she'd experienced earlier that evening.
"I've never made any secret of wanting you. Maybe what
really makes you angry is that you want me, too."

In one swift motion he bent, sat his glass on the floor
and then rose again, his mouth taking hers. There was
nothing controlled about the kiss. It was wet and deep,
explicit in its demand. And far too easily it ignited embers
of their earlier desire. He crowded nearer, until they were
pressed together—chests, hips, legs, while his mouth ate
at hers. And she knew, with twin feelings of passion and
fear, that this time would end differently than the last.

He wrapped his arms more tightly around her, his
tongue probing at hers, and dimly she felt his hands at her
back. Her arms raised to twine around his neck, and held.
Their mouths twisted together, fierce and hungry for the
taste of each other. The kiss was rough, wild and unre-
strained. And it was the wildness that excited her the most.
The hint of shredding control that torched her own.

His flavor was heady, darkly seductive, and she could
feel her muscles going lax. This was the real threat of him,
always had been. She'd recognized his power even in the
café in New Orleans. This was a man who could make her
want.

His mouth went to her jawline, to her throat, and her

neck arched. She knew the danger of wanting, the futility of it. Nothing lasted. Nothing was worth sacrificing her hard-won control. But...she'd never experienced anything like this. Even as her limbs grew weaker, something coiled tighter and hotter inside her, pulsing for release. She shuddered as his teeth closed over the sensitive cord of her throat.

Her dress loosened and Nick pushed it down. Her eyes fluttered open. She hadn't realized he'd unzipped it. He reared back a little, and his hands went to her bare breasts, fingers stroking her nipples to tight taut knots.

"You're beautiful, *mon ange*. Sexy. You can't know how I've wanted you." Their gazes met, held. "But you will."

The rasped words were still prickling across her nerves when he lowered his head and drew her nipple into his mouth. The pleasure was immediate and electric. A whimper escaped her lips and her eyes closed, weighted shut. She pulled him closer, arched so he could take more of her breast into his mouth, then moaned when he did.

His hands were everywhere. Smoothing over the fabric covering her hips, then finding the hem and slipping beneath it. He switched his attention to her other breast even as one deft hand glided along her silk-clad leg until it found where the nylon ended on her thigh, and brushed the skin above it.

Her hips jerked helplessly and he lifted his head. Her nipples were wet from his mouth, aching, and she fumbled for the buttons on his shirt, desperate for contact. He let her undress him, his other hand joining the first, brushing the bare skin of her inner thighs with light deft strokes.

She'd freed the majority of the buttons on his shirt, but couldn't find the will to complete the act. Instead, her fingers greedily glided over his skin, tangling in the dark mat of hair covering his chest.

Touching him was as gut-wrenchingly sexy as having his hands on her. His wide shoulders blocked the shaft of moonlight, leaving them in shadows. She tested the padded muscle beneath her fingers, leaned forward to scrape one tight pec with her teeth. His body jolted, and his hands slid to cup her bottom. She gave a satisfied smile. This time there would be no question of either of them holding back. If her control was going to shatter, so was his.

She flicked her tongue at one of his small flat nipples as his hands kneaded her flesh, and she trailed her own hands over the tight smooth skin stretched over his ribs, carefully skirting the bandage. There wasn't a spare ounce of flesh on him, and her hands traced a return journey, stroking sinew, angles and hard male flesh.

He stroked a finger along the elastic of her panties, close, tantalizingly closer to the apex of her thighs. The bold touch shocked her, tempted her. She was beyond thinking of logic and consequences, beyond holding back. None of what she'd known about sex had prepared her for this mind-numbing flood of sensation, this *wanting*, that radiated through her system in waves of need.

She reached for Nick's belt, loosened it, before he pulled away, knelt down to tug her panties down her legs.

"Step out of them, *ma petite*." The seductive command drifted to her and she obeyed mindlessly, drawing her breath in as he pushed the dress up to bunch at her hips.

Desire pounded through her, and she gripped his shoulders, trying to pull him up her body. The feeling was fierce, demanding. This longing couldn't be satisfied until he was inside her, thick and heavy, driving them both to madness.

But rather than obey her urgings, he remained kneeling and, leaning forward, pressed his mouth to her core.

The shock of the intimate kiss drove the breath from her lungs. The unfamiliarity of the act would have had her backing away, but she was locked in place between Nick and the pillar behind her. His mouth was hot on her sensitive flesh, the tip of his tongue tracing the seam of her cleft with long heated strokes.

Her hands went to his shoulders, meaning to push him away. Instead they clung for support as her knees weakened. He pushed her legs farther apart, tilted her hips to his satisfaction and probed her with his tongue.

Bolts of sensation speared through her, and a high wild cry was ripped from her throat. The pleasure was so exquisite it balanced on the keen edge of pain. Every flick of his tongue, every deft stroke sent wild spirals of need zinging through her. She tangled her hands in his hair, digging her fingers into his scalp, unaware of the tightness of her grip. There was an ache deep inside her, one only he could assuage, but she didn't have the words to tell him that. She could only twist against him mindlessly, seeking an end to the sensual torment.

He entered her with one finger, stroking deeply, and Sara's teeth clamped down on her lower lip. That finger was joined by another, and the tip of his tongue swirled over her clitoris, causing her to jerk helplessly against him. The dual assault staggered her system, the rhythmic thrusting coupled with the quick stabbing motions of his tongue torching what was left of her control. She was sobbing now, her breath heaving, her hips pressing closer for more contact. Deeper. More. Oh, please, more.

Then a sudden shock as the thrill snapped through her, overheating circuits, scorching nerve endings. A moan ripped out of her, as a long liquid wash of pleasure tossed her high, swamped her system.

Weak and trembling, she would have sunk to the floor if he hadn't supported her. He slid up her body, his hands hard and demanding. "*'Tite chatte.* Mine." He dropped a kiss on her mouth, then found the sensitive area beneath her ear.

Her limbs felt drugged. She forced her eyes open, looked into his and felt an unexpected flicker of desire return. His face was stamped with arousal, his nostrils flared. Color flushed across his cheekbones. He looked savagely male, and his body fairly shuddered with tension.

The signs of his need were a kind of aphrodisiac. She finished unbuckling his belt, then slowly worked the zipper over his straining manhood. He wore a pair of dark, form-fitting boxers, and they did nothing to hide his erection.

Renewed desire thrummed in her veins. Slowly she worked him free of the briefs and took him in her hands.

He cursed in French. His meaning was unclear, but not his intent. A smile curved her lips as she stroked the hard, pulsing length of him. He fumbled in his pocket, retrieved a condom. Ripping the package with his teeth, he withdrew the rolled latex, placed it over the head of his shaft, then reached for her hands, guided them. She knew instinctively what he wanted, but her fingers turned clumsy, the act unfamiliar. She unrolled the condom down the length of his hardness, taking long enough in the process that a groan escaped him. The sound became strangled in his throat when she finished and wrapped her hand around his length, squeezing gently.

"*Mon Dieu,* you're killing me." Despite the guttural words, his hand covered hers, showing her the motion that pleasured him, groaning again when she imitated it. He shoved her dress higher, cupped her hips to lift her, and stepped between her spread thighs.

"Wrap your legs around me."

Uncertain of the position, she did as he demanded, then stilled when she felt the head of his shaft probing between her legs. There was a flash of fear; he was huge and it had been a long time for her. That instinct had her trying to close against him, but it was impossible. He pressed against her opening, the liquid dampness of his earlier ministrations and her own desire easing his way. He stopped, breathing hard, seeming to fight for control. Then he withdrew almost all the way, and pushed slowly, inexorably inside her, until he was buried to the hilt.

She made a small sound of distress at the completeness of his invasion, and he stilled, giving her body time to adjust. She felt impaled by him, helpless, the pose leaving her vulnerable. The dark silk of his voice flowed over her as he whispered in her ear, erotic words of sex and wanting, in a mixture of French and English. She shivered against him, relaxing by increments. One of his hands went to her breast, teased the nipple, then squeezed it gently. His mouth went to the side of her neck, doing secret sensual things that made her body quiver and her hands clutch him closer.

He took the time to arouse her all over again, but this time was different. This time she had the throbbing length of him pressed deep inside her. It was a promise that soon had her moving against him—tentatively at first, then with an instinctive motion that drew him ever deeper.

His hands went to her hips, held her steady as he thrust hard, wringing a cry from her. Sensation exploded at the contact, convulsing her. He thrust again, and again, too quickly for her to catch her breath. She panted as she clung to him, her ankles crawling higher to press into his hips. Nick pounded rhythmically into her, not allowing the inner spasms to halt. They eddied wider and stronger, shuddering through her as her body demanded release. She writhed against him as he surged into her over and over, the pleasure building and coiling tighter until his name was wrung from her lips, a demand, a plea.

He gave one last violent thrust and she abruptly shattered, spinning in a vortex of pleasure. His hips hammered hers until a groan was wrenched from him, his mouth going in search of hers.

And when she floated back down to reality from the heights they'd reached, he was there to catch her.

Nick waited with utter stillness at the isolated table at the small outdoor restaurant. The breeze blowing off the lake was strong; most of the diners had opted to dine indoors. But the wildness of the elements never bothered him. Perhaps because he possessed more than a hint of wildness himself.

He reached for his glass of water and sipped. His father and grandmother had tried to stamp that quality from him, but had failed. It was as much a part of him as the black hair and eyes. He didn't give it much consideration because he'd long since learned to control it. At least he thought he had, until last night.

He'd hoped that making love to Sara would quench the fire she'd ignited in his blood, but instead he'd been left with an unquenchable desire for more. Broodingly, he waved the approaching waiter away. He didn't lose control with women—not ever. But Sara wasn't like the other nameless, faceless females who had passed through his life without leaving a mark. He'd known she wouldn't be. Her response to him had stripped away the polished, civilized veneer he cultivated, leaving the most primitive man beneath.

They'd slept very little last night. Each time they'd made love, she'd gone willingly into his arms. All the experience had proved was that emotion, long suppressed, could strike at any time with a furious bite. Uncomfortably, he shifted in his chair. Trying to tuck the uncharacteristic feelings away worked only until he touched her again. Caught the scent of her shampoo. Then they reared again with a force that couldn't be denied.

It was beginning to occur to him that handling Mannen wouldn't be the trickiest part of this assignment. Grappling with these long-dormant feelings would surely be the biggest challenge Nick had ever faced.

A waiter showed Victor Mannen toward the table, and Nick glanced down at his watch. Twenty minutes late. Just long enough to make a point about who wielded the power in their relationship. When Mannen held out his hand in greeting, Nick didn't move, merely arched his brows. Mannen allowed it to drop to his side, not a flicker of expression crossing his face.

Nick waited for the waiter to leave and for the other man to seat himself before saying evenly, "If you ever keep me waiting again, you'll be looking for a new partner."

Mannen paused in the act of reaching for his menu. He recovered admirably. "Forgive my tardiness. Something came up that required my attention."

Baring his teeth, Nick leaned forward. "You were playing games, *mon ami,* and I'm the wrong kind of man to play them with. I'm no one's lackey and you need me much more than I need you. Don't make that mistake again."

Mannen pursed his lips. Nick couldn't tell if he was irritated or intrigued. "You'll have to forgive me. I'm unused to dealing with associates of your…sensibilities." He grew still when Nick reached in his jacket pocket, withdrew what looked like a slim gold pen and laid it on the table, one end pointing directly at Mannen.

"You'll have to forgive *me.* I'm not the trusting sort." Nick waited sixty seconds, until a small red light flickered from the pen's top. He picked up the pen, replaced it in his pocket. Giving a shrug at the other man's expression, he said, "You could have been wired."

His eyes going cold, Mannen noted, "So could you."

Nick spread his arms. "I assume you're checking that out as we speak."

A small smile crossed Mannen's lips. He reached into his pocket, took out something that resembled a calculator. "I'm told it has the ability to pick up security devices from twenty feet away."

As the other man replaced it, Nick gave a small smile and made a show of relaxing. "We both share a similar need to feel...secure."

Mannen inclined his head. "I have found it pays to be proactive in these matters."

Picking up his menu, Nick opened it and observed, "I can understand why. You've acquired some unfortunate attention. After you were seen speaking to us last night, my friend was approached by an assistant state attorney inquiring about you."

It wasn't difficult to read Mannen's expression this time. His lips pressed together and his fingers tightened on his menu. "Yes, that is unfortunate, but I can assure you there is nothing to fear. With the appropriate amount of caution I'm certain we can manage to do business without undue interference." He scanned the list of entrées quickly before folding it and setting it aside. "I can recommend the pressed duck. It's quite good. The chef here trained in Paris."

Nick kept his eyes on the menu until the waiter came back and stood beside their table, his pen poised above his tablet. "May I recite our specials tonight, gentlemen?"

Mannen set down his menu with a decided air. "That won't be necessary. I'll have the pressed duck, and my friend..."

He paused expectantly, and Nick nodded. "Make that two."

"And please bring us a bottle of 1989 Château Palmer Margaux, if you will." When the waiter picked up their menus and turned away, Victor looked at Nick. "I hope the wine meets with your approval."

He leaned back, nodded. "I have several bottles of it in my cellar."

Mannen looked pleased. "Another connoisseur. It occurs to me, Michel, that we may have more in common than I had originally thought."

Nick stroked the side of his water glass idly. "I can think of several things. The foremost being a strong desire to stay out of one of your American prisons."

Propping his fingers together, Mannen nodded. "Of course."

"Because of the interest you've generated, however, anyone associated with you is likely to draw similar scrutiny."

"My dear Michel..." Mannen reached for his water glass, raised it. "If you're going to use that to try to drive your price up you're going to be sadly disappointed."

Nick shook his head. "Just making an observation, my friend. I have enough associates in the area to make the transaction go quite smoothly even if I can't oversee it personally. My fee more than covers all such expenses. However, if I need to pay off some officials, that would be an unforseen cost I would expect you to absorb."

Mannen set down his glass. "Of course, but I don't think you'll need to worry about that. I have several officials in different agencies who look out for my interests. Now—" he took a moment to meticulously straighten his cuffs "—why don't you give me an idea of what is involved in an operation of this size?"

Spotting the waiter approaching them, Nick delayed answering until he'd presented the wine, deferentially allowing Mannen to sample its bouquet and pronounce it satisfactory. After he'd filled two wineglasses and retreated, Nick said, "There will be four shipments, and each will port at a different Chicago terminal. They'll be spaced two days apart. That allows us to move the cargo at night, transport it to a holding building somewhere in the area, and disperse it before the next shipment comes in. Do you have enough buyers lined up?''

Mannen appeared to be savoring the wine. "That is my end of this association, is it not?''

Nick made an apologetic gesture. "As you say. I just need to know if I should plan a longer time between the shipments.''

"Why can't you get a place large enough to hold the entire cargo?''

To listen to their conversation, Nick thought, no one would suspect they were discussing human lives, about to be shattered for one man's ambition. "I can," he replied. "But the people get spooked if they're held for long. A two-day window gives us time to take some phony snapshots, present them with a set of doctored papers and lull them into thinking things are progressing as planned. If they have time to start to question motives, things get ugly in a hurry. People get hurt, and that costs you money.''

Mannen considered this. "Perhaps you're right. I imagine it's easier to control smaller groups, as well. But there's no need to worry. I have everything in hand.''

"All right. I've got the ships lined up, but will still need to arrange transport from the docks and find a building of the proper size in an isolated location. It will need to be primitively outfitted, cots and rest rooms. Someone on hand who can provide medical services, if necessary. A kitchen.''

Raising his eyebrows, Mannen observed, "That seems like a lot of trouble.''

"They have to be fed, and ordering out for a couple hundred at a time isn't feasible.'' He gazed at the man steadily. "I thought you'd had some experience with this before."

"I have, of course. But I've eliminated a middleman on this end who dealt with some of those details."

Nick gave an approving nod. "Cost effective. Lowering your overhead means increased profit."

Mannen's pale eyes glinted. "I need increased profits. You're more expensive than some of your competitors."

Picking up his wineglass, Nick noted coolly, "As for that...I actually have fewer competitors these days. Hinrich and Roven contacted me before I arrived here. They were...unhappy they'd been replaced. They'll no longer be available for any business transactions you have in mind."

The other man stared at him for an instant, then chuckled with real amusement. He raised his glass, tipped it toward Nick in a salute. "Mr. Falcol, I really believe the two of us shall get along famously."

Nick finished his call and tucked the cell phone back in his pocket. Kim asked, "Well? How did my baby perform?"

He smiled at her wording. "As promised. The wireless microphone is every bit as good as you claimed. Martin and Kwilisz said they could even pick up the sound of the tables inside being cleared."

She looked smug. "Told you it was worth the money."

"And you were right." Wire was a misnomer for the device he'd had taped to his chest. In actuality it was a thin loop of plastic encasing the listening instrument. State of the art, it didn't cause any fluctuations in voltage that an oscilloscope could pick up. The fact that the entire device and all its parts were made of plastic meant that not even a sweep with a metal detector would discover it.

And of course, if Mannen had found it, it was highly unlikely that Nick would be having this conversation.

"How far away was the van?"

"It was in the parking lot, so..." He made a quick estimate. "Fifty yards, I suppose."

"Did you get everything you needed?"

He slipped his hands in his trouser pockets and prowled the room. "Maybe. I want more. I wish I could be sure that the money he wired to my account could be traced back to him. I'm not satisfied I have enough evidence yet." He glanced around, and finally asked the question that had been on his mind since he'd walked in the door. "Where's Sara?"

"She's in her room."

Nick watched Kim, giving her credit for her bland stare. She'd be perfectly aware it was *their* room. He suspected she had questions about their relationship, but she was too well trained to voice them.

"How long has she been alone?"

There was a hint of annoyance in Kim's tone. "Not long. Less than twenty minutes."

Nick gave her a hard stare and turned for the stairway. "That's twenty minutes too long."

"Where is she going to go, Nick?" The question trailed after him as he took the steps two at a time. "You've got enough men on the perimeter of the property to prevent a small invasion."

He didn't answer. He couldn't. But tomorrow, he decided, making a savage note to himself, he and Kim would have a long talk about following his instructions exactly.

The first thing he observed after entering the room was the open window. His gut clenched hard and he began to cross to it, then caught a movement from the corner of his eye. He turned to see Sara coming from the adjoining bathroom.

She stopped short when she saw him, her gaze flicking from him to the window. "Hope it doesn't bother you to leave it open."

"No." The knot in his stomach eased, as a measure of relief spread through him. He used the routine of readying himself for bed to cover his reaction.

When he slipped into bed he rolled to his side and curved his body to hers, spoon fashion. Her narrow back was toward him, his arm around her waist and pressed gently on her belly. His mouth went to her shoulder, and he could feel her shiver in response. "Are you still sore?"

It was an intimate question, one a man asked a woman he'd loved hard and well. A woman he wanted, quite desperately, to love again. She gave a jerky half nod, and he drew a breath, released it. Ordering his clamoring hormones to subside, he cuddled her closer to him. "Then sleep, *'tite chatte.*"

He took a measure of satisfaction that she did, eventually, do just that. She was growing accustomed to his touch, to his body close to hers through the night. The fact that it meant so much to him was a matter far better left unspoken.

He slid his hand over the curve of her hip, lightly enough to avoid waking her. Sex with Sara had been even more intense than he'd imagined. And although he wasn't ready to agree with Luc that his judgment was impaired regarding her, Nick could admit, silently at least, that his fascination had begun long before he'd actually met her. From almost the moment he'd started tracking her, in fact.

Luc was right. Obsession was an alarmingly apt description for the feeling Sara evoked in him. And Nick was damned if he knew what he was going to do about it.

Chapter 10

Nick fell into step beside Sara the next morning as she began jogging her second lap around the property.

"Good idea to keep up with your training. I was going to suggest it myself."

"Well, there's not a whole lot else to do around here, is there?" Her tone was short. It hadn't escaped her notice that several staff members had appeared since their arrival; more staff, she suspected, than three people in a home even this size could use. She'd counted five would-be gardeners alone. "Tell me, do you have to pay your men extra when they pull double duty—lawn work and security?"

Nick gave an unapologetic shrug. "I don't kid myself that sleeping with me has cured your desire to disappear again. I'm not going to take that chance."

She pressed her lips together and stared straight ahead. She was unsurprised by his allusion to her desire for escape. She wasn't so nonchalant at his mention of their lovemaking.

Sex, she corrected herself, concentrating on her stride. Because that was all it was, all it could be. There was no doubt that however much the experience had shattered her, it would hardly have affected Nick the same way. He was a man with a great deal of expertise in the area.

Because she didn't want to consider how he'd arrived at that expertise, she pushed herself harder, focusing on rhythmic breathing the way he'd taught her. He ran easily by her side in silence for a time. She wondered if the exercise hurt his injury, but didn't ask. If ever there was a man who oozed self-sufficiency, it was Nick.

She examined the perimeter of the property as they jogged. It was second nature for her to plan for escape. After being on the run for six years she couldn't even enter a building without checking for the location of the exits. But this situation offered more difficulties than most. There were too many people around during the day, and at night... She could feel warmth seep to her cheeks at the thought. At night there was Nick.

Sleeping next to her in bed, holding her close might be an effective deterrent to her leaving, but it was dangerously effective in other ways, as well. His touch was becoming too familiar, and it occurred to her, with a jarring bolt of shock, that he'd probably planned that, as well. He was constantly touching her casually, on the hand, the shoulder, or stroking a finger down her arm. She'd never liked people getting too close to her physically, and the knowledge that he'd managed to slip beneath decade-old defenses was terrifying.

They rounded a corner of the property and turned in tandem. Sara was slowing, but she thought she ran more easily than she had in the Keys. Nick had yet to breathe heavily, and she knew the workout barely qualified as such for him. And yet less than forty-eight hours before, his breathing had been ragged, perspiration sheening his body.

A shiver rippled down her spine in reaction to the sensual memory. It helped, when remembering the helpless desire she'd felt in his arms, to recall the desire hadn't been one-sided. They'd barely slept at all that night. Restraint had been shredded on both sides. And while she'd survived for the last several years by maintaining that quality, her control didn't even come close to matching his.

There was a seductive kind of pleasure in the knowledge, a certainty that she hadn't been the only one blind-sided by the pleasure, left gasping and overwhelmed by the force of their passion. The knowledge wasn't much, but it was something.

His voice curled through her system, so low and silky she thought for a moment it came from memories of that night. "Tell me what you're thinking, *chérie*."

She wasn't about to give voice to her thoughts, although she had an uncomfortable feeling that he could read them too well. Several moments passed before she finally said, "I don't see a good ending in all this. At least not for me."

"Mannen didn't recognize you the other night. You're as safe here as I promised you'd be."

Safe, she thought, was a relative term. There was no safety here from the conflicting emotions Nick caused in her. But she couldn't hold him responsible for them. No, those she'd have to deal with herself.

"But when this is over, what then? Nothing will have changed. Justice will have more against Mannen, but I'll still have to testify against him. Then it's back to what they laughably call protective custody, because regardless of whether Mannen spends pre-trial time free or in jail, his reach is long." She broke off, emotion working through her. She didn't speak again until she could be sure her voice would be steady. "Of course, after testifying, there's always the witness protection program. Also under the Department of Justice.'' She gave a humorless smile. ''You could say I'll have come full circle.''

Nick stopped and reached for her hand, bringing her to a halt. ''I promised to protect you. There's no time limit on that.''

His expression was a little frightening, a fierce, ruthless mask. A mental image flashed across her mind of the way he must have looked on missions for the Green Berets. But he couldn't keep her away from the consequences of this thing when it played out, even if he truly wanted to. And for the life of her, she couldn't think of a reason for him to try.

Cupping her nape in his hand, he drew her closer and rested his forehead against hers. ''I wish you could trust me. Just a little.''

She went into his embrace without protest, gave in to the temptation to lean, just for a moment. Her response was muffled against his chest, but reverberated through them both.

''So do I.''

The house didn't come equipped with a gym, so Nick had had two of his men haul some mattresses into the center of a large solarium. She worked with him for over an hour on the moves he'd shown her in the Keys, but her heart wasn't in it. Her thoughts were still chasing one after the other, in a never-ending puzzle to which there was no solution.

''Pay attention.'' His voice was sharp. Nick had always taken the training very seriously. ''The minute you lose your concentration, you could be dead.''

He looped an arm around her neck from behind, and she didn't even stop to think. Her foot slammed down on top of his and she drove her elbow back into his ribs. She twisted in his grip, ramming her thumb where his eye would be if he hadn't suddenly let go of her.

There was a satisfied smile on his face. "I stand corrected. Maybe you do remember a few things I taught you."

Sara was feeling a bit smug herself. "Now let's practice that blow you showed me that causes instant diarrhea when it's landed."

His teeth gleamed and he backed away, scooping up a couple of towels and tossing her one. "Not on me. And you've done enough for one day. You didn't panic when I came up behind you a moment ago."

She was swiping the towel over her face, and her movements faltered at the words. Lowering the towel, she stared at him, stricken. It hadn't even occurred to her. He'd grabbed her and immediately her attention had been focused on getting the best of him, a competitive edge. But the familiar panic hadn't reared, fueled by old ghosts.

When she didn't respond, his smile faded. She didn't doubt that he'd been gentling her to his touch like a horse shaman did to a wild mare. It was one more example of how he'd chipped away at her well-constructed armor. Perhaps she no longer had to fear how she would defend herself from an attacker.

But her growing susceptibility to Nick Doucet was even more terrifying.

While Sara showered, Nick stayed downstairs to call Luc.

"Any messages from Whitmore?"

"Three yesterday. And the tone is getting shorter. I think he's getting pissed. Probably because he's wasted a lot of manpower searching for where you stashed Parker."

Nick's brows rose. "He has, huh?"

"Oh, yeah. He's got feelers out all over the Continent. You let him trace you as far as Brussels, didn't you?"

"It seemed the thing to do at the time."

"Well, like I said, he isn't happy and he wants you to call him."

"I'll let you do that." The messages Whitmore had left were delivered to an e-mail account Luc had set up. Efforts to trace the address would be met with as much success as locators on calls made from their offices. LeNoue was an electronics wizard. It was best to let him control the contacts from that end. Nick's cell phone service didn't allow for locator traces, but it was difficult to keep up with the government's technical skills. There was no use taking chances.

He had no doubt that Whitmore had agents watching every movement Mannen made. Which meant he, as Michel Falcol, would come under scrutiny, as well. He wasn't concerned. The Falcol identity was as impenetrable for Justice as it was for Mannen. Nick hadn't given Whitmore any details of his plan—it'd be inconvenient for the man to disavow knowledge of activities he'd been briefed on. And Whitmore would no more expect to find Sara in Chicago than Mannen would.

Luc's voice interrupted his thoughts. "So should I send him your love?"

Strolling toward the window, Nick looked out over the rolling expanse of lawn. "You might remind him that he gave me a job to do. I'll be the one to decide how it gets done."

"He's going to want to know about the girl."

"She's twenty-three, hardly a girl." And older, far older, than her years. "She's safe. That's all he needs to know."

"And Mannen?"

"Things are progressing as planned. I'll update him in a few more days."

"That's it?"

"That's all you need to share with Whitmore. Between you and me, I think Mannen is planning to flee the country."

A long whistle was heard on the line. "Got proof of that?"

Nick shook his head, unmindful that his friend couldn't see the action. "Just some things he's said. He's not worried at all about the charges currently pending against him. I know there's an assistant state attorney pretty anxious to match his voice prints to a tape recording of him hiring an assassin. And Whitmore claimed Justice is close to untangling his offshore accounts and hanging a money laundering charge on him. But I don't see Mannen sweating any of it at all."

"Maybe he knows he can afford to buy himself out of the trouble," Luc suggested.

"Or maybe he's looking to make a huge profit on this job and find a country without an extradition treaty with the States. He placed an order for eight hundred illegals. He stands to sell each for a cool thirty, forty thousand each. Subtract my fee and expenses and he still stands to clear between twenty to thirty million. Not a bad nest egg for someone looking to disappear and start over."

"You might be on to something. Want me to do some checking into that?"

Nick remembered Sara's words earlier that day. *I don't see a good ending in all of this.* "Yeah. Let me know whatever you find out."

As he tucked the phone away, Sara came into the room. Her gaze raked him. "You haven't cleaned up yet."

"No." Her hair was damp, and left to dry in layers around her face. Regardless of the new color, the cut suited her. She'd donned a casual cotton dress that left her limbs bare. Her skin still bore the kiss of the sun from their time in the Keys, and he was blindsided by the desire to stroke his hand along the length of her legs again. He swallowed, fighting the knee-jerk reaction. She looked completely different than she had in New Orleans when they'd first met, but her effect on him was the same. The woman had started affecting him long before he'd ever met her.

With a mental curse, he turned away. There were priorities to adhere to, and he wasn't going to be able to do his job if he allowed himself to be led around by his hormones. But the reminder fell flat. It wasn't just any woman who had come close to managing such a feat, it was *this* woman. Only Sara. And that realization filled Nick with approximately the same emotion as having a live grenade tossed at his head.

Dammit, it shouldn't be so hard to do his job without feelings entering into it, had never been this impossible before. He'd been a machine for the last five years, taking one assignment after another, establishing a reputation as a dependable operative. It was a damn inconvenient time to start feeling. And, he thought savagely, he certainly didn't need to start wanting now, with a deep vicious urge that churned relentlessly.

Despite the thoughts, or perhaps because of them, he took the phone from his pocket. "You know, there may be some good to come out of all this." Ignoring her expression, he held the phone out to her. "It's untraceable. If you want to contact your family, you could."

Her face grew still, then bloodless. Wondering at her reaction, he went to her. "It's been years, Sara. Don't you want to talk to your mother?"

He noted the effort it took her to swallow, and the way she was eyeing the phone as if he were offering her a live tarantula.

"You know, not everyone has a family like yours," she murmured.

Thinking of some of the dysfunctional relatives with whom he shared a bloodline, he gave a wry smile. "I sincerely hope not."

She backed away when he would have put the phone in her hands, and clasped her fingers behind her back. "I haven't spoken to my mother for eight years." Her voice was flat, with no noticeable note of regret. He was getting the idea that this topic had been a grave mistake.

"A lot can change in eight years."

Her lips twisted in something that didn't resemble a smile. "Not that much, they can't." With visible eagerness to change the subject, she asked, "Do you have plans for today?"

He would have liked to have interpreted her question as a desire to spend time with him, but he was beginning to know her too well. Cocking a brow, he asked, "Bored?"

"To death. I'm not used to having a lot of time on my hands. There's nothing to do here but watch TV. Can you believe in a house this size there's not a library?"

Intrigued, he asked, "You like to read?"

Her shrug was embarrassed. "I'm not totally ignorant, although I don't have a diploma to prove it."

"You're not ignorant at all." His flat statement was no more than fact. She was touchy about not graduating from high school, but he knew of few people with her age and experience who could have pulled off what she had for the last six years. That took creativity, ingenuity and a wisdom far beyond her years.

He considered her request. He had appointments with four different Realtors to look at some properties for purchase. But if Nick was followed today as he made the rounds, it would look odd for him to have taken his lover along on that type of business. The less involved Sara got in this end of things, the better.

He looked at her face and felt an unusual tug in his chest. "I don't see why you have to stay in all day. You and Kim could go somewhere. A bookstore, maybe."

He was rewarded for his suggestion with an incredulous smile. "Really?"

The impact hit him square in the chest with the force of a brick. Her smiles were much too infrequent to be taken lightly. Feeling slightly strangled, he cleared his throat. "Sure. Just let me arrange it."

He watched her leave the room with a spring to her step, and mentally began planning the arrangements. It shouldn't present much risk. If Kim was with her every second, there would be few opportunities for Sara to slip away.

It was doubtful whether she'd notice the white utility van that would follow them closely. Its ConEd markings would make it blend in with the cityscape, but if she observed it and guessed its true purpose, that wouldn't matter.

Even if she objected, she'd understand the need behind it.

The Chicago skies opened up late that evening and pummeled the ground with leaden fists. Sara stood before the open window of the bedroom and watched the lightning dance across the heavens. She'd always found a curious sort of solace in observing nature's tantrums. Perhaps she enjoyed the reminder that there were some things free of man's manipulation.

When the door opened behind her she turned her head, saw Nick standing there. He moved into the room, closing the door behind him.

"Wicked weather."

She hadn't turned on any lights. It wasn't until he moved closer that she saw he was drenched. He'd raked his hair back with a careless hand, but his clothes were plastered against him.

"I like to watch it."

He shrugged, peeling off his sodden shirt. "You should close the window a bit. You'll catch your death, as my *grand-mère* is fond of saying."

She heard the scrape of a zipper, and a chill skated over her skin. Anticipation and trepidation drummed a duet in her veins. It would be difficult, if not impossible, to return to the way their relationship had been before it turned sexual. Even more difficult to pretend that she wanted it to.

She had no illusions about how this arrangement would end. But whatever twist of fate had brought Nick Doucet into her life, she was certain that, for better or worse, she would never meet anyone like him again.

That thought was as much relief as torment. She knew somehow that no one else would ever have this kind of effect on her. It was too powerful, too inevitable, too… overwhelming. There was security in the knowledge that she'd never feel this kind of blind need again, even filled as she was with uncertainties. And there was also a stabbing sense of pain.

Sharp little needles of rain slashed through the screen, whipped by the rising wind. She welcomed the sting. Her skin was hot, despite the occasional shiver that worked down her spine. The physical reaction had more to do with arousal than cold. She could hear the sounds of Nick readying for bed. In a few moments his arms would be around her again, and this time she would turn to him, invite his touch. There was a funny little zap of sexual hunger at the thought. There were still unanswered questions in this mess, plenty of them, but there was no question of her wanting him. Of taking what she could get for the short time allowed her.

She slipped into bed, and moments later felt the mattress dip beneath his weight. His approach had been silent.

"Mannen is having a large gathering at his house tomorrow night. He's expecting us there." His hand stroked down her leg, kneaded the muscles lightly, as if he could chase away the tension that had suddenly pierced her.

"What's the occasion?"

"He's a patron of the local opera house. It sounds like some benefactor thing that gets his name in the social pages. Who knows? Maybe it gives him an opportunity to thumb his nose at his detractors. That would be his style."

So tomorrow she'd have to meet the man again. Sara took a deep breath, released it. At least it would be in another large group. And this time wouldn't be such a shock to the system. She'd be prepared, at least mentally. Emotionally was another matter.

"Okay."

He brushed a light kiss over her shoulder. "It will be easier this time, *chérie.*"

She turned toward him and his arms wrapped around her, bringing her close. A kiss was whispered across her lips. He lifted his mouth from hers a fraction and murmured, "Will you make love with me tonight, *mon ange?*"

In answer, she arched against him, near enough that he would feel her heart pounding, would read the response in her body. His mouth pressed hers open, and his tongue made a bold, sensual sweep inside. She felt the waves of need begin, cresting higher with each taste, as the kiss changed from soft to deep. Wet. Hard. When he lifted his mouth from hers, his voice was satisfyingly ragged.

"You must have let the rain in." He stroked a moist area with his finger. "Your nightgown is damp." Rolling from the bed, he strode to the window, and before she could summon a protest, pulled the sash down almost completely.

She swallowed, every vestige of her building desire dashed in an instant. He was back in bed in just a few moments, his hands drawing the nightgown over her head. But she couldn't stop staring in the direction of the window.

It was almost closed.

Not quite. Logic came to the rescue, shaky but reasonable. It was open a little. It would take nothing at all to widen the expanse. Nick drew her back into his arms, but she couldn't seem to relax again. Which was ridiculous, really. The window wasn't completely shut.

Sneaky little fingers of panic were creeping up her spine. She was determined to ignore them. Closing her eyes, she slid a hand into Nick's hair, pulled his mouth to hers and tried to lose herself in his kiss. The rain would stop. It couldn't go on for much longer. And then there would be no reason not to have the window open. Scraping her teeth over his bottom lip, she couldn't appreciate the sound of approval he made because the panic was sprinting up her spine now. *Later,* she promised herself, as Nick stroked her back. *Maybe even soon. A few minutes, perhaps.*

"You're tense," he murmured, his hand kneading the cluster of nerves at her lower back. "*Chérie,* what's wrong?"

"Nothing." The word sounded thready, lacking the conviction she was striving to summon. This was stupid. She wasn't this weak. She refused to be. His mouth sampled hers, a sensual invitation. She turned her face away, her breath coming in gasps. And she knew that in another moment she was going to embarrass herself by flying into a dozen pieces.

She pulled away from him, strode to the window and

threw the sash up, as high as it would go. She was ashamed by the deep gulps of air she had to take to ease her strangled lungs. And humiliated, with a bone-deep mortification, when Nick sat on the edge of the bed, watching her silently.

"I'm sorry," she said when she was able. Her hands still clutched the windowsill in a death grip. It would be a while before she'd be able to let go. "I...it's hot in here."

"No, *chérie,* it's not."

The denial, spoken gently, squeezed her lungs even harder. "I just like it open. I sleep better that way."

"There's a difference, isn't there, between wanting it open and *needing* it open?"

She drew in a shuddering breath and he approached her. He didn't touch her, a fact she was grateful for. She didn't think she could bear that.

"Tell me."

The words were an invitation, not a command. It wasn't an invitation she expected to accept. Only her mother had ever heard all the details, and she just hadn't given a damn.

But Nick settled his shoulders against the wall next to Sara and didn't look away. It was that quiet air of acceptance that finally penetrated her silence.

"My mother...she liked a good time, and booze and men were always a part of that equation." The rain was still falling outside, but it had quieted to a soothing rhythm that calmed Sara's racing pulse. "I never knew my father. Janie, my mother, had a short attention span. She didn't stick with guys for long. She must have had a dozen living with us over the years. I got used to being careful and I got used to never being alone with any of them."

She wiped away a drop of moisture on the sill with her index finger, and let the memories come and the inner darkness take over. "The last one lived with us the longest—almost two years. I never saw my mom as wild for a guy as she was for him. You can probably guess the rest.''

Her shoulder jerked in a poor excuse for a shrug. Sara didn't look at Nick; she couldn't. She didn't want to see pity on his face and she couldn't bear to see revulsion. Her voice became steadier, the recitation more matter-of-fact. ''He was slimy…always trying to touch me or rub against me when he could. He used to tell me…''

Come and get it, little girl. Uncle Jesse's the best there is. I'll treat ya good. Real good.

She plowed through the memory and continued. ''He convinced her she'd be better off taking the extra money to work third shift at the diner. That left him home alone with me.'' Sara had used every reason she could come up with not to go home at night. When she couldn't stay with a friend, she would always stay late at the library. ''I just needed to get inside and to my room. He left me alone until he got enough beer in him. Then he'd come upstairs.''

Open the door, ya 'lil bitch. Y'know ya want it.

''I put locks on my door three different times. He'd take them off while I was out. So I always left the window in my room open. Took the screen off it so I could crawl out onto the garage roof when I needed to. He was afraid of heights.'' She'd spent more than one night perched on the roof, she remembered—when he'd slam the window shut and lock it in a fit of rage. She'd never minded. Once outside she'd always known she was safe. But she had to be able to get outside.

''One night I walked in and he didn't say a word. I went to my room and heard him on the stairs. I ran to the window as he came up behind me…and he'd nailed it shut.''

A deep weariness filled her, one that came not from the physical but the mental. ''I didn't make it easy for him, but he was big, over six foot, and he had a lot of pent-up hostility from all the times I'd gotten away before.''

She still remembered the hope she'd harbored. The tiny piece of faith as she experienced that drunken attack, the long hours until morning. ''I met my mother at the door when she came home.'' Sara pressed her lips together, remembering the look on the woman's face when she'd seen her, bruised and bloody. ''I tried to tell her what had happened. She took one of her high heels and beat me with it.'' One hand went to her scalp, fingering the scar that could still throb like a fresh wound. ''She said I was a no-good whore, and told me to get out. She wasn't going to put up with me teasing and tempting her man.''

''What's his name?''

Disoriented, Sara looked at Nick. He'd been silent so long she'd lost herself in the litany and hadn't sensed the change in him. But she noticed it now. Menace was emanating from him in waves. ''It doesn't matter....''

''His name.''

She took a deep breath, let it out. ''Jesse Carson. He's dead. I kept up with the local news by the Internet. He was knifed outside a bar less than a year later.''

''He's lucky.''

Blinking at Nick, Sara watched him visibly search for control. Wonderingly, she stepped forward, put her hand on his chest, felt the deep shudders as he donned the awesome mantle of restraint.

''It was a long time ago,'' she whispered. It had been an unspeakable trauma, had shaped who she became. But the man's attack hadn't been as traumatic as her mother's betrayal. It would have been easier to forgive had she been drunk, but Janie had just gotten off work. She'd been sober and she'd been enraged.

Because Nick seemed to need it, Sara rested her head

against his chest. Her fingers stroked his side, skirting the bandage he still wore there.

"Wasn't there someone you could have gone to? At school? The police?" he choked out.

"I didn't think I'd have a lot of credibility. I was kind of a problem kid. I'd been in trouble before...had run away twice, and the police had hauled me back. But I didn't figure my mother would be reporting me missing this time, that no one would care where I'd gone." And she'd been right—no one had.

The memories were tugging her too close to the brink of emptiness, which she'd lived with for too long. It had been Sean who'd helped keep the abyss from swallowing her whole. Sean who had healed something inside her that she'd thought was broken forever. She would always regret failing to do the same for him. He'd never talked about what had sent him to the streets, but she'd sensed that whatever it had been had damaged him in some deep, irreparable way. His kindness to her, his relationship with her, had caused his death. And there was no regret in this world that could weigh heavier than that.

She didn't know how long Nick held her that night. Long enough for the memory-induced tension to fade and exhaustion to take its place. Long enough for the rain outside to slow to the occasional audible drop against the window.

Long enough, she thought, to chase away a ghost or two from her past.

Chapter 11

Nick gripped the windowsill and breathed as deeply of the fresh night air as he'd watched Sara do hours before. She'd fallen asleep, finally, but slumber hadn't been so kind to him. The story she'd relayed haunted him, left him wound too tightly to relax.

A helpless kind of rage circled in his gut. For a man unused to feeling at all, it was an unsettling emotion. Sara had been able to stir all kinds of unfamiliar feelings in him, even long before he'd met her.

She'd been raped.

Ugly words for an unspeakably ugly act. She'd been little more than a child and had been violated in the cruelest kind of way.

There was a deeply primitive part of him that wished Carson was still alive. Wished he'd have the opportunity to track the man down and make him pay, one torturous second at a time, with his worthless life. The fact that the satisfaction would be denied to him was only partly to blame for the level of frustration Nick felt right now.

The clouds parted then, drifting across the sky and allowing a sliver of moonlight through. He couldn't remember the number of times he'd wondered about Sara when he'd been tracking her. Couldn't recall when his task of finding her had become more like the obsession Luc had called it. He'd been a step behind her for months before he'd finally traced her to New Orleans. The irony of discovering her in his hometown hadn't been lost on him. She'd been someone different in every town she'd left. In Biloxi she'd been a gum-cracking airhead with a weakness for flashy rings. In Atlanta she'd become a studious wallflower who'd constantly had her nose in a book. And in New Orleans she'd been a waitress with nervous mannerisms at odds with the cool, measuring look in her eyes—a waitress who collected statues of cats.

The rain had cooled the night air, but he welcomed its chill. He felt like he was burning from the inside out. He'd known that the odd sort of kinship he'd started to feel was the most dangerous kind of distraction. But he hadn't been able to will it away. He'd chosen to live in life's sewers, dealing with human garbage, but circumstances hadn't given her a choice.

Every week he'd spent on her trail, his fascination had grown. The similarities between them had been impossible to ignore. So Nick found himself wondering if she even knew anymore which of the identities she donned was most familiar. Whether she felt like she'd lost a little piece of herself with every disguise.

A tiny sound came from the bed and he turned his head sharply. Sara stirred, but didn't waken. He studied her in the darkness, wishing he could undo things that were impossible to undo, halt events that had already been set in motion.

He hadn't needed the words earlier to know that it hadn't been the violence Carson had done to her that had wounded her most powerfully, but her mother's reaction to it. Sara had been betrayed by the one who should have protected her, and betrayed in a different way by Mannen.

The time was long past when Nick could have fooled himself into believing he had this situation under control. A blade of terror edged along his heart at the acknowledgment. In the last five years he'd never given himself reason to doubt the outcome of an assignment. With sixty-six deaths on his conscience, he vowed to never let feeling enter a mission again. But he was dangerously close to that precipice here, battling emotions far better left unidentified.

He could only hope, for both Sara's and his sake, that he won the skirmish.

Sara clung tightly to Nick's tux-clad arm and tried to will the nerves away. "You're getting a lot of mileage out of that tuxedo."

A five-piece band played music from the forties as he guided her through the throngs of people and scanned the crowded room for their host. "We men don't have the same need as women to not be seen in the same thing twice." He glanced at her, his smile teasing. "That's why it doesn't bother us to wear identical monkey suits to every event that comes along."

She didn't point out that such events had never filled up her calendar until she'd met him. "I'm not the type to need a lot of clothes. You arranged for the wardrobe, remember."

His gaze was openly admiring. "And a fine job I did, too."

The dress was an ice-blue waterfall of silk that brushed the tops of her sandal-clad feet. She was draped in diamonds again, solitaire studs, with a necklace fashioned like a shimmering collar. When she'd put them on she'd felt like a little girl playing dress-up. The feeling had intensified when Kim had helped her with her hair, sweeping it up in a style that Sara would have sworn it was too short for. But then, she didn't have a lot of experience with readying herself for fancy events. If her stomach hadn't been alive with nerves, maybe she would have tried to enjoy the situation just a little.

She spotted Mannen across the room, surrounded by a group of people. Her chest tightened. "It appears you were right. His notoriety hasn't seemed to deter his guests."

"Just the opposite, probably."

When she sent Nick an inquiring glance, he shrugged. "Human nature being what it is, a lot of these people probably enjoy rubbing shoulders with someone who is tainted by scandal like Mannen. It gives them something to gossip about and makes them feel daring when they go back to their own lives."

She surprised them both by laughing. "You're a cynic. Why am I not surprised?"

"I'm a realist," he corrected, but he was smiling crookedly down at her. "Or perhaps a fatalist. At any rate, there's enough of a crowd here to make you feel comfortable, isn't there?"

Comfort was a relative term, she thought, as they slowly made their way around the large room. Her heart was knocking so hard at the wall of her chest that she could stand in as the band's percussionist. But she felt slightly more secure that she wouldn't be recognized by Mannen. Clothes had a way of framing a person, setting impressions in others' minds. That's why she'd always given her wardrobe careful consideration each time she'd chosen a new identity. She couldn't believe anyone would ever recognize her dressed as she was right now.

That thought should have smoothed jagged nerves, but only succeeded in holding them in check. When Nick handed her a wineglass, she sipped too eagerly, and choked a little. She knew from his raised brows that he suspected she'd gone for some liquid courage, and she wasn't ashamed to admit it. It wasn't every day she was forced to look her would-be killer in the face and make nice.

"Don't drink so much that you forget your cover." Nick whispered the words in an undertone as he nuzzled her ear. If she could have prevented the all too visible shudder his action sent skating down her spine, she would have.

"Michel," she drawled, "yoah such a tease." Giving him an arch look, she flicked an imaginary bit of lint from his lapel. "If yoah going to lecture, maybe Ah'll find a more accommodating escort."

The smile on Nick's mouth was slight, but there was a glint of pure amusement in his eyes. "I'd be a fool to take a chance like that, Raeanne, darling."

As they slowly moved through the room, halting to exchange introductions or chatter with other guests, Sara noted the way Nick's gaze continually scanned the area. He was used to sizing a place up, she thought, as well as everyone in it. She appreciated the quality, because she shared it herself.

"Shall we dance?"

Not if she could help it. "Maybe later." She held up her glass, which was still half-full, a handy excuse.

"No time like the present." Nick whisked the glass out of her hand and set both it and his on a nearby table. Sara threw a look at the surprised people sitting there and tried not to drag her feet as he drew her into his arms.

"I can't dance."

He raised her hand up to his shoulder and caught the other one in his. "What did you say?"

Her teeth clenched. "I said I don't know how to…"

Her words were rendered meaningless when he swirled her around the floor with a few deft movements.

They were in the midst of swaying couples, and she had no idea how they'd gotten there. "You must be mistaken," Nick said with a self-satisfied smile. "You *are* dancing. Waltzing, to be precise."

She made the mistake of looking down, and immediately stumbled. His arm tightened around her, his hand pressing against her lower back. "Haven't you ever heard the warning 'don't look down'?"

"I thought that referred to heights," she said automatically.

"Goes for dancing, too. Look at me." Her gaze raised to his. "There. Keep your eyes on me and you'll do fine. All you have to do is feel the music and let me guide you to the rhythm. Do you feel it?"

What she *felt* was threatening to undo all the good that had been done with the deep breathing exercises she'd been practicing. Her nerves reared, began scampering again.

Nick was holding her close. Sending a surreptitious glance around at the other couples, she decided they were dancing nearer than most. But he might have had to take that avenue to avoid having his feet brutalized by hers. Sensation radiated from the spread of his fingers on her back. His shoulders looked a yard wide in the dark cloth, a perfect foil for his inky hair and eyes. And since she'd seen him in a tux so recently, the sight of him in one now shouldn't do such strange things to her pulse.

Of course, she reflected, as his fingers brushed her bare back, perhaps she had a deeper appreciation of that well-honed body packed in black-and-white tailoring now that she had a vivid mental image of him out of it.

The provocative thought had her stumbling again, this

time in embarrassment. He gathered her even closer, seeming unaware that her body had gone stiff against his.

The recollection, once summoned, couldn't be banished. Of Nick's shoulders, blocking out the moonlight; of his shirt half-off; of his hair mussed by her fingers and his chest damp from his exertions. Of his hips pounding against hers in a rhythm she'd been helpless to deny.

"Chérie." The word sounded at her ear. She closed her eyes and arched her neck, and his lips found the pulse there, beating wildly. He'd recognize her reaction, would probably even guess its cause. She couldn't bring herself to care.

The music ended. Nick released her, but kept his arm around her waist as he guided her from the dance floor. He snagged a wineglass from a waiter going by and took a long swallow.

Sara looked at him uncertainly. His face looked as if it had been carved from stone. In that instant his eyes met hers. He took another drink, then offered the glass to her. "You go to my head far faster than any liquor could."

The compliment had her eyes widening. "Maybe we should get some food in you."

"Maybe we should. Because right now your mouth is looking like a particularly tasty morsel."

Confused pleasure spread through her with a flush. She'd never learned the art of flirtation, the teasing give-and-take of lighthearted banter, with something else layered beneath. Tongue-tied, she merely stared at him. And watched him take a long deep breath.

"Let's get some air." His intent was clear, and her blood began to slow, to throb. Her body was all too familiar with the promise his embrace offered. And all too willing to experience it again.

But as they cut across the room toward the open terrace

doors, their host left the clutch of people he was conversing with and approached them.

"Michel, good of you to come. And your lovely companion." Mannen turned to her, smiled genially. And Sara's blood abruptly cooled.

His tuxedo had a silver vest that was the same color as his hair. It was his eyes, though, that held her attention. They resembled a shark's—flat, without feeling. "May I call you Raeanne?"

"Please do." It was an effort to keep a smile on her lips, a drawl in her voice. He took her hand in his and an icy finger of fear licked down her spine. Dimly, she was aware of Nick's arm tightening around her waist. She was grateful for it. Her knees had gone to jelly.

"Michel seems quite taken with you." Mannen flicked an amused glance toward Nick. "I noticed it the last time we met. How long have you known each other?"

Sara looked at Nick and drew an odd sort of strength from his rugged profile. "Nineteen days." She was in familiar territory now. Nick had made her practice the story often enough. Caressingly, she stroked the hand he had resting on her hip. "I've never met anyone quite like him."

"You have an impressive home." Nick's gaze roamed the area.

"Thank you. I do like my comfort."

The space he deemed comfortable would easily have housed a dozen families. The lavish estate made Nick and Sara's temporary quarters seem paltry by contrast. The rare and the collectible was displayed everywhere—museum quality, but without warmth. There was something cold in the space that had nothing to do with the temperature and everything to do with the man standing before them. The house bore the stamp of his personality, and was permeated with the chill he emanated.

"You've invited an interesting collection of guests."

At the words, Mannen turned in the direction Nick was gazing and stilled. If she hadn't been watching so carefully, Sara would have missed the expression that flickered across his face and was gone. It had seemed almost like glee.

She looked at the group that had just entered the room, and recognized the two women who had spoken to her at the fund-raiser—Meghan Patterson and the state attorney, Addison Jacobs. Sara wondered who their escorts were. Nick had seemed certain that one was a cop, so that was sure to be the big man with the short-cropped dark hair and careful eyes. He bent down then, whispered something to Meghan, and she turned and smiled at him.

"I enjoy keeping things interesting." Mannen raised a finger, and a waiter immediately came to his side. He lifted a glass from the tray, brought it to his lips.

"Who are the men?" Nick asked.

Mannen smiled serenely. "Thorns in my side. Detective Gabe Connally is the dark-haired gentleman. The blond man with our esteemed state attorney is Dare McKay, an investigative journalist."

"As I said, an odd collection of guests." Nick's voice was hard. "Why would you invite that kind of scrutiny?"

His eyes cold, Mannen said, "How does that old saying go? Keep your friends close, and your enemies closer? I have nothing to hide. And before long, those four will find their suspicions…laid to rest."

Sara's gaze shot to his. Had she imagined the threat in his words? His expression remained impassive. But she had the impression of something dark and malevolent behind that smooth, genial mask.

A woman came up then and whispered in his ear. Mannen gave them a rueful look. "I'm sorry. I must attend to something in the kitchen. I would like to have the two of

you visit again so we can have a more intimate gathering.''
His brows raised, he looked from one to the other. ''Sometime later this week, perhaps?''

''You have my number,'' Nick said.

As she watched him walk away, Sara had a strong desire to wash. ''I don't know how many more times I can stand being near him,'' she murmured, her revulsion evident in her voice.

Nick's hand went to her back, his fingers rubbing soothingly. ''You'll never have to face him alone. Just remember that.''

But she would, at some point, have to face him. As herself, not as Raeanne Backstrom. In a trial she'd have to sit on the stand and tell her story, knowing all the time that he was behind the deaths of her friends, that he'd long plotted her own. And knowing that he wouldn't rest until he'd succeeded.

''Don't look now,'' she said as an aside, as she looked beyond Nick's shoulder, ''but we're about to have more company.''

''Hello again. We met a couple nights ago, at the fundraiser.''

Sara smiled at the woman and her party. ''Of course, Ah remember. Meghan and Addison, right? Darling—'' she turned to Nick, shifting seamlessly into her role ''—you recall me mentioning them, don't you?''

During the round of introductions, she studied the group as nerves twitched in her stomach. The detective, Connally, had an expression that could have been etched from granite, and the same quick assessing look that she'd often seen in Nick's eyes. McKay had the face of a glorious saint and the eyes of a beguiling sinner. And it was apparent, within thirty seconds of meeting, that she and Nick were being schmoozed.

The four were slick, Sara would give them that. If she

didn't have a naturally suspicious mind she might have thought friendliness was all that motivated them. They made the effort to chat casually for a bit, during which time Raeanne was called upon to admire Meghan's engagement ring and hear a few details of the upcoming wedding.

Sara cast a wary look at Connally. She would never have imagined the stone-faced cop with the petite blond woman, but the only time she saw his stoic countenance relax at all was when he looked at his fiancée. Sara was equally surprised to hear McKay speak about shopping for rings with Addie, as he called the assistant state attorney. As the conversation swirled around her, Sara felt a sense of disorientation. It all seemed so...normal. Yet it was completely divorced from anything she could contemplate for her future. Whether Mannen ended up in prison or not, she'd never be safe again. And that kind of uncertainty wasn't the sort she could invite anyone to share.

With a subtle maneuvering that elicited her respect, Sara was flanked by the women and engaged in idle chatter, while Nick was subjected to what amounted to little more than an interrogation.

"So you just got to the States recently?" This was from Dare, as he tucked his hands in his pockets and rocked back on his heels. "First visit?"

"No, but I haven't been here for a couple years."

"Fly private?"

Sara's attention was split between the women's conversation and the men's. From Connally's question, she'd bet that he'd already checked out the public passenger lists at the airport.

"Yes, I enjoy the comfort my own jet affords." Nick's answers were smooth—all of them. Yes, this trip was for pleasure only. No, he had no business interests in the

States, but the tech stock here was likely to rebound, wasn't it?

"Do you and Mannen share stock tips?" Dare gave him an affable grin. "He probably has some hot commodities." He gestured around the room. "From the looks of this place, he's loaded."

"I understand he's become involved in another venture recently," Connally murmured.

As Sara gave up pretending not to listen to the conversation, Nick responded to the detective's remark. "I'm sure whatever he involves himself in is very lucrative."

"His business interests are always worth looking into." Gabe's comment weighed heavily in the air. Sara wondered if she was imagining the meaning behind them.

A few minutes later the group excused themselves and drifted away. Sara waited until Nick had led her off before letting out a long breath. "My nerves are never going to last."

He glanced around. "Your nerves are steel—they'd have to be to get through what you have the last few years. But we're definitely going to have to be careful. The interest of Connally and McKay, not to mention Jacobs, can complicate everything."

A skitter of unease chased through her system. "They'll be looking into our covers, won't they?"

"Poring over them, most likely. They'll stand—I'm not worried about that. But when they do a little digging into Michel Falcol's background—" he shrugged "—they'll be watching me as closely as they do Mannen."

"What's that mean?"

"It means, *chérie*—" he pulled her into his arms and danced her out to the dance floor "—that I better take what I can when the opportunity presents itself."

The opportunity presented itself less than an hour later. Nick thought the time had been spent pleasurably enough.

Sara was relaxing in his arms, and when she wasn't watching their feet, she had a natural grace that helped her to match the rhythm he set.

He bent his head, nipped at her earlobe. "Follow my lead."

"I thought that's what I'd been doing."

His arm tightened around her waist. "We're going to take advantage of a distraction. Right...now."

He danced her off the floor and bent down to press a warm kiss on her lips. Against them he whispered, "Mannen's busy with Connally and the others. We've got some time."

She may not have understood, but she didn't ask questions as he guided her with seeming nonchalance from the room. A quick glance showed the space was empty, but he wasn't about to take any chances. He nuzzled her neck as they walked farther down the hall. Anyone noticing them would think they were seeking a little privacy.

When he came to the second door on the right, Nick reached into his pocket and palmed a small remote device. He pointed it at the door, and a small red light blinked furiously for several seconds, before turning to a green steady glow. There was a barely audible click. With a quick glance around, he replaced the remote and withdrew the gold pen. He pushed the door open an inch and played the device over the space. There was no response. He opened the door and stepped inside, pulling Sara in behind him.

"This is Mannen's office!" she hissed.

"So it is." The intelligence he'd gathered had been correct. The office was right where it was supposed to be, and there were no security devices besides the electronic lock on the door. The man obviously felt protected in his own home.

"What are we doing in here?"

He took some latex gloves from his pocket and snapped them on. "I'm going on a search. You're going to wait patiently and not touch anything." He reengaged the lock with a push of a button on the console. If anyone came they would at least be alerted by the sound of the code being keyed in on the other side of the wall.

Scanning the room quickly, he decided to start with the computer. There was a low hum when he turned it on, and slipped an encryption disk into the CD carousel. It was a sweet piece of software, and utterly necessary in this case. Without Luc's expertise he didn't trust himself to break the code-protected files.

The disk made that unnecessary. It attacked the start-up data in the hard drive, sifting through patterns until it found one that appeared with some frequency. As the eight-character password popped up on the screen, Nick memorized it, used it, extracted the disk and put in a blank one. Then he began downloading files.

He didn't bother to read them. He couldn't afford to. There'd be time for that later. Checking his watch, he noted that they'd been inside for five minutes. They could afford only a couple more.

He looked at Sara. Her eyes were huge in her face.

"How do we get out of here?" she whispered anxiously.

Since that part would be the trickiest of this exercise, he thought it prudent not to answer. He waited impatiently for the files to finish downloading, then extracted the CD and slipped it into his pocket. The computer was then shut down, and he got up, taking care to replace the chair in its former position.

"Ready?" He quickly crossed the room toward her.

Her voice was shaky. "Definitely."

"Wait just a second." Striding to the door, he used the remote to disengage the lock, and pulled the door open a fraction. When he determined there was no one in the vicinity, he waved a hand for her to join him. She did so eagerly, a little too eagerly. Hearing a small sound, he turned to see that she'd stumbled, caught her heel on the hem of her dress. "Easy," he breathed.

A moment later she'd reached his side, and checking the hallway again, he ushered her out, closing the door behind them and taking off the gloves. If those computer files turned up anything interesting, it could be a nice bonus to the file he was gathering on Mannen. It had been a risk, but one he'd thought worth taking. His life was comprised of weighing chances, figuring the odds.

With a glance at the silent woman beside him, he recalled that she still represented the biggest risk he'd ever taken. And the outcome of that particular venture was still far from decided.

"You're a natural at subterfuge." Nick folded his jacket over the back of a chair and began undoing the buttons of his shirt.

Sara gave him a sideways glance as she sat on the bed and slipped off her sandals. "I've had to be."

He shrugged out of the shirt and threw it carelessly on top of the coat. Of course she had. As had he. But he could walk away from a job at any time and become Nick Doucet again. She didn't have that option. He didn't see a way for her to ever have it.

She went into the bathroom and turned on the water. If he could give her one thing, he thought savagely, unzipping his pants and stepping out of them, it would be to allow her that chance at a normal life. One where she wouldn't have to fear anyone. Anything. One where she could learn to walk down a street without looking over her shoulder.

Something most people were able to do without ever giving it a second thought.

Naked, he walked to the bathroom and stopped inside the doorway. She had just finished washing her face and was patting it dry with a towel. The room smelled of her—the aroma of her perfume and her shampoo. He drew in her scent now, in a greedy, guilty swallow, and was pierced with a blade of need.

Setting the towel aside, she reached behind her to her zipper. He stepped forward and she stilled, their gazes locking in the mirror. Replacing her hands with his, he slowly unzipped her dress. Her slender back was bared, an inch at a time, and he leaned forward to drop a kiss against one shoulder blade.

She gave a quick little shiver at the contact, and his gut clenched in a violent surge of satisfaction. Maybe she didn't completely trust him, but she couldn't prevent her reaction to him. The knowledge had blood pooling in his loins.

He parted the silky fabric and, hooking a finger in each of the narrow straps, drew them down her arms. The dress puddled around her feet, and she stepped out of it, pushed it aside with one foot.

She was wearing a sheer bra and panties that left little to the imagination. The French, Nick thought with approval, had excellent taste in lingerie. His hands went to her hair, his gaze on hers in the mirror, and he started drawing out the pins. One after another strands fell like sleek bits of silk against his knuckles. When he'd removed them all, he threaded his fingers through her hair and kneaded her scalp.

He'd experienced both duty and desire, but he'd never known them to entwine, entangle until the result was uncertain. He knew better than to veer from his mission, but

Sara presented a complication that couldn't be denied. And she was one he wouldn't deny himself.

His hands went to the clasp on her bra, released it. She moistened her lips, and he detected a flush of what could have been desire or embarrassment flood her cheeks. "You're perfectly made, *mon ange*." He rubbed the back of his fingers along the sides of her breasts and watched the small nipples peak at the contact. The evidence of her arousal was irresistible. He turned her in his arms and caught her mouth with his.

Her hands came to his chest, stroked. The contact was electric. His tongue probed her mouth, slow and deep, and when her tongue flicked against his, then away, he was suffused with heat.

He took one breast in his hand, feeling the nipple stab his palm. Tearing his lips from hers, he went in search of the small nub and took it in his mouth.

He suckled her, lashing her nipple with his tongue, the taste of her flesh driving spikes of need through his system. She gave a low thin cry and arched against him. He leaned her farther back over his arm and took more.

He wanted to excite her. He wanted to satisfy her in a way no other man ever could. And to that end he pleasured her with all the skill of his experience. He didn't think of it as seduction. He was as much the seduced as the seducer. Sara's spell over him was complete.

She squirmed against him, and his free hand found her hip, glided around to cup her silk-encased mound. The fabric was damp with her moisture, and the discovery was erotic. Slipping his fingers beneath the silk, he stroked her satiny heat.

A groan was ripped from his throat. He raised his head, leaving her nipple glistening and tight. "You're hot. Wet. *Non*." Her hand fluttered over his, as if she were going to push it away. "Don't. Do you know what it does to a man when a woman responds to him as you do?'' His erection was rock hard against her hip. There was no missing the effect her response had on him. He waited until her body relaxed against his again, waited for her hand to raise to his arm, then stroked a finger inside her and felt the delicate pulsations of her inner muscles close around it.

She gave a sharp high cry, the sound calling to something elemental inside him. Every pulse in his body throbbed like a wound. The light in the room was too bright; it danced in his eyes. He pushed her panties aside with his other hand and rubbed her moist softness even as he probed deeper.

Sara arched against his hand, forcing him to the rhythm her body set. His lips went to her neck, and he shuddered against her. Tiny little demons from hell were riding his control with wicked, jagged spurs. He blinked, tried to focus, but all he could see was her.

He could feel her tensing beneath his touch, her hips moving more frantically. *''Non,''* he whispered, the word dragged out of him. ''Wait, *ma petite.''* When he withdrew his touch she moaned, and he kissed the sound from her mouth. He dragged her panties over her hips and down her legs. Turning her around, he braced her hands on the vanity top. He stroked the round firm globes of her buttocks, moved between her legs. ''I want to be inside you. You're so silky and tight.'' He guided himself into her womanly opening and his restraint began to fray as he pressed that first inch inside. He halted, feeling the delicate adjustments as her sensitive flesh yielded to his intrusion. He watched her face in the mirror as he rolled his hips and buried himself deeper. ''I want to see you come. I want to feel it.''

A sob ripped out of her. Her fingers were clutching the edge of the counter and she rubbed her hips against him, aiding his entry. He gulped in a deep breath, took her hips in his hands and drove into her with a harsh groan.

The rhythm he set torched any thought of control. She climaxed in moments, her body convulsing around him, milking his own response. He exploded an instant later, pouring himself inside her. And for the first time in more years than he could count, he felt complete.

Chapter 12

Nick and Kim were at the breakfast table when Sara got up the next morning. She slipped into a chair next to him, strangely reluctant to meet his warm gaze.

"You slept late."

"Must have been all the dancing you made me do."

"Nick danced?" Kim's voice was incredulous.

He gave the woman a quelling look. "I can dance."

"*Can,* yes. It's your willingness to do so that's surprising."

Sara reached for the coffeepot and poured a steaming cup. She felt oddly in need of fortification this morning.

"So did you find out anything of interest last night?"

Kim's question was surely meant for Nick, but it reminded Sara of something she'd wanted to mention. "I got a bad feeling when Mannen was talking about Connally, McKay and the women." She screwed up her brow, trying to remember the man's exact wording. "The way he said 'laid to rest.' I got a distinct impression he was talking about more than allaying their suspicions."

"He has some scores he intends to settle," Nick agreed grimly. "There's too much public scrutiny right now for him to move against his enemies, but he's definitely planning something. I'm more convinced than ever that he won't be hanging around much longer to see what charges stick."

"Just long enough for the big score," Kim said. She stabbed her fork at the last bite of waffle on her plate and lifted it to her lips. After swallowing, she added, "How much longer before you move on him?"

Sara caught Nick's sidelong glance her way. "That depends on what we get from the disks. And I'd like to get him recorded at least once more."

A shaft of pain lanced through her. To cover it, Sara reached for a piece of toast. She didn't need any reminders that their time together was rapidly coming to an end. With Mannen in custody, Nick's job would be over. The danger to her wouldn't lessen appreciably, but protecting her had never been his prime duty. And despite his promises, she couldn't see a reason why he'd bother to keep his vows. She wasn't his problem. He seemed to want her, but she didn't fool herself into believing that would last. Before long, she'd be on her own again.

The wave of desolation that overcame her at the thought was hard to battle. She steeled herself against the feeling. There was always a price for letting oneself want. She'd known that, just as she'd known she'd have to deal with the resulting loss. She'd kept her expectations low all her life so as to cushion herself from just this sort of disappointment.

She washed the toast down with a gulp of coffee, barely noticing when Kim left the table. With Nick out of the picture, there would no longer be a choice between him and Justice. The agency would be no less a threat to her then, with the mole Mannen had inside. It was time, past

time, for her to begin making plans for how she was going
to deal with it.

Nick reached a finger beneath her chin, turning her to
face him. A soft kiss was pressed to her mouth. He tasted
like coffee sweetened by maple syrup. "Good morning."

"Good morning." It was an effort, but she managed to
meet his gaze, and immediately recognized the look of lazy
male satisfaction apparent in it.

"I let you sleep. I thought you needed it." A smile
crooked his mouth. "Or rather, I thought I owed you
some."

She reached for her coffee with a hand that wasn't quite
steady. "I'm fine."

"I didn't use protection the first time last night."

His bald statement had her hand jerking, sending coffee
sloshing over the side of the cup. Setting it down quickly,
she used her napkin to soak up the resulting spill. "I know.
I mean...it's all right. I'm on the pill." She'd escaped
Carson's attack without a pregnancy to further complicate
her life, and she'd started taking precautions shortly after
she ran away. It would have been hideously irresponsible
to bring a child into the kind of life she was forced to lead.

It wasn't a topic she felt at ease discussing with Nick,
not now, not last night. Perhaps if she could even come
close to matching him in experience, such an intimate discussion wouldn't have her feeling awkward and inade-
quate.

The feelings were intensified when he said, "That's
never happened before. Ever."

The words had her gaze flying to his. "I'm a bastard,"
Nick stated quietly. "My teenaged father didn't care
enough about my mother to marry her, and *she* didn't care
enough to keep *me*." His mouth twisted self-deprecatingly.
"A Doucet could be born outside marriage, but one could
never be raised outside the family."

Sara was fascinated despite herself at this tiny sliver of his past. "Your father raised you alone?"

"My father let my grandmother raise me, and he went about doing what he does best—running through women and money with equal fervor. Though I am the only child he had. He's a great disappointment to my grandfather," Nick added.

"And to you?" she dared to ask.

He took the soaked napkin she was clutching in her hand and set it aside. "I never allowed myself to be disappointed." The words were such an eerie echo of her earlier thoughts that she could only stare. "I'm telling you this just so you know. I've never let that happen before. Not when I was seventeen...not ever. And no child of mine would ever be raised without me in its life."

She strove for an even tone. "Well, like I say, there's no reason to worry."

"You misunderstood me, *chérie,* if you thought I was worried."

She was saved from replying to his cryptic comment when he raised his head, listening. A moment later, she heard the sound, too. His cell phone was ringing.

"Excuse me, would you please?"

She nodded and he went into the next room. Because she discovered her fingers were shaking, she curled them tightly into her palms. She didn't know what to make of the information he'd just given her. Knew only that his reference to his loss of control last night was doing a fine job of shredding her own composure.

"Dammit, what did I tell you?"

The lash of Nick's voice startled her. She turned to look into the next room. He was pacing with the phone clutched to his ear, and the expression on his face was thunderous.

"I already told you how this was going to be played."

Sara was listening unabashedly now, slipping from her

chair to move closer when he paced farther away. Was he
talking to Mannen? She discarded the thought in the next
moment. He wouldn't speak to the man in that tone. He
was too well trained to slip out of his role. So it was
someone else, someone he was truly angry at.

Doubts circled, gnawing vicious little holes in her stomach. The caller could be Whitmore. Did he have Nick's
number? Was he still trying to convince him to turn her
over to the department? There was no way to be sure. It
could just as easily be someone else he worked with, although if it were any of the staff he had helping him out
on this job she doubted they would use a phone to contact
him.

She doubted that he'd sound that furious, either.

He listened for a long time. When he spoke again his
tone was no less terse, but there was a note of acceptance
in it. "You may be on to something. I'm not saying I
approve of your disobeying orders, understand, but I'll
take a look at what you've got. Noon. There's a bar on
Thirty-fifth and Troost called the Horseshoe Grill. Be
there."

As she heard him prepare to end the conversation, Sara
slipped back into her chair. A few moments later, when
he came striding into the room again, she was sipping coffee. "Who was that?"

"No one important."

It had sounded important to her, but it was obvious he
wasn't going to share the conversation with her. "Can I
convince you to come along to the bookstore with me today? Kim and I found one that has something for every
taste."

"Not today." As if realizing how abrupt he sounded,
he added, "I have a meeting. But tonight...you and I need
to sit down and have a long talk."

Anxiety rose in a wave. "Sounds serious."

He came up behind her and rested his hands on her shoulders, kneaded gently. "It is."

"I don't see a bookstore anywhere near here. Are you sure you have the address right?"

At Kim's question, Sara acted confused. "I thought so. Do you mind if we look just a bit longer? Then if we don't find it in the next block or two we can go back to that place we found yesterday."

"Bookstores aren't my idea of shopping," the other woman muttered. "Now, a shoe sale marked fifty percent off—that's shopping."

Sara barely heard her. Her focus was on the sign two doors down: The Horseshoe Grill. Uncertainty churned in her stomach. It was ridiculous to feel like she was betraying a trust. Nick hadn't seen fit to explain himself to her, so was it so wrong to check things out on her own? She wanted, she *needed*, to be sure he wasn't meeting someone from Justice.

She needed to believe that he wasn't dealing with Whitmore.

The man had been full of assurances when she'd met him six years ago, but things had gone wrong, horribly wrong, anyway. He might have risen higher in the department by now, but that didn't mean the agency was any safer, at least for her.

They were drawing even with the restaurant. In a nonchalant tone, she said, "Okay if we stop in here for a soda?"

Kim looked at the place, then scanned the street. After a moment, she shrugged. "All right by me." They entered and Sara's gaze immediately went in search of Nick. Unerringly, she picked him out at a rear table. With his back to the wall he was able to see all arrivals. It would only be a moment before he noticed them.

The other man's back was to her.

The hostess approached them, blocking Sara's view. While Kim spoke to the woman, Sara took a step closer, stared harder. It wasn't Mannen with Nick. The man was shorter, broader, with brown hair. Whitmore had brown hair. At least he had the last time she'd seen him. But hadn't it been streaked with gray?

Kim was looking at her curiously. The hostess was walking in another direction, leading them toward their table. Sara took another step, and then another. If she could just see the man's profile, she could be certain. Whitmore had a hooked nose that would be impossible to…

Nick picked that moment to look up, and the expression on his face stopped her in her tracks. In the next instant his lips were moving in what she somehow knew were curses, and he was rising from the table. Kim saw him, and grabbed Sara's arm. Nick's guest turned and Sara was finally able to get a look at him.

It wasn't Whitmore at all. But recognition slammed into her all the same. The battered features, the square jaw, those pale gray eyes… Sara staggered back as reality hit her with the force of a death blow.

It was the man who'd tried to kill her in New Orleans. The man Nick had assured her she'd never see again.

Nick's expression was a tight hard mask as he strode toward her. Kim was talking, but Sara couldn't make out the words. She couldn't hear anything above the roaring in her ears, the pounding in her blood.

Instinct took over. It had been dulled perhaps in the last several days, but it rose inside her now, sharp as a spear. She whirled on Kim and curved her hand into position, dealing her a blow guaranteed to neutralize her.

Nick yelled something she couldn't make out, and lunged toward her. Sara pushed Kim's doubled-over body toward him and spun away. Running a few steps, she grabbed a tray of food from a shocked waitress and threw it in Nick's direction. Then she ran full out, not bothering to look back. She slammed through the kitchen door. She'd worked in enough restaurants to know building codes guaranteed a second exit.

There was a chorus of angry shouts from the cooks and the wait staff in the kitchen, but Sara didn't hesitate. Dodging people and counters, she sped out the back door.

She knew better than to turn around, to slow. She darted down the alley and into the back door of another store, then out the front of it. And when she got on the street, breath heaving through her lungs, she sprinted to one of the taxis lining the curb and yanked the door open.

Leaping inside, she leaned forward and yelled, "Drive!"

The last thing she saw as they moved into traffic was Nick standing in the cloud of their exhaust.

"Where to?" The driver leaned forward, turned on the meter. Its ticking sliced through her panic-induced haze, delivering yet another realization.

She didn't have any money.

Lowering her head to her hands, Sara forced herself to think. She didn't even have a purse. With no keys, money or identification, she'd hardly needed one. Nick had seen to that.

The thought of him summoned a wave of nausea. Reaction was setting in, shudders racking her system. Confusion clouded her thinking. Nick had told her...what had he said? That the scene in New Orleans had been a ruse. That the man who had pretended to attack her had left the country. But that didn't explain why Nick had been arguing with him on the phone this morning. Or why the man was here, in Chicago, when Nick had said he wouldn't be returning to the States.

"Lady, you gotta give me an address."

She drew a breath, tried to concentrate. "Give me a minute to think." When she'd seen the man with Nick, she'd reacted, thought receding, to be replaced with survival instinct. Logic was returning now, and with it, emotion. She wished she could talk to Nick, hear his explanation. There may well be a simple reason for...

Even as the thought formed, she regarded it with shock. Was she actually making *excuses* for the man now? That should show her just how close he'd gotten to her, how completely he'd destroyed the defenses she'd spent years building. It really didn't matter if he'd lied to her about the attack in New Orleans or not. She'd allowed him to get too close to her. Sara took a deep breath. She couldn't chance trusting him again, and she certainly couldn't trust her own feelings.

There was really no decision to make here at all. The thought slyly slipped through the welter of emotion. This was a bigger matter than whether or not she could trust Nick. If she could allow herself to. She was *free*. A curious sense of calm settled over her then. There had been no way out of the situation she and Nick had been engaged in. No way to escape Mannen in this lifetime, except by death. Fate, perhaps, had finally balanced out the cards in her life and decided she was owed a break. Regardless of the ache in her heart, it was one she wasn't going to waste. "Take me to a pawnshop," she told the driver. "A reputable one."

The small storefront the driver pulled up to twenty minutes later was tucked away in a building that had seen better days. But the neighborhood seemed decent enough, if slightly deteriorated. Sara had a heated discussion with the driver, who was unwilling to wait for her, even with the meter running. When he learned she didn't have the money to pay him, wouldn't until she'd conducted her business inside, the discussion increased in volume. It cost her a promise of triple the fare to convince him to let her out of the car.

A bell rang as she pushed open the door to the shop. A tall thin man with a fringe of gray hair looked up from the betting sheets he had spread across the glass counter. "Can I help you?"

Sara reached up, took the earrings from her ears. "I want to sell these." Because there wasn't a bare spot on the counter, she set them on the paper.

After giving her a sweeping glance from head to toe, he picked up one of the earrings and gave it a cursory look. "I ain't no jeweler. But I could take a chance. Give you two hundred for them." He smiled, revealing nicotine-stained teeth.

"They're worth twenty times that." She had no idea of the value, but she'd lived on the streets long enough to know when she was being hosed.

"So you say, but there ain't no way for me to tell for sure. Three hundred's as high as I can go."

"Fine." She snatched them out of his hand and turned to leave. "I'm sure I can get a better deal from your competitor down the street." The threat was a stab in the dark. She had no idea how far it was to the next shop, but from the man's reaction, there must have been another in the vicinity.

"Hey, now, where ya going in such a hurry?" Those yellow teeth were bared again. "There's no use wasting your time with Pete. Guy's a thief, even if he is my cousin. C'mon back here," he coaxed, as she halted on her way to the door. "Let's take another look." This time he reached beneath the counter and pulled out a jeweler's loupe, taking his time examining the earrings.

When he lowered it, he hitched up his pants with his

free hand and said, "Look high quality, but they could be stolen. I'm taking a big risk here, if they are. Cops come to my place, accuse me of receiving stolen property—"

Sara interrupted him unapologetically. "Two thousand."

"With the risk I'm assuming here? If you want that kind of money you came to the wrong place. One."

The cab driver tapped his horn impatiently. Sara looked at the earrings in the man's somewhat less than sanitary hand. A mental image flashed across her mind, a mirror reflection of her figure wrapped in Nick's arms, naked except for the earrings. The memory seared like the stroke of a hot blade. "All right," she said, cutting short both the negotiation and the mental picture. "One."

The driver was measurably happier when she returned, the fifty she handed him curbing most of his impatience. She mentally flipped through her options. The airport was out; tickets were too difficult to obtain without identification, and she wasn't up to the elaborate ruse she'd have to construct to try and purchase one.

She almost decided on heading to the bus depot, before rejecting the idea in the next moment. Nick would be expecting her to try to flee the city, so he'd have the major transit centers covered. She leaned forward and asked the driver, "How far is the next town that would have its own bus depot?"

The driver scratched his head. "Well, there's a station in Joliet."

"How much would it cost to have you drive me there?"

The look he sent her in the rearview mirror was incredulous. "Lady, it'd be a lot cheaper to just take a bus there from here, y'know?"

She drew in a deep breath, let it out slowly. "I'm growing fond of your company. How much?"

"To Joliet?" The price he named would put a sizable

dent in the amount of money she had stuffed in her pants pocket. But she couldn't let that fact deter her. ''Then let's do it.'' She sank back against the seat cushions and watched the scenery pass by with less speed than she would have liked. She willed her impatience away. Soon enough she'd be putting Chicago, and Victor Mannen, behind her once again, this time forever.

The pain in her chest reminded her that she was also putting miles between her and Nick Doucet.

Sara stared out the window at the Joliet bus station. She peered in all directions, but saw nothing out of the ordinary. Somehow she doubted Nick would come after her in the limo, but she'd feel better if she knew what kind of vehicle she should be looking for.

In the next moment she shook off her nerves. There was no way for him to cover Chicago and all its surrounding towns. She was almost home free.

An ironic smile twisted her lips as she counted out the bills to pay the driver. Home was a relative term. And in the next few hours she needed to decide where her next ''home'' would be. She got out of the cab and crossed the parking lot toward the depot. Her identities were always chosen after combing a county's death records for a female who would have been around her age if she'd lived. It took further digging to narrow the search to one who'd been born in a different county or state, and some careful research to find out whether the two locations were cross-referenced.

It would work best to choose a city, do the research there, then move on to another town hundreds of miles away and send for a birth certificate. Sara decided she'd been wise to choose to travel by bus, after all. She passed the vehicles in the handicapped spots and ascended the curb. It wouldn't take long to go through the rest of her money. Especially while she was waiting for—

He loomed out of nowhere. One moment she had her eye on the steps ahead leading to the depot building, and the next Nick had appeared from behind a nearby van. Immediately she whirled to sprint away.

In less than four strides he was at her side, his arms wrapped around, rendering useless the training he'd given her. Her feet were free, though, and she kicked frantically even as she opened her mouth to scream.

Before she could emit a sound, she was picked up and tossed in the back of a white utility van, and the door was shut behind them. When she tried to scramble to her feet, Nick sprawled on top of her.

"Go."

At Nick's command the driver pulled away. Sara struggled beneath him, trying to throw him off.

"You need to listen to me." His voice was harsh, to cover the underlying layer of urgency. "I know how it looked. How it seems. But there's an explanation."

"Get off me." Her own voice shook with rage. She worked a hand free and made a bridge of her palm, then rammed it upward. Quick reflexes were all that saved him from a broken nose or worse. He caught her wrist in his hand and wrestled it back to the floor of the van. The ease with which he managed the feat seemed to infuriate her further.

"You'll listen," he said grimly, "if I have to keep you in here all day."

"You've explained a lot of things over the last several days, Nick," she snapped. "It's getting increasingly difficult to sustain belief. You said that man was *gone*."

"I remember what I said." He felt an uncharacteristic thread of panic, one that had started unraveling the moment he'd looked up from that table and seen her staring at him, knowing what she'd think. And certain that one too many lies along the way had strained her shaky trust too much for her to give him the benefit of the doubt.

"The man you saw was Luc LeNoue, a colleague of mine. He did leave the country. He was told—" his tone took on a note of grimness "—to stay out for the course of this job. He was supposed to be in France."

Her chin was tilted at a familiar angle. "How did you find me?"

"That doesn't matter. Let me explain about Luc. I know it must have frightened you to see him again, but—"

"How did you find me?" she repeated flatly.

He drew in a breath, aware that his answer wasn't going to help his cause any. "Your shoes. I had tracking devices planted in every pair when I ordered them. The men in this van have the monitoring equipment necessary to trace your movements."

Her eyes, her voice, went glacial. "How very enterprising of you. And so much more effective than a leash and chain."

He shifted his weight, making their contact that much more intimate. There was a layer of desperation in his gut now. He couldn't have said why it was so important to make her understand. "Everything I told you in the Keys is the truth. I didn't expect Luc here, but he was able to uncover something about Mannen that might put this case to rest."

She turned her face away, and the gesture was like a punch to the jaw. It told him better than words that there was nothing he could say that she would listen to right now, or believe.

Which meant that the bond he thought they'd forged hadn't been deep enough, strong enough to hold her when freedom beckoned. And he knew he had only himself to blame for that.

Chapter 13

Kim and Luc wore abashed looks when Nick followed Sara into the house. She didn't spare a glance for either one of them before striding to the stairway and mounting the steps toward the bedroom. The sight of that slender spine shot with steel made Nick's gut clench. He tore his gaze away from Sara and used it to stare down his employees.

Kim broke first. "Ah…I'll go upstairs and stand watch."

"You do that. Will you need to be armed first?"

Wincing at the reference to the effortless manner in which Sara had disabled her, Kim backed away, shaking her head. "That won't happen again." She turned to follow Sara, only to stop in midstride. "I forgot." Looking over her shoulder, she said, "Mannen called twice since we got back. He says it's urgent." She shot Nick a pacifying glance. "Maybe this thing is going to break soon, huh?"

Tension was rapping at the back of his skull. He'd forgotten for a while that he'd sent the phone with Kim. The one in the van had allowed him to communicate with the operatives he'd dispatched to the house before taking off after Sara.

Kim hurried up the stairs. He allowed her to make her escape. His true wrath was saved for the man who even now was looking as though he wished he'd stayed on the other side of the ocean.

Striding into the drawing room, Nick headed straight to the bar and poured two fingers of Scotch. Luc followed him into the room with all the enthusiasm of a prisoner approaching the gallows.

"Believe me, I know what you're going to say."

Nick tossed back the first shot and let the liquor sear a wicked path to his stomach. "Then you won't be surprised when I kick your ass clear across the Atlantic."

"I know I screwed up and I don't blame you for tearing into me. If it makes you feel any better, I'm as disgusted with me as you are."

Tipping the bottle to his glass, Nick filled it again. "Somehow I doubt that could be possible."

The man shrugged, his tone placating. "It all turned out okay, though, right? You found her. I knew you were too damn careful not to have a foolproof backup plan." Something in Nick's eyes must have warned him. He actually took a step away. "But why don't I get to the point? Like I told you in the restaurant, I found something I think we can use on Mannen."

Nick's attention still had an annoying habit of straying to the woman upstairs. With a conscious effort, he shifted it. "Tell me what you found."

Surer of his footing now, the man complied. "I started with the countries without extradition treaties with the United States, but decided that was too restrictive. I can't see Mannen retiring to live in comfort in Libya. So then I broadened the search to countries where he'd be at ease, if he had a new identity. Started with a couple dozen, then narrowed it down to places he's visited in the last few years. Hit pay dirt a couple days ago. Want to take a wild guess?''

Despite himself, Nick felt a flicker of interest. ''Italy.''

There was a moment of stunned silence, then Luc shook his head wonderingly. ''Damn. You are good. How'd you figure it?''

''He considers himself cultured—a connoisseur of art, wine and opera. Italy fits on all counts. It's also welcoming to wealthy Americans looking to relocate and spread their money around.''

''That's how I figured it, too. Sent out some feelers and found a rather large estate outside Milan has just changed hands among very mysterious circumstances. The owner is already beginning to ship his belongings.'' Before Nick could ask, Luc admitted, ''I haven't gotten that far yet. If it's Mannen, he'd route the packages through different countries to disguise their origin. But that's my next item of business.''

''Maybe you'll find something to help you on this.'' Nick reached into his pocket and withdrew the CD on which he'd downloaded Mannen's files. ''I'd planned to give it to you at the restaurant.'' He explained how he'd gotten it, and was rewarded with a look of sheer joy on the man's face.

''You got to his computer? Ah…you're a god, Nick. I always knew it.'' Luc practically sprinted across the floor to snatch the file from his hand.

''I'm still going to kick your ass.''

''For a peek into the man's files I'll buy you the boots.''

Although his tension hadn't lessened appreciably, Nick pushed his glass aside. The liquor wasn't helping. With a void this wide yawning inside him, it would be dangerous to try to fill it with booze, at any rate.

"So…ah…" Luc appeared to be unusually tongue-tied. That was rarely a good sign. "I guess that was a real shock to Parker. To see me again like that."

A shock. Bitter humor twisted through Nick. "You could say that."

"Maybe it's for the best, though. You know." With more guts than sense he rushed on, even after Nick's gaze landed on him. "Doesn't really matter whether Mannen goes to prison or not, he's not the type to give up. Anyone who gets tangled up with Parker becomes a target, too."

"You're just full of wisdom today, aren't you, Luc?" The man was saved from answering by the ringing of the cell phone in the next room. With a sense of inevitability, Nick went to answer it.

"Michel, I left messages."

If there was a hint of rebuke in Mannen's voice on the line, it was well hidden.

"Have you? I've just walked in the door, I'm afraid. Haven't spoken to anyone yet."

"No matter. I was wondering if you'd be free tonight. I have some thoughts about a way to shield our relationship from unwelcome scrutiny." His reference to the undisguised interest of Connally, Jacobs and McKay was thinly veiled.

"I'd be interested to hear any ideas you have, of course."

"Perhaps we could discuss them after dinner at my home this evening. Bring your lovely friend. I have an exquisite collection of Italian sculpture she may enjoy while we discuss business."

After a few more seconds of conversation, Nick broke the connection. Luc was watching him avidly. "Well? Got something going for this evening?"

"Looks like it. Mannen wants another meeting."

"Maybe you'll get lucky and wind this thing down sooner than you thought."

There was no reason for the sentence to remind Nick, yet again, of Sara. Of something precious lost before it could really be claimed.

"Yeah," he agreed, his voice expressionless. "That'd be real lucky."

Sara would rather be force-fed splinters of glass than see Victor Mannen again, let alone be expected to dine with him, pretending to admire his belongings. The lone consolation was that the nerve-scraping scene would take her mind off Nick. And off the doubts that were jackhammering in her head.

One bold thought stood out above the others, demanding her attention. Nick had mentioned that he and Mannen would discuss business this evening. Which meant she'd be alone, at least for several minutes. If the opportunity arose to slip away, she'd be on the run again without a second thought. And this time she'd know enough to do it minus her shoes.

Nick's hand was on her back as they mounted the marble steps to Mannen's home. She felt as cold as the stone beneath her feet. She was grateful for the icy numbness encasing her, but knew it couldn't be expected to last for long. When it melted and left her emotions raw and battered once again, she wanted to be far, far away from Nick Doucet. The last several hours had proved she couldn't trust her feelings when it came to him.

The door opened before they could ring the bell. Light spilled out behind Mannen as he greeted them. "Michel and Raeanne. I'm pleased you could make it." Sara fought to keep her smile in place as he took her hand between his. Revulsion crawled in her veins.

"And Ah'm pleased to be able to see more of yoah lovely home."

"Raeanne was quite taken with it the other night," Nick said, as they strolled through the foyer.

"I'm delighted you like it. I've always enjoyed surrounding myself with the best."

They followed him into a dining room, where a polished cherry table was set for three. Mannen withdrew a bottle of wine from a brass ice bucket and filled three crystal goblets. Handing them each a glass, he retained one for himself.

"We have a half hour before the first course will be served. Allow me to show you some of my most prized belongings." He gave them an indulgent smile. "I'm afraid I'm quite vain about my collections."

His mansion had reminded Sara of a museum the first time she'd seen it, but she was forced to revise her opinion now. It more closely resembled a mausoleum. Without the throngs of people that had filled the home the last time they'd been there, the area was lifeless. There was something eerie about the glass-encased shelving built to enshrine riches that would be enjoyed by only one man.

She acted suitably impressed by the centuries-old carpets and Fabergé eggs. Her head swirled with his talk of Grueby statues and Han horses. Nick had to carry on the bulk of the conversation because she was totally out of her element. It was enough, she hoped, that she acted dazzled.

They'd gone through several of the rooms on the lower floor before Mannen looked at his watch. "I believe we have time before dinner to show you one more thing." He turned and walked down the hall. In the direction of his office.

Sara kept her gaze trained on the back of Mannen's impeccably tailored suit. She wanted, badly, to look at Nick, to get his reaction. But in the next moment she remembered there wouldn't be one, at least not a visible one. A knot the size of a fist clenched hard in her stomach. He was a master at a shielding his true emotions. She knew that better than anyone.

Mannen used his body to shield their view as he keyed in the code to the security system. In the next moment, he was pushing the door open and turning on the light.

"I'm especially proud of this piece." He showed them to a statue of a horse that sat on a table next to a leather sofa. "I acquired it only last year. Rumors suggest it's a lost piece from the bronzes of Miklagard." He picked it up and caressed it with the greedy touch of a lecher stroking a woman. "I like to think that Emperor Nero once held this in his hands as he ordered the slaughter of those who opposed him."

"It's beautiful," Sara said dutifully.

He set it down on the table again, using the care of a mother with her child. "Thank you, my dear, but as you should know, beauty can't always be trusted."

She blinked. "Excuse me?"

He turned to face her then, and in his hand he held a lethal looking semiautomatic. And it was pointed right at her heart.

"Mannen, what the hell are you doing?" Nick's voice held just the right amount of incredulity, just the right amount of command. Even now, he was firmly entrenched in his role.

Sara swayed, her gaze narrowed on the barrel of the gun. Pieces of the past flashed across her mind, forming a terrifying collage of violence. *His order to his associate in the restaurant that night…the sound of the shot…* But it wasn't the stranger's crumpled body that shifted into focus next, it was those of her friends. *The lifeless bodies, the river of blood on the floor…*

"I have wondered, Michel, if you know just what kind

of woman you've been keeping company with.'' When Nick would have made a move toward him, Mannen stepped to the side, the gun still pointing at Sara. "I confess I've wondered myself since I entered this room after the party the other night and found that your lovely friend had been in here."

"What? Are you crazy?"

Mannen backed away from them slowly, all the way to his desk, where he picked something up. Sara's throat closed. From the man's fingers dangled several ice-blue threads.

Memory came with a sick sense of terror. She'd caught her heel in her hem, had had to work it loose. She'd never noticed the frayed threads her dress had shed. Such a little thing, she thought, to guarantee her death.

"Don't be a fool. What would Raeanne want in here? She wouldn't know a Miklagard from a Ming."

"You're quite right," Mannen agreed equably. The gun never wavered. "The only thing in here of interest is the computer. And after some checking I decided that a flit-headed socialite probably has very little talent in that area. Which led me to deduce, Mr. Falcol—" the gun slowly swung toward Nick "—that the interest was yours. You were quite good. My associate still isn't sure how you breached the security on it, but he can say with some certainty that it *was* breached." Despite his words, Mannen's tone was far from admiring. He was furious.

Amazingly, Nick gave a rueful shrug. "Under the circumstances, I can appreciate your displeasure. But when I see an opportunity, I take it. That's the kind of man I am. For the same reason, I never walk into the web of a powerful man without at least one bargaining chip."

The other man's eyes glinted. "My computer files."

"That, and the witness your men missed six years ago."

Sara's gasp was ripped from her lungs. The walls of the

room seemed to rush in on her. Nick's voice came from a distance, dispassionate and matter-of-fact. "Take a good look at her, Victor. Tell me what you see."

The man's gaze swung to her, assessing and wary. She was incapable of protesting. Sorrow and rage barreled through her with the force of a locomotive. "You bastard!"

Nick's hands slipped into his pockets. His eyes seemed strangely intent as they returned her gaze. "I admitted as much to you, did I not? I know I promised to help you kill the man, but you have to admit the possibility isn't financially prudent for me."

She frowned, his words as disorienting as the rest of the horrifying scene.

Mannen was eyeing her narrowly. "Parker?"

"The question I have, *mon ami*, is whether she is worth more to you or to Justice. I rather thought you'd be the most appreciative."

"You were going to auction her off to the highest bidder?" There was anger but acceptance in Mannen's tone. While he might not appreciate the mercenary action, he would understand it.

Nick gave a negligible shrug. "A man does what he must."

"You understand that I would need proof of her identity."

She was standing in Victor Mannen's office listening to him and Nick discuss her murder. It was a waking nightmare. In the midst of a pool of shattered trust, pounding betrayal, Sara groped wildly for understanding. Nick... Justice...Mannen... How were the three really entwined? The questions had dogged her since she was in the Keys. And she was no closer to the truth now.

"There are ways of obtaining proof once she's dead."

At Nick's encouragement, Mannen focused on her once

more. Sara swayed on her feet as reality funneled in, becoming more and more narrow until it included only that gun. The dark lethal hole in the barrel.

"Remember New Orleans, *ma petite.*"

Nick's words managed to distract her from her certain death. Mannen's finger tightened on the trigger. Sara's gaze swung to Nick, caught the blur of his movement even as Mannen detected it from the corner of his eye. Nick rammed the other man, knocking him off balance, and Sara dove out of the way. The gun jerked, fired.

There was a solid crash as the two fell to the floor, grappling for the gun. Guided by instinct alone, she ran to the bronze, lifted it and turned back to the pair. Standing above Mannen, she poised the heavy piece above his skull, her hands shaking with restraint.

The men abruptly stilled. Mannen's eyes were glued to the threat above him. With very little force, his most prized possession would crush his skull. It was a delicious little irony that wasn't lost on Sara.

"It's all right, *mon ange.*" Nick's voice floated through the room, curled around her system. "You can put it down." She didn't question the gun he'd drawn from his ankle holster. She was buried beneath the avalanche of the past, the horror, the gut-rending pain of losing all she'd held dear. All to this man. This one man cowering beneath her, arm still outstretched for his gun, which had landed beside him.

Reaction gripped her, shaking her hard from the inside out. It would be so easy to let go of the statue. Put paid to so many lives lost in vain.

"Put it down, Sara. Take a step back. Now another. Set it on the table."

She wasn't even aware that she'd obeyed that low command until the statue was out of her hands. Only then did she look at Nick and see the spreading stain soaking his shirt.

"You're hit." The realization pierced her mental fog as nothing else could. Distantly, she heard the front door burst open, the sound of running footsteps.

"It's over, Mannen." Nick had stepped outside his role now. His voice was flat and merciless. He never took his gaze from the man on the floor, who was inching ever closer to the gun beside him. "I'll think of you doing life. Wearing prison blues. Eating in the mess hall with the lowest kind of scum. You'll all be the same in there, won't you?" He gave a chilling smile. "Enjoy your new friends."

The sound of the door to the office being kicked in was lost in the deafening roar of the gunshot.

It seemed an odd place to hold a debriefing. Nick was sitting up in the hospital bed, bare-chested save for the bandages that swathed his shoulder. His face was stamped with impatience, but it was the tubes and machines he was hooked to that drew Sara's gaze time and again. Mannen's first shot had grazed him several inches below his previous wound, which had reopened yet again. With the blood loss he'd suffered, his vitals still weren't stable enough to satisfy the medical staff. The doctor had indicated Nick would be staying several days, despite Nick's protests.

Paul Whitmore was just as imposing as she remembered, and his hair decidedly more gray. She'd spent long hours surrounded by him and his agents already, repeating her story endlessly. Although he'd been understanding in a gruff sort of way, she'd be more than willing to see the last of him.

Gabe Connally and Meghan Patterson had joined the odd mix of occupants in the room, as had Addison Jacobs and Dare McKay. The four surrounded Nick's bed, while

Sara stood a little ways apart. It was better...far better if she didn't get too close to the man. She thought she had just enough composure to make it through this last meeting, but distance would help maintain it.

"Okay, you've got five minutes." Whitmore's voice was brusque. "And McKay, if I read one word about any of this that hasn't been okayed by me first, I'm coming after you."

Sara noted a layer of steel below the reporter's affability. "You kept your word, Whitmore. I'll keep mine."

The man nodded curtly. "Five minutes," he repeated, then left the room.

"Call in a few favors, McKay?" Nick said.

"Some would refer to his actions as blackmailing a government agent," the woman by his side noted dryly.

"Addie's right," Dare agreed, lacing his fingers with hers. "Whitmore isn't anxious to have the media pick up the story about the mole Mannen had in Justice for the last eight years."

"How about the one he has there now?" Sara's question took the group by surprise. "At least I have to assume Mannen would have someone to replace his contact before he had him killed."

Gabe gave a low whistle. "That might be another reason Whitmore was so eager to cooperate."

"I never promised not to do any digging into that," Dare mused. He shot Sara a wicked grin. "Thanks for the tip."

"I wouldn't mind a look at that wireless receiver you used," Gabe told Nick. "Must be state of the art. The men you had in the van near Mannen's house could tell exactly what was going down. They were able to alert the Chicago Police for backup, but it looked to me like you had things pretty well under control when we got there."

"I can't say I wasn't looking forward to seeing Mannen

behind bars," Addie mused, "but seeing him dead works for me."

Nick's gaze met Sara's. "With the noise when the reinforcements arrived, I didn't even see him go for the gun. I wouldn't have expected him to use it on himself."

Silent communication sparked between them. She remembered Nick's voice, hypnotic and low, urging her to step away from an act that would have haunted her forever. And that same voice reminded Mannen of how much he'd had. And how much he was about to lose.

"It's best this way." Gabe gave voice to the words, exchanging a glance with Dare. "With his money he'd have been a threat even in prison." He looked down at Meghan, stroking a hand over her hair, and Sara felt a funny little jolt of realization.

With Mannen gone, she was free.

Her mouth abruptly went dry, and she moved to the wall, leaned against it, needing the support. During her grueling sessions with Whitmore, that one fact had remained tantalizingly unformed. But it was crystal clear now, and the recognition of it was staggering. For the first time in eight years, she could stop running.

She released a shuddering breath, and saw Nick watching her reaction. And knew that despite everything that had gone on between them, she'd never be able to repay him for what he'd given her.

Meghan stepped forward, touched Nick's hand. "I don't pretend to understand everything that went on, but I want to thank you for your part in it."

Nick's lips curved, the woman's sincerity summoning a shadow of a smile. "From what I'm hearing, you four already had the guy on the run. I was just the final act."

Gabe glanced at his watch. "Our five minutes are up. Whitmore's due in here any second breathing fire." His words compelled the group to move.

Dare drifted by Sara. "I'll bet you have quite a story to tell."

"Stay away from her, McKay."

The threat in Nick's words wasn't negated in the least by the fact that he was lying in bed.

Dare gave an innocent shrug. "Do I have those words tattooed on my forehead or something?"

Addie leaned forward, kissed the area in question. "No, but you will after the wedding." And amid good-natured laughter, they left the room, to be followed, moments later, by Sara.

She heard her name being called, but hurried down the hallway. It wasn't like she didn't have things to do, she assured herself when that sick and hollow feeling in her stomach threatened to swamp her. She had a future, finally. She had a life, thanks to Nick.

She didn't want to consider at that moment just how empty it loomed.

"Sara!"

The sound was an explosion, accompanied by the sudden bustling of medical staff. Bewildered, she turned, then stared, disbelieving.

"Mr. Falcol, you have to get back to bed." The nurse bullying Nick toward his room had a determined look in her eye and snap to her voice. "Orderly! I need some help here."

"Sara!" Nick nudged the woman aside, swayed a bit, then started down the hallway wearing nothing but the stark bandages at his shoulder and side, and wrinkled dress pants, half-zipped.

She watched as the nurse and a large orderly attempted to take hold of Nick, as he shrugged them off and lurched toward her.

Driven to move, Sara hurried back to him. "What are you doing? You're not supposed to be out of bed." She tried to check his bandages for signs of renewed bleeding, but he caught her close, his arms steel bands around her body.

"Don't go." The words were a demand, a plea. Sara tried to look at him, but he had her wrapped too tightly, her face pressed to his heaving chest. His voice became little more than a jagged whisper. "Don't leave, *chérie.*"

"Lady, help us get him back in bed where he belongs," the outraged nurse ordered.

Nick didn't make it a choice. He simply refused to let go of her while he was forced back to his room. While the nurse reinstated the IVs with a less than gentle touch, Nick gripped Sara's hand tightly enough to have her bones protesting, his eyes fixed on hers, dark and intense.

Only when the woman left the room, muttering dire threats for Nick's welfare should he try that again, did his hand relax around Sara's, as if he was just then noticing his grasp.

"What did you think you were doing a minute ago?" Real anger was bubbling through her. "You may have really hurt yourself. The last thing you need is for one of those wounds to reopen."

He raised her fingers to his lips in silent apology, never releasing her from his gaze. "Where were you going?"

Because she didn't have an answer to the question, she avoided it. "I didn't think there was anything left to say."

"I've plenty left to say, *chérie.* I just didn't know how little time you would give me to say it."

Her smile felt forced. "You're right. I was taking the easy way out. I warned you that I was a coward." She stopped, drew a fortifying breath. "The magnitude of the whole thing just hit me. What you did for me at Mannen's, I mean. A week ago...a day ago I couldn't even imagine a positive ending to this. And now I'm free, in a way I've never been before. And I have you to thank for that."

His thumb skated across her palm. "I was afraid when I told Mannen who you were that you would think I'd betrayed you again."

Sara could feel a flush work up her cheeks. Of course she'd thought exactly that at first. "I figured out what you were up to after a few minutes."

"Deceit has been a way of life for me for too many years to count," he murmured. "First with the Green Berets, and then as an operative. The ends quite regularly justify the means in my assignments."

There was a stabbing pain somewhere in the vicinity of her chest. His assignments. He couldn't have defined their relationship any more clearly had he tried.

He interlocked their fingers, almost distracting her from the rest of his words. "I learned the hard way in Special Ops that the longer a mission lasts, the greater the likelihood that objectivity is compromised." She recognized old guilt in his voice, and the ghosts in his eyes. "I should have seen it happening this time. Because the longer I spent on your trail, the more intrigued I became. It was like looking in a mirror. I began to wonder if you lost a bit of yourself with each cover you took on. I know what that's like, you see. To wake up in a strange place, using a strange name, with nothing tangible in your life to use as an anchor."

She wanted to shout at him to stop. His murmured confession was caustic, like stripping off a surface of skin, and she was afraid, very much afraid, of what would be revealed to him. Warily, she searched his eyes. And caught herself, just in time, before she was pulled into their fathomless dark depths. "I was just a job."

"Luc told me I was obsessed and although I denied it, he was right. I can't tell you when you became more." He trailed a finger over her knuckles. "Maybe when I realized I wasn't going to trust your safety to Justice.

Maybe when I figured out just how much I wanted you to trust me, instead.''

Her breath strangled in her lungs. Something like hope unfurled inside her, blanketing her familiar caution. "I was never certain how you did it. But no matter how strong my defenses were, you managed to sneak inside them, over and over again. No one's ever gotten that close to me, even with me fighting it every step of the way.''

"That kind of vulnerability is terrifying.''

He might have plucked the thought from her mind. "Yes.''

"I know because I'm experiencing something approaching terror myself right now.''

She tugged at her hand, but it was held fast. "You?'' she scoffed. "I doubt you've ever known a moment's fear in your life. While I...'' It took a ridiculous amount of courage to push aside her well-worn guard. Even more to allow rein to the emotion she was most comfortable keeping tucked away. "Because of you I have my life back. I can go anywhere, be anything. And all I can think of...'' here her voice cracked despite her best efforts "...is how empty it looks. How alone.''

Nick's voice was unsteady. "It won't be empty, *chérie,* if there's room for us both in it. I'm in love with you.'' Her eyes widened in disbelief, but the fierce expression on his face convinced her she'd heard him correctly. "I didn't want to be. God knows, I fought it. It was the toughest battle in my life, and one I'm happy to lose. Because I can't tame the emotion I have for you. I lost the will to even try.''

He brushed a kiss across her knuckles and her pulse stuttered. "Come back with me, to New Orleans. My family home has never held much of a family, but we can start one, beginning with just the two of us.'' His smile was as beguiling as his words. "*Grand-mère* will be pleased.''

There were tiny bubbles of joy rising in her veins. The feeling was too new, too unfamiliar, to be easily identified. "I love you," she said unsteadily. "But even more...I trust you." She saw Nick swallow hard, and knew that the words meant as much to him as they did to her. "If New Orleans is where your life is, then that's where we'll go."

His lips approached hers, hovered. "That's what I'm telling, you, *chérie*. You are my life."

And as their lips met, the words sounded very much like a promise.

Epilogue

Celeste Doucet's gardens were breathtaking at sunset. The three couples still lounged at the patio table where they'd dined earlier that evening. Sara, Addie and Meghan sat near their husbands, all contentedly full after the big meal. Six pairs of alert eyes kept watch on the scene playing out before them.

"It's my turn to pick a flower for *Grand-mère* Celeste." Three-year-old Callie McKay's voice had an imperious tone that had all the adults grinning. As usual, the Connally boys acquiesced to her demand, with Danny helping her choose just the right bloom and four-year-old Nathan adding his advice.

"How beautiful it is, little one." Celeste exclaimed over the mangled bloom Callie handed her, stroking her palm over the child's golden hair. "And how thoughtful."

"I picked it all myself."

"I helped," Nathan insisted.

"And so you did." The older woman put a frail hand

on the boy's dark head. "All three of you did wonderfully."

"Danny's always so good with the two of them," Sara observed.

Meghan shifted to a more comfortable position, earning her a concerned glance from Gabe. She was only six months pregnant, and it was already becoming difficult to keep the man from hovering. "The age difference between Danny and Nathan keeps things fairly calm, unless Nate enters Danny's room without permission." She shared a droll glance with her husband. "Then there's a minor war." The two of them had started adoption procedures for Danny the moment they'd returned from their honeymoon. But a piece of paper hadn't been necessary. Danny was their son, as much as the one who'd been borne to them.

"All I can say is you're a brave woman to go through childbirth again after the last time," Addie told Meghan. "Aren't you afraid to go back to that hospital?"

The six of them grinned at the memory. Gabe had set the facility on its ear with his frantic demands when Meghan's water had broken.

"I heard there's a security guard at the door with Gabe's picture and orders to tranquilize him on sight," Dare said lazily.

Nick laughed. "And you were so much better, *mon ami?* Weren't you the one who ended up in a hospital bed beside your wife?"

"Sympathy pains are a documented medical phenomenon," Dare pointed out.

"*You're* a documented medical phenomenon," Gabe retorted, while everyone else laughed at the memory.

A close-knit relationship had developed among the three couples, sparked at first by their pursuit of Mannen, and later by friendship. A year after the case climaxed Justice had discovered Mannen's latest mole in the agency, and the three couples had met in Chicago again. Six months later the criminal's tangled ownership of Golden Enterprises had been unraveled, and all his associates in the venture had been arrested and charged. That had called for another celebration, and since then, at least twice a year they made a point of all getting together.

As the conversation went on around her, Sara's attention drifted. She couldn't look away from the scene the children made clustered around Celeste. Despite the older woman's failing health, she seemed energized by the children. Sean's grandmother had passed away the previous winter, reminding Sara just how precious each day with Nick's grandmother was. Unexpectedly, Sara's eyes began to burn. She knew Nick wanted a family. That was one of the reasons he'd retired from field work to a much less risky position directing several teams of operatives. He hadn't pushed her while she'd made the first tentative steps toward reaching out to her mother. The relationship there was never going to be close, but time might help heal the breach between them to some degree. Nick had been equally patient as Sara pursued her general equivalent diploma and entered college majoring in social work. But now, looking at Celeste's face, she could feel her priorities shifting.

She looked up at her husband, smiled as he lowered his head for a quick kiss, and said to him softly, "I think I'm ready."

She didn't have to explain her meaning. His eyes widened for a moment, before he hugged her close. "You will be a wonderful mother, *mon ange.*"

Despite his low, intimate tone, Dare overheard him. "You guys are going to start a family?"

Nick's grin was smug. "*Oui.* Very soon."

"Get the security guards ready."

"Call for an additional hospital bed."

Nick couldn't tear his gaze away from Sara. His treasure. His wife. To his companions he said, "I must thank you for the invaluable experience you've already provided on what *not* to do at the hospital."

"Hey." Gabe reached forward, snagged another beer from the cooler. "That's what friends are for."

* * * * *

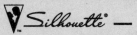

Silhouette®

INTIMATE MOMENTS™

In February 2002

MERLINE LOVELACE

brings back
the men—and women—of

CODE NAME: DANGER

Beginning with

HOT AS ICE, IM #1129
He was frozen in time! And she was
just the woman to thaw him out....

Follow the adventures and loves of the
members of the Omega Agency.
Because love is a risky business.

Also look for

DANGEROUS TO HOLD in February 2002
DANGEROUS TO KNOW in July 2002

to see where **CODE NAME: DANGER** began

Available at your favorite retail outlet.

 *Silhouette*®

Where love comes alive™

If you enjoyed what you just read,
then we've got an offer you can't resist!

Take 2 bestselling
love stories FREE!
Plus get a FREE surprise gift!